**W9-ABJ-676**

**Date: 2/21/12**

**FIC ROHMER**
**Rohmer, Sax,**
**The bride of Fu Manchu /**

PALM BEACH COUNTY
LIBRARY SYSTEM
3650 SUMMIT BLVD.
WEST PALM BEACH, FL 33406

# THE BRIDE OF
# FU MANCHU

# The Adventures of
# Nayland Smith

●

# THE BRIDE OF FU MANCHU

SAX ROHMER

The American Reprint Company

MATTITUCK

# THE BRIDE OF FU MANCHU

Copyright © 1933 by Sax Rohmer
Republished by Special Arrangement

Library of Congress Catalog Card Number 81-70797
International Standard Book Number 0-89190-801-3

All of the characters in this book are fictitious,
and any resemblance to actual persons,
living or dead, is purely coincidental.

Printed in the United States of America

*To Order, Contact:*
AMERICAN REPRINT COMPANY
Box 1200
Mattituck, New York 11952

# CHAPTER I

# FLEURETTE

ALL the way around the rugged headland, and beyond, as I sat at the wheel of the easy-running craft, I found myself worrying about Petrie. He was supposed to be looking after *me*. I thought that somebody should be looking after him. He took his responsibilities with a deadly seriousness; and this strange epidemic which had led the French authorities to call upon his expert knowledge was taxing him to the limit. At luncheon I thought he had looked positively ill; but he had insisted upon returning to his laboratory.

He seemed to imagine that the reputation of the Royal Society was in his keeping.

I had hoped that the rock-bound cove which I had noted would afford harbourage for the motor-boat. Nevertheless, I was pleasantly surprised when I found that it did.

The little craft made safe, I waded in and began to swim through nearly still water around that smaller promontory beyond which lay the bay and beach of Ste. Claire de la Roche. Probably a desire to test my fitness underlay the job; if I could not explore Ste. Claire from the land side, I was determined to invade it, nevertheless.

The water was quite warm, and it had that queer odour of stagnation peculiar to this all but tideless sea. I swam around the point, and twenty yards out from the beach my feet touched bottom.

At the same moment I saw her. . . .

She was seated on the smooth sand, her back towards me, and she was combing her hair. As I stumbled, groped, and began to make my way inland, I told myself that this sole inhabitant of Ste. Claire was probably one of those fabulous creatures, a mermaid—or should I say, a siren.

I halted, wading ashore, and watched her.

Her arms, her shoulders and her back were beautiful. Riviera salt and sun had tanned her to a most delectable

5

shade of brown. Her wavy hair was of a rich, red mahogany colour. This was all I could see of the mermaid from my position in the sea.

I made the shore without disturbing her.

It became apparent, then, that she was not a mermaid: a pair of straight, strong and very shapely brown legs discredited the mermaid theory. She was a human girl with a perfect figure and glorious hair, wearing one of those bathing suits fashionable in Cannes.

What it was, at this moment, which swamped admiration and brought *fear*—which urged me to go back—to go back—I could not imagine. I fought against this singular revulsion, reminding myself that I was newly convalescent from a dangerous illness. This alone, I argued, accounted for the sudden, weird chill which had touched me.

Why, otherwise, should I be afraid of a pretty girl?

I moved forward.

And as I began to walk up the gently sloping beach, she heard me, and turned.

I found myself staring, almost in a frightened way, at the most perfect face I thought I had ever seen. Those arms and shoulders were so daintily modelled that I had been prepared for disillusionment: instead, I found glamour.

She was bronzed by the sun and at the moment innocent of make-up. She had most exquisitely chiselled features. Her lips were slightly parted, showing the whitest little teeth. Big, darkly-fringed eyes—and they were blue as the Mediterranean—were opened widely, as if my sudden appearance had alarmed her.

I may have dreamed, as some men do, of flawless beauty, but I had never expected to meet it; when:

"How did *you* get here?" the vision asked, and rolled over on to one elbow, looking up at me.

Her voice had a melodious resonance which suggested training, and her cool acceptance of my appearance helped to put me more at ease.

"I just swam ashore," I replied. "I hope I didn't frighten you?"

"Nothing frightens me," she answered, in that cool, low tone, her unflinching eyes—the eyes of a child, but of a very clever and very inquisitive child—fixed upon me. "I was certainly surprised."

"I'm sorry. I suppose I should have warned you."

Her steady regard never wavered; it was becoming disconcerting. She was quite young, as the undisguised contours

6

of her body revealed, but about her very beauty there hovered some aura of mysteriousness which her typically nonchalant manner could not dispel. Then suddenly I saw, and it greatly relieved me to see, a tiny dimple appear in her firm round chin. She smiled—and her smile made me her slave.

"Please explain," she said; "this isn't an accident, is it?"

"No," I confessed; "it's a plot."

She shifted to a more easy position, resting both elbows on the sand, and cupping her chin in two hands.

"What do you mean 'a plot'?" she asked, suddenly serious again.

I sat down, peculiarly conscious of my angular ugliness.

"I wanted to have a look at Ste. Claire," I replied. "It used to be open to inspection and it's a spot of some historical interest. I found the road barred. And I was told that a certain Mahdi Bey had bought the place and had seen fit to close it to the public. I heard that the enclosed property ran down to the sea, so I explored and saw this little bay."

"And what were you going to do?" she asked, looking me over in a manner which struck me as almost supercilious.

"Well. . . ." I hesitated, hoping for another smile. "I had planned to climb up to Ste. Claire, and if I should be discovered, explain that I had been carried away by the current which works around the headland, and been compelled to swim ashore."

I watched eagerly for the dimple. But no dimple came. Instead, I saw a strange, far-away expression creep over the girl's face. In some odd manner it transformed her; spiritually, she seemed to have withdrawn—to a greater distance, to another land; almost, I thought, to another world. Her youth, her remarkable beauty, were transfigured as though by the occult brush of a dead Master. Momentarily, I experienced again that insane desire to run away.

Then she spoke. Her phrases were common-place enough, but her voice, too, was far-away; her eyes seemed to be looking right through me, to be fixed upon some very distant object.

"You sound enterprising," she said. "What is your name?"

"Alan Sterling," I answered, with a start.

I had an uncanny feeling that the question had not come from the girl, herself, although her lips had framed the words.

"I suppose you live somewhere near here?"

"Yes, I do."

"Alan Sterling," she repeated; "isn't that Scotch?"

7

"Yes, my father was a Scotsman—Dr. Andrew Sterling—but he settled in the Middle West of America, where I was born."

The mahogany curls were shaken violently. It was, I thought, an act of rebellion against the fey mood which had claimed her. She rose to her knees, confronting me; her fingers played with the sand. The rebellion had succeeded. She seemed to have drawn near again, to have become human, and adorable. Her next words confirmed my uncanny impression that in mind and spirit she had really been far away.

"Did you say you were American?" she asked.

Rather uncomfortably I answered:

"I was born in America. But I took my degree in Edinburgh, so that really I don't quite know what I am."

"Don't you?"

She sank down upon the sand, looking like a lovely idol.

"And now please tell me *your* name," I said; "I have told you mine."

"Fleurette."

"But Fleurette what?"

"Fleurette nothing. Just Fleurette."

"But, Mahdi Bey—"

I suppose my thoughts were conveyed without further words, for:

"Mahdi Bey," Fleurette replied, "is—"

And then she ceased, abruptly. Her glance strayed away somewhere over my shoulder. I had a distinct impression that she was listening—listening intently for some distant sound.

"Mahdi Bey," I prompted—

Fleurette glanced at me swiftly.

"Really, Mr. Sterling," she said, "I must run. I mustn't be caught talking to you."

"Why?" I exclaimed. "I was hoping you would show me over Ste. Claire."

She shook her head, almost angrily.

"As you came out of the sea, please go back again. You can't come with me."

"I don't understand why—"

"Because it would be dangerous."

Composedly she tucked a comb back into a bag which lay upon the sand beside her, picked up a bathing cap and stood up.

8

"You don't seem to bother about the possibility of my being drowned!"

"You have a motor-boat just around the headland," she replied, glancing at me over one golden shoulder. "I heard your engine."

This was a revelation.

"No wonder you weren't frightened when I came ashore."

"I am never frightened. In fact, I am rather inhuman, in all sorts of ways. Did you ever hear of Derceto?"

Her abrupt changes of topics, as of moods, were bewildering, but:

"Vaguely," I answered. "Wasn't she a sort of fish goddess?"

"Yes. Think of me, not as Fleurette, but as Derceto. Then you may understand."

The words conveyed nothing at the time, although I was destined often to think about them, later. And what I should have said next I don't know. But the whole of my thoughts, which were chaotic, became suddenly focused . . . upon a sound.

To this day I find myself unable to describe it, although, as will presently appear, before a very long time had elapsed I was called upon to do so. It more closely resembled the note of a bell than anything else yet it was not the note of a bell. It was incredibly high. It seemed at once to come from everywhere and from nowhere. A tiny sound it was, but of almost unendurable sweetness: it might be likened to a fairy trumpet blown close beside one's ear.

I started, violently, looking all around me. And, as I did so, Fleurette, giving me no parting word, no glance, darted away!

Amazed beyond words, I watched her slim brown figure bounding up a rocky path, until, at a bend high above, Fleurette became invisible. She never once looked back.

And then—the desire to get away, and as soon as possible, from the beach of Ste. Claire de la Roche, claimed me again, urgently. . . .

## CHAPTER II

# A PURPLE CLOUD

WHEN presently I climbed on board the motor-boat and pushed off, I found myself to be in a state of nervous excitement. But as I headed back for the landing-place below Petrie's tiny villa, I grew more and more irritated by my memories.

Fleurette was not only the most delightful but also the most mysterious creature who had ever crossed my path; and the more I thought about her, reveiwing that odd conversation, the nearer I drew to what seemed to be an unavoidable conclusion. Of course, she had been lying to me—acting the whole time. A beautiful girl in the household of a wealthy Egyptian—in what capacity was she there?

Common sense supplied the answer. It was one I hated to accept—but I could see no alternative. The queer sound which had terminated that stolen interview, I preferred not to think about. It didn't seem to fit in. . . .

As I secured the boat to the ring and started a long, hot climb up to the Villa Jasmin, I found myself wondering if I should ever see Fleurette again, and, more particularly, if she wanted to see *me*.

I supposed Mme. Dubonnet had gone into the village to do her midday shopping, which included an apéritif with one of her cronies outside a certain little café. Petrie, I knew, would be hard at work in the laboratory at the bottom of the garden.

Mixing myself a cool drink, I sat down on the flower-draped veranda, and allowed my glance to stray over the well-stocked little kitchen-garden. Beyond and below were more flower-covered walls and red roofs breaking through the green of palm and vine, and still beyond was a distant prospect of the jewel-like Mediterranean.

I reflected that this was a very pleasant spot in which to recuperate. And then I began to think about Fleurette.

No doubt my swim had overtired me, but stretched out there in a deck-chair, the hot sun making my skin tingle agreeably, I presently fell asleep. And almost immediately, as I suppose, I began to dream.

I dreamed that I lay in just such a deck-chair, under an equally hot sun, on a balcony or platform of an incredibly high building. I have since decided that it was the Empire State Building in New York. I was endowed with telescopic vision. Other great buildings there were, with mile after mile of straight avenues stretching away to the distant sea.

The sky was sapphire blue, and a heat haze danced over the great city which lay at my feet.

Then there came a curious, high sound. It reminded me of something I had heard before—but of something which in my dream I could not place. A cloud appeared, no larger than my hand, on the horizon, miles and miles away—over that blue ocean. It was a purple cloud; and it spread out, fan-wise, and the sections of the fan grew ever larger. So that, presently, half of the sky was shadowed.

And then, a tiny glittering point, corresponding, I thought, to the spot where the hinge of this purple shadow-fan should have been, I saw a strange jewel. The fan continued to open, to obscure more and more of the sky.

It was advancing towards me, this shadowy thing, and now, the jewel took shape.

I saw that it was a dragon, or sea-serpent, moving at incredible speed towards me. Upon its awful, crested head, a man rode. He wore a yellow robe which, in the light focused upon him, for the sun was away to my left as I dreamed, became a golden robe.

His yellow face glittered also, like gold, and he wore a cap surmounted by some kind of gleaming bead. He was, I saw, a Chinaman.

And I thought that his face had the majesty of Satan— that this was the Emperor of the Underworld come to claim a doomed city.

So much I saw, and then I realized that the dragon carried a second rider: a woman, robed in queenly white and wearing a jewelled diadem. Her beauty dazzled me, seeming more than human. But I knew her. . . .

It was Fleurette.

The purple shadow-fan obscured all the sky and complete darkness came. The darkness reached me, and where there had been sunshine was shadow. I shuddered and opened my eyes, staring up, rather wildly, I suppose.

Dr. Petrie had just stepped on to the veranda. His shadow touched me where I lay.

"Hullo, Sterling," he said briskly. "What's wrong? Been overdoing it again?"

I struggled upright. Then, in a moment, I became fully awake. And as I looked up at Petrie, seated on the low wall beside a big wine jar which had been converted into a flower-pot, I realized that this was a very sick man.

He wore no hat, and his dark hair, liberally streaked with grey, was untidy—which I knew to be unusual. He was smoking a cigarette and staring at me in that penetrating way which medical men cultivate. But his eyes were unnaturally bright, although deep shadows lay beneath them.

"Been for a swim," I replied; "fell asleep and dreamed horribly."

Dr. Petrie shook his head, and knocked ash from his cigarette into the soil in the wine jar.

"Blackwater-fever plays hell even with a constitution like yours," he replied gravely. "Really, Sterling, you mustn't take liberties for a while."

In pursuit of my profession, that of an orchid hunter, I had been knocked out by a severe attack of blackwater on the Upper Amazon. My native boys left me where I lay, and I owed my life to a German prospector who, guided by kindly Providence, found me and brought me down to Manaos.

"Liberties be damned, doctor," I growled, standing up to mix him a drink. "If ever a man took liberties with his health, that man is yourself! You're worked to death!"

"Listen," he said, checking me. "Forget me and my health. I'm getting seriously worried."

"Not another case?"

He nodded.

"Admitted early this morning."

"Who is it this time?"

"Another open-air worker, Sterling, a jobbing gardener. He was working in a villa, leased by some Americans as a matter of fact, on the slope just this side of Ste. Claire de la Roche—"

"Ste. Claire de la Roche," I echoed.

"Yes—the place you are so keen to explore."

"D'you think you can save him?"

He frowned doubtfully.

"Cartier and the other French doctors are getting in a perfect panic," he replied. "If the truth leaks out, the Riviera will be deserted. And they know it! I'm rather pessimistic myself. I lost another patient to-day."

"What!"

Petrie ran his fingers through his hair.

"You see," he went on, "diagnosis is so tremendously difficult. I found *trypanosomes* in the blood of the first patient I examined here; and although I never saw a *tsetse* fly in France, I was forced to diagnose Sleeping sickness. I risked Bayer's 205"—he smiled modestly—"with one or two modifications of my own; and by some miracle the patient pulled through."

"Why a miracle? It's the accepted treatment, isn't it?"

He stared at me, and I thought how haggard he looked.

"It's one of 'em," he replied—"for Sleeping sickness. But this was *not* Sleeping sickness!"

"What!"

"Hence the miracle. You see, I made cultures; and under the microscope they gave me a shock; I discovered that these parasites didn't really conform to any species so far classified. They were members of the Sleeping sickness family, but *new* members. Then—just before the death of another patient at the hospital—I made a great discovery, on which I have been working ever since—"

"*Over* working!"

"Forget it." He was carried away by his subject. "D'you know what I found, Sterling? I found *bacillus pestis* adhering to one of the parasites!"

"*Bacillus pestis?*"

"Plague!"

"Good God!"

"But—here's the big point: the *trypanosomes* (the parasites which cause Sleeping sickness) were a new variety, as I have mentioned. *So was the Plague bacillus.* It presented obviously new features! Crowning wonder—although you may not appreciate it—parasite and *bacillus* affiliated, and working in perfect harmony!"

"You've swamped me, doctor," I confessed. "But I have a hazy idea that there's something tremendous behind this."

"Tremendous? There's something *awful*. Nature is upsetting her own laws—as we know them."

This, from Dr. Petrie, gave me something to think about.

My father had been invited to lecture at Edinburgh—his old university—during Petrie's first year, and a close friendship had sprung up between the keen student and the visiting lecturer. They had corresponded ever since.

During my own Edinburgh days, the doctor was established in practice in Cairo; but I spent part of one vacation as his guest in London. And another fast friendship resulted. He had returned from Egypt on that occasion to receive the medal of the Royal Society for his researches in tropical medicine. I remember how disappointed I had been to learn that his wife, of whose charm I had heard many rumours, was not accompanying him on this flying journey.

His present visit—also intended to be a brief one—had been prolonged at the urgent request of the French authorities. Petrie's reputation had grown greater with the passage of years, and learning that he was in London, they had begged him to look into this strange epidemic which threatened southern France, placing the Villa Jasmin at his disposal. . . .

Three weeks later I was invalided home from Brazil. Petrie, who had had the news from my father, met the ship at Lisbon and carried me off to the Villa Jasmin to recuperate under his own watchful eye.

I fear I had proved to be a refractory patient.

"You didn't see the other case, did you?" Petrie asked suddenly.

"No."

"Well." He set down his glass. "I wish you would come along to the hospital with me. You must have met with some queer diseases on the Amazon, and you know the Uganda Sleeping sickness. There's this awful grin—proof of some sort of final paroxysm—and, particularly what Cartier calls the *Black stigmata*. Your bulb hunting has taken you into a few unwholesome places; have you ever come across anything like it?"

I began to fill my pipe.

"Never, doctor," I replied.

The sound of a distant gun boomed through the hot silence. A French battleship was entering Villefranche Harbour. . . .

## CHAPTER III

# THE BLOODSTAINED LEAVES

"GOOD God! it's ghastly! Cover him up again, doctor. I shall dream of that face."

14

I found myself wondering why Providence, though apparently beneficent, should permit such horrors to visit poor humanity. The man in the little mortuary—he had been engaged in a local vineyard—had not yet reached middle age when this new and dreadful pestilence had cut him off.

"This," said Petrie, "is the really singular feature."

He touched the dead man's forehead. It was of a dark purple colour from the scalp to the brows. The sun-browned face was set in a grin of dreadful malignancy and the eyes were rolled upward so that only their whites showed.

"What I have come to recognize as the characteristic sign," Petrie added. "Subcutaneous haemorrhage; but strangely localized. It's like a purple shadow, isn't it? And when it reaches the eyes—finish."

"What a ghastly face! I have seen nothing like it, anywhere!"

We came out.

"Nor have I!" Petrie confessed. "The earlier symptoms are closely allied with those of Sleeping sickness but extraordinarily rapid in their stages. Glandular swellings always in the armpit. This final stage—the *Black stigmata,* the purple shadow, which I have managed to avert in some of the other cases, is quite beyond my experience. That's where the plague comes in.

"But now for the most mysterious thing of all—in which I am hoping you can really help me. . . ."

If anyone had invited me to name Dr. Petrie's outstanding characteristic, I should have said Modesty.

Having run the car into its garage, Petrie led the way down the steep rocky path to a shed a hundred yards from the villa, which he had fitted up as a laboratory.

We entered. The laboratory was really an enlarged gardener's hut which the absent owner of Villa Jasmin had converted into a small studio. It had a glass window running along the whole of one side. A white-topped table now occupied a great part of the space before it, and there was a working bench in a corner opposite the door. In racks were rows of test-tubes, each bearing a neatly-written label, and there were files of specimen slides near the big microscope.

I noted the new pane of glass in a section of window which had been cut out one night less than a month ago when some strange burglar had broken in and explored the place. Since that time, Petrie had had steel shop-blinds fitted to the interior of the windows, which could be closed and locked at night.

He had never secured any clue to the identity of the intruder or formed any reasonable theory as to what his object could have been.

At that moment, several of the windows were open, and sunlight streamed into the place. There was a constant humming of bees in the garden outside. Petrie took up a little sealed tube, removed the stopper and shook out the contents of the tube into a glass tray. He turned to me, a strange expression upon his haggard brown face.

"Can you identify this, Sterling?" he asked. "It's more in your line than in mine."

I found it to consist of several bruised leaves, originally reddish purple in colour, attached to long stalks. I took up a lens and examined them carefully, the doctor watching me in silence. I saw, now, that there were pollen-like fragments adhering to a sticky substance exuded by the leaves.

There were some curious brown blotches too, which at first I took to be part of the colouring, but which closer examination showed to be due to a stain.

"It's *drosophyllum*," I murmured—"one of the fly-catching varieties, but a tropical species I have not come across before—"

Petrie did not interrupt me, and:

"There are stains of what looks like dark brown mud," I went on, "and minute shiny fragments of what might be pollen—"

"It isn't pollen," Petrie broke in. "It's bits of the wing and body of some very hairy insect. But what I'm anxious to know, Sterling, is this—"

I put down the lens and turned to the speaker curiously. His expression was grimly serious.

"Should you expect to find that plant in Europe?"

"No, it isn't a European variety. It could not possibly grow even as far North as this."

"Good. That point is settled."

"How do you account for the stains?"

"I don't know how to account for them," Petrie replied slowly, "but I have found out what they are."

"What are they?"

"Blood!—and what's more, human blood."

"Human blood!"

I stopped, at a loss for words.

"I can see I am puzzling you, Sterling. Let me try to explain."

16

Petrie replaced the fragments in the tube and sealed it down tightly.

"It occurred to me this morning," he went on, "after you had gone, to investigate the spot where our latest patient had been at work. I thought there might be some peculiar local condition there which would give me a new clue. When I arrived, I found it was a piece of steeply terraced kitchen-garden—not unlike our own, here. It ended in a low wall beyond which was a clear drop into the gorge which connects Ste. Claire with the sea.

"He had been at work up to sunset last evening about half-way down, near a water tank. He was taken ill during the night, and early this morning developed characteristic symptoms.

"I stood there—it was perfectly still; the people to whom the villa is leased are staying in Monte Carlo at present—and I listened for insects. I had gone prepared to capture any that appeared."

He pointed to an equipment which lay upon a small table.

"I got several healthy mosquitoes and other odds and ends. (Later examination showed no trace of parasite in any of them.) I was just coming away when, lying in a little trench where the man had apparently been at work up to the time that he knocked off—I happened to notice that."

He pointed to the tube containing the purple leaves.

"It was bruised and crushed partly into the soil."

He paused, then:

"Except for the fragments I have pointed out," he added, "there was nothing on the leaves. Possibly a passing lizard had licked them. . . . I spent the following hour searching the neighbourhood for the plant on which they grew. I drew blank."

We were silent for some time.

"Do you think there is some connexion," I asked slowly, "between this plant and the epidemic?"

Petrie nodded.

"Of course," I admitted, "it's certainly strange. If I could credit the idea—which I can't—that such a species could grow wild in Europe, I should be the first to agree with you. Your theory is that the thing possesses the properties of a carrier, or host, of these strange germs; so that anyone plucking a piece and smelling it for instance, immediately becomes infected?"

"That was not my theory," Petrie replied thoughtfully.

17

"It isn't a bad one, nevertheless. But it doesn't explain the bloodstains."

He hesitated.

"I had a very queer letter from Nayland Smith today," he added. "I have been thinking about it ever since."

Sir Denis Nayland Smith, ex-Assistant Commissioner of Metropolitan Police, was one of Petrie's oldest friends, I knew, but:

"This is rather outside his province, isn't it?" I suggested.

"You haven't met him," Petrie replied, labouring his words as it seemed. "But I think you will. Nayland Smith has one of the few first-class brains in Europe, and *nothing* is outside his—"

He ceased speaking, staggered, and clutched at the table edge. I saw him shudder violently.

"Look, here, doctor," I cried, grasping his shoulders, "you are sickening for 'flu or something. You're overdoing it. Give the thing a rest, and—"

He shook me off. His manner was wild. He groped his way to a cupboard, prepared a draught with unsteady hands, and drank it. Then, from a drawer he took out a tube containing a small quantity of white powder.

"I have called it '654'," he said, his eyes feverishly bright. "I haven't the pluck to try it on a human patient. But even if Mother Nature has turned topsy-turvy, I believe this may puzzle her!"

Watching him anxiously:

"Strictly speaking, you ought to be in bed," I said. "Your life is valuable."

"Get out," he replied, summoning up the ghost of a smile. "Get out, Sterling. My life's my own, and while it lasts I have work to do. . . ."


CHAPTER IV

# SQUINTING EYES


I SPENT the latter part of the afternoon delving in works of reference which I had not consulted for many months, in an

endeavour to identify more exactly the leaves so mysteriously
found by Petrie.

To an accompaniment of clattering pans, old Mme. Dubonnet was preparing our evening meal in the kitchen, and
humming some melancholy tune very cheerily.

Petrie was a source of great anxiety. I had considered
'phoning for Dr. Cartier, but finally had dismissed the idea.
That my friend was ill he had been unable to disguise: but
he was a Doctor of Medicine and I was not. Furthermore,
he was my host.

That he was worried about his wife in Cairo, I knew. Only
the day before, he had said, "I hope she doesn't take it into
her head to come over—much as I should like to see her."
Now, I shared that hope. His present appearance would
shock the woman who loved him.

Fleurette—Fleurette of the dimpled chin—more than once
intruded her image between me and the printed page. I tried
to push these memories aside.

Fleurette was the mistress of a wealthy Egyptian. Despite
her name, she was not French. She was, perhaps, an actress.
Why had I not thought of that before? Her beautifully
modulated voice—her composure. "Think of me as Derceto. . . ."

"In *Byblis gigantea,* according to Zopf, insect-catching is
merely incipient," I read.

She could be no older than eighteen—indeed, she might
be younger than that. . . .

And so the afternoon wore on.

Faint buzzing of the Kohler engine and a sudden shaft
of light across the slopes below, first drew my attention to
approaching dusk. Petrie had turned up the laboratory
lamps.

I was deep in a German work which promised information,
and now, mechanically, I switched on the table lamp.
Hundreds of grasshoppers were chirping in the garden; I
could hear the purr of a speed-boat. Mme. Dubonnet continued to sing. It was a typical Riviera evening.

The shadow of that great crag which almost overhung the
Villa Jasmin lay across part of the kitchen-garden visible
from my window, and soon would have claimed all our tiny
domain. I continued my studies, jumping from reference to
reference and constantly consulting the index. I believed I
was at last on the right track.

How long a time elapsed between the moment when I
saw the light turned up in the laboratory and the inter-

ruption, I found great difficulty in determining afterwards. But the interruption was uncanny.

Mme. Dubonnet, working in the kitchen, French fashion, with windows hermetically sealed, noticed nothing.

Already, on this momentous day, I had heard a sound baffling description; and it was written—for the day was one never to be forgotten—that I should hear another.

As I paused to light a fresh cigarette, from somewhere outside—I thought from the Corniche road above—came a cry, very low, but penetrating.

It possessed a quality of fear which chilled me like a sudden menace. It was a sort of mournful wail on three minor notes. But a shot at close quarters could not have been more electrical in its effect.

I dropped my cigarette and jumped up.

What was it?

It was unlike anything I had ever heard. But there was danger in it, creeping peril. I leaned upon the table, staring from the window, upward in the direction from which the cry seemed to have come.

And as I did so, I saw something.

I have explained that a beam of light from the laboratory window cut across the shadow below. On the edge of this light something moved for a moment—for no more than a moment—but instantly drew my glance downward.

I looked. . . .

A pair of sunken, squinting eyes, set in a yellow face so evilly hideous that I was tempted then, and for some time later, to doubt the evidence of my senses, watched me!

Of the body belonging to this head I could see nothing; it was enveloped in shadow. I saw just that evil mask watching me; then—it was gone!

As I stood staring from the window, stupid with a kind of horrified amazement, I heard footsteps racing down the path from the road which led to the door of Villa Jasmin.

Turning, I ran out on to the veranda.

I reached it at the same moment as the new arrival—a tall, lean man, with iron-grey crisply virile hair, and keen eager eyes. He had the sort of skin which tells of years spent in the tropics. He wore no hat, but a heavy topcoat was thrown across his shoulders, cloakwise. Above all, he radiated a kind of vital energy which was intensely stimulating.

"Quick," he said—his mode of address reminded me of a machine-gun—"where is Dr. Petrie? My name is Nayland Smith."

"I'm glad you have come, Sir Denis," I replied; and indeed I spoke sincerely. "The doctor referred to you only to-day. My name is Alan Sterling."

"I know it is," he said, and shook hands briskly; then: "Where is Petrie?" he repeated. "Is he with you?"

"He is in the laboratory, Sir Denis. I'll show you the way." Sir Denis nodded, and we stepped off the veranda.

"Did you hear that awful cry?" I added.

He stopped. We had just begun to descend the slope.

"*You* heard it?" he rapped in his staccato fashion.

"I did. I have never heard anything like it in my life!"

"*I* have! Let's hurry."

There was something very strange in his manner, something which I ascribed to that wailing sound which had electrified me. Definitely, Sir Denis Nayland Smith was not a man susceptible to panic, but some fearful urgency drove him to-night.

I was about to speak of that malignant yellow face, when, as we came in sight of the lighted windows of the laboratory:

"How long has Petrie been in there?" Nayland Smith asked.

"All the afternoon. He's up to his eyes in work on these mysterious cases—about which, perhaps, you know?"

"I do," he replied. "Wait a moment."

He grasped my arm and pulled me up just at the edge of the patch of shadow. He stood still and I could tell that he was listening intently.

"Where's the door?" he asked, suddenly.

"At the farther end."

"Right."

He set off at a run, and I followed past the lighted window. Petrie was not at the table nor at the bench. I was puzzled to account for this, and, already, vaguely fearful. A premonition gripped me, a premonition of something horrible. Then, I had my hand on the door and had thrown it open. I entered, Sir Denis close behind me.

"Good God! . . . Petrie, old man. . . ."

Nayland Smith had sprung in and was already on his knees beside the doctor.

Petrie lay in the shadow of his working-bench, in fact, half under it, one outstretched hand still convulsively gripping its edge!

I saw that the apparently rigid fingers grasped a hypodermic syringe. Near to his upraised hand was a vessel

21

containing a small quantity of some milky fluid; and the tube of white powder which he had shown to me lay splintered, broken by his fall, on the floor a foot away.

In those few fleeting seconds I saw Sir Denis Nayland Smith, for the first and last time in my knowledge of him, fighting to subdue his emotions. His head dropped into his upraised hands, his fingers clutched his hair.

Then, he had conquered. He stood up.

"Lift him!" he said, hoarsely—"out here, into the light."

I was half stunned. Horror and sorrow had me by the throat. But I helped to move Petrie farther into the middle of the floor where a central light shone down upon him. One glance told me the truth—if I had ever doubted it.

A sort of cloud was creeping from his disordered hair, down over his brow.

"Heaven help him!" I whispered. "Look—look! . . . the purple shadow!"

CHAPTER V

# THE BLACK STIGMATA

THE laboratory was very silent. Through the windows which still remained open I could hear the hum of the Kohler engine in its little shed at the bottom of the garden—the chirping of crickets, the clucking of hens.

There was a couch littered with books and chemical paraphernalia. Sir Denis and I cleared it and laid Petrie there.

I had telephoned Dr. Cartier from the villa.

The ghastly purple shadow was creeping farther down my poor friend's brow.

"Shut the door, Sterling," said Nayland Smith sharply.

I did so.

"Stand by," he went on, and pointed.

Petrie, who wore a woollen pullover with long sleeves when he was working late, had evidently made an attempt to peel it off just before coma had claimed him.

"You see what he meant to do," Nayland Smith went on. "God knows what the consequences will be, but it's his only chance. He must have been fighting it off all day. The swelling in his armpit warned him that the crisis had come."

He examined the milky liquid in a small glass measure.

"Have you any idea what this *is?*"

I indicated the broken tube and scattered white powder on the floor.

"A preparation of his own—to which I have heard him refer as '654'. He believed it was a remedy, but he was afraid to risk it on a patient."

"I wonder?" Sir Denis murmured—"I wonder—"

Stooping, I picked up a fragment of glass to which one of Petrie's neatly-written labels still adhered.

"Look here, Sir Denis!"

He read aloud:

"'654'. 1 grm. in 10 c.c. distilled water: intravenous."

He stared at me hard, then:

"It's kill or cure," he rapped. "We have no choice."

"Shouldn't we wait for Dr. Cartier?"

"Wait!" His angry glare startled me. "With luck, he'll be here in three-quarters of an hour. And life or death in this thing is a matter of *minutes!* No! Petrie must have his chance. I'm not an expert—but I can do my best. . . ."

I experienced some difficulty in assisting at what followed; but Nayland Smith, his course set, made the injection as coolly as though he had been used to such work for half a lifetime. When it was done:

"If Petrie survives," he said quietly, "his own skill will have saved him—not ours. Lay that rug over him. It strikes one as chilly in here."

The man's self-mastery was almost super-human.

He crossed to close the windows—to hide his face from me. Even that iron control had its breaking-point. And suddenly the dead silence which fell with the shutting of the windows was broken by the buzzing of an insect.

I couldn't see the thing, which evidently Sir Denis had disturbed, but it was flying about the place with feverish activity. Something else seemed to have arrested Sir Denis's attention: he was staring down at the table.

"H'm!" he muttered. "Very queer!"

Then, the noise of the busy insect evidently reached his ears. He turned in a flash and his expression was remarkable.

"What's that, Sterling?" he snapped. "Do you hear it?"

"Clearly. There's a gad-fly buzzing about."

"Gad-fly—nothing! I have recently spent many hours in the laboratory of the School of Tropical Medicine. That's why I'm here! Listen. Did you ever hear a gad-fly that made that noise?"

His manner was so strange that it chilled me. I stood still, listening. And presently in the sound made by that invisible, restless insect, I detected a difference. It emitted a queer *sawing* note. I stared across at Nayland Smith.

"You've been in Uganda," he said. "Did you never hear it?"

At which moment and before I had time to reply, I caught a glimpse of the fly which caused this peculiar sound. It was smaller than I had supposed. Narrowly missing the speaker's head, it swooped down on to the table behind him, and settled upon something which lay there—something which had already attracted Sir Denis's attention.

"Don't move," I whispered. "It's just behind you."

"Get it," he replied, in an equally low tone. "A book, a roll of paper—anything; but for God's sake don't miss it. . . ."

I took up a copy of *La Revue de Monte-Carlo*. One of poor Petrie's hobbies was a roulette system which he had never succeeded in perfecting. I rolled it and stepped quietly forward.

Nayland Smith stood quite still. Beside him, my improvised swatter raised, I saw the insect distinctly. It had long, narrow, brownish wings and a curiously hairy head. In the very moment that I dashed the roll of paper down I recognized the object upon which it had settled.

It was a spray of that purple-leaved *drosophyllum*, identical, except that it was freshly cut, with a fragment which I knew to be sealed in a tube somewhere in Petrie's collection!

"Make sure," said Sir Denis, turning.

I repeated the blow. Behind us, on the couch, Petrie lay motionless. Sir Denis bent over the dead insect.

"Don't you know what this is, Sterling?" he demanded.

"No. Flies are a bit outside my province. But I can tell you something about the purple leaves."

Taking the roll of paper from me, he moved the dead fly farther forward upon the polished table-top where direct light fell upon it; then:

"Hullo!" he exclaimed.

He snatched up a lens which lay near by and bent over the insect, peering down absorbedly.

I turned and looked towards the couch where Petrie lay, and I studied his haggard features. I could detect no evidence of life. The purple shadow showed like a bruise on his forehead; but I thought that it had not increased.

Yet, I believed he was doomed, already dying, and my

thoughts jumped feverishly to that strange plant upon the table—and from the plant to the yellow face which so recently had leered at me out of the darkness.

Was it conceivable—could it be—that some *human agency* directed this pestilence?

I turned, looking beyond the bent, motionless figure of Nayland Smith, out into the dusk—and a desire to close the steel shutters suddenly possessed me.

This operation I completed without drawing a single comment from Sir Denis. But, as that menacing dusk was shut out, he stood upright and confronted me.

"Sterling," he said, and there was something in his steady gaze which definitely startled me—"have you, as a botanist, ever come across a true *genus-hybrid?*"

"You mean a thing between a lily and a rose—or an oak growing apples?"

"Exactly."

"In a natural state, never—although some curious hybrids have been reported from time to time. But many freaks of this kind can be *cultivated,* of course. The Japanese are experts."

"Cultivated? I agree. But Nature, in my experience, sticks to the common law. Now here, Sterling"—he indicated the table—"lies an insect which, from the sound it made when flying, I took to be a *tsetse fly—*"

"A *tsetse?* Good heavens! *Here?*"

He smiled grimly.

"Well outside its supposed area," he admitted, "and above its usual elevation. I thought you might have recognized its note, as you have travelled in the fly-belt. However, I was right—up to a point. It definitely possesses certain characteristics of *glossina,* the *tsetse* fly! notably, the wings, which are typical. You see, I have been taking an intensive course of this subject! But can you imagine, Sterling, that it has the legs and head of an incredibly large *sand-fly?* The thing is a nightmare, an anachronism; it's a sort of giant *flying flea!*"

His words awakened a memory. What had Petrie said to me, earlier in the day? . . . that "even if Nature is turning topsy-turvy I think I can puzzle her! . . ."

"Sir Denis," I broke in, "I think you should know that Petrie found, in the blood of a patient, some similar freak—a sort of hybrid germ, which I lack the knowledge to describe to you. He found Sleeping sickness and Plague combined—"

"Good God!"

I thought that that lean, sun-baked face momentarily grew yet more angular.

"You know," he interrupted, "that *tsetse* carries Sleeping sickness? Sand-fly is suspect in several directions. But the rat-flea (and this is more like a flea than a sand-fly) is the proved cause of Plague infection. . . . Am I going mad?"

He suddenly crossed and bent over Petrie. He examined him carefully and in detail. The fact dawned upon me that Sir Denis Nayland Smith had more than a smattering of the medical art. I watched in silence whilst finally he took the temperature of the unconscious man.

"There's no change," he reported. " '654' seems already to have checked its progress. But this coma. . . . Dare we hope?"

"I don't know what to hope, or what to believe, Sir Denis!"

He nodded.

"Nor do I. The nature of my job forced me to pick up some elements of medicine; but this is a specialist's case. However, tell me about these leaves—the leaves which seemed to attract the fly. . . ."

I told him briefly all that I knew of the insect-catching plant.

"The specimen which Petrie has preserved," I concluded, "bears traces of human blood."

Sir Denis suddenly grabbed the lens again and bent over the purple leaves on the table-top. A moment he looked, then turned.

"So does this!" he declared. "*Fresh* blood."

I was dumb for a matter of seconds; then:

"The insect which I partly crushed?" I suggested.

He shook his head irritably.

"Quantity too great. These leaves have been *sprayed* with blood!"

"How, in heaven's name, did they get here? And how did the damnable fly get here?"

He suddenly clapped his hands upon my shoulders, and stared at me fixedly.

"You're a man of strong nerve, Sterling," he said, "and so I can tell you. They were *brought here*. And"—he pointed to the still body on the couch—"for *that* purpose."

"But—"

"There are no 'buts'. I left the car in which I had been driven over from Cannes some distance back on the road to-night, and walked ahead to look for this villa, the exact

location of which my driver didn't know. I had nearly
reached the way in, when I heard a sound."

"I heard it too."

"I know you did. But to you it meant nothing—except
that it was horrible; to me, it meant a lot. You see, I had
heard it before."

"What was it? I shall never forget it!"

"It was the signal used by certain Burmans, loosely known
as *dacoits*, to give warning one to another. If poor old Petrie
had come across this new species of *tsetse* fly—he would
have begun to think. If he had heard that cry . . . he
would have *known!*

"He would have known what?" I asked, aware of a growing excitement communicated to me by the speaker.

"He would have known what he was up against." He
raised his fists in a gesture almost of despair. "We are chil-
dren!" he exclaimed vehemently, momentarily taken out of
himself. "What do you know of botany, and what does
Petrie know of medicine beside Dr. Fu Manchu!"

"Dr. Fu Manchu?" I echoed.

"A synonym for Satan—evil immutable; apparently eternal."

"Sir Denis," I began—

But he turned aside, abruptly, bending again over the
motionless body of his old friend.

"Poor Kâramanèh!" he murmured.

He was silent awhile, then, without looking around:

"Do you know his wife, Sterling?" he asked.

"No, Sir Denis; we have never met—"

"She is still young, as we count years to-day. She was a
child when Petrie married her—and she is the most beautiful
woman I have ever known. . . ."

As he spoke I seemed to hear a soft voice saying, "Think
of me as Derceto" . . . Fleurette. Fleurette was the most
beautiful woman I had ever *seen.* . . .

"She was chosen by a Master—who rarely makes mis-
takes."

His manner and his words were so strange, that I may
be forgiven for misunderstanding.

"A master? Do you mean a painter?"

At that, he turned, and smiled. His smile was the most
boyish and disarming I had ever met with in a grown man.

"Yes, Sterling, a painter! His canvas, the world; his
colours, the human races. . . ."

This was mystery capping mystery, and certainly I should

27

never have left the matter there; but at this moment we were interrupted by a series of short staccato shrieks.

I ran to the door. I had recognized the voice.

"Who is it?" Sir Denis snapped.

"Mme. Dubonnet."

"Housekeeper?"

"Yes."

"Keep her out."

I threw the door open and the terrified woman tottered into my arms.

"M. Sterling," she panted, hysterically—"something terrible has happened! I know, I know—something terrible has happened!"

"Don't worry, Mme. Dubonnet," I said, and endeavoured to lead her away. "Dr. Petrie—"

"But I must tell the doctor—it concerns him. As I looked up from my casserole dish I see at the window just above me—a face—a dreadful yellow face with cross eyes. . . ."

"Rather a quandary, Sterling," Sir Denis cut in, standing squarely between the excited woman and the insensible man on the couch. "One of those murderous devils is hanging about the place. . . ."

Dimly I heard the sound of an insistent motor horn on the Corniche road above, nearing the head of that narrow by-way debouched from the Corniche which led down to the Villa Jasmin.

"The ambulance from the hospital!" Sir Denis exclaimed in relief.

## CHAPTER VI

### " 6 5 4 "

MME. DUBONNET, still shaking nervously, was escorted back to her quarters. Petrie, we told her, was down with a severe attack of influenza and must be moved immediately. The appearance of the yellow face at the window, mendacity had failed to explain; and the old lady announced that she would lock herself in the kitchen until such time as someone could take her home.

She was left lamenting—"Oh, the poor, dear kind doctor! ..."

Cartier had come in person, with two orderlies and a driver. The bearded, round-faced little man exhibited such perfect consternation on beholding Dr. Petrie, that it must have been funny had it not been tragic. He dropped to his knees, bending over the insensible man.

"The *black stigmata!*" he muttered, touching the purple-shadowed brow—"I am too late! The coma. Soon—in an hour, or less, the final convulsions . . . the end! God! it is terrible. He is a dead man!"

"I'm not so sure," Sir Denis interrupted. "Forgive me, doctor; my name is Nayland Smith. I have ventured to give an injection—"

Dr. Cartier stood up excitedly.

"What injection?" he demanded.

"I don't know," Sir Denis replied, calmly.

"What is this?"

"I don't know. I used a preparation of Petrie's which he called '654'."

" '654'!"

Dr. Cartier dropped upon his knees again beside the insensible man.

"How long," he demanded, "since the shadow appeared?"

"Difficult to say, doctor," I replied. "He was alone here. But it hasn't increased."

"How long since the injection?"

Nayland Smith shot out a lean brown wrist and glanced at a gun-metal watch in a leather strap.

"Forty-three minutes," he reported.

Cartier sprang to his feet again.

"Dr. Smith!" he cried excitedly—and I saw Sir Denis suppress a smile—"this is triumph! From the time that the *ecchymosis* appears, it never ceases to creep down to the eyes! It has remained static for forty-three minutes, you tell me? This is triumph!"

"Let us dare to hope so," said Sir Denis gravely.

When all arrangements had been completed and the good Dr. Cartier had grasped the astounding fact that Nayland Smith was not a confrère but a super-policeman:

"It's very important," Sir Denis whispered to me, "that this place be watched to-night. We have to take into consideration"—he gripped my arm—"the possibility that they may fail to save Petrie. The formula for '654' *must* be somewhere here!"

But we had searched for it in vain; nor was it on his person.

The driver of the car in which Sir Denis had come, agreed, on terms, to mount guard over the laboratory. He remained in ignorance of the nature of Petrie's illness; but Dr. Cartier assured us there was no danger of direct infection at this stage.

And so, poor Petrie having been rushed to the isolation ward, Nayland Smith going with the ambulance, I drove Mme. Dubonnet home, leaving the chauffeur from Cannes on guard. Returning, I gave the man freedom of the dinner which Fate had decreed that Petrie and I were not to eat, lent him a repeater, and set out in turn for the hospital.

This secret war against the strange plague, which threatened to strip the Blue Coast of visitors and prosperity, had aroused the enthusiasm of the whole of that small hospital staff.

Petrie, with other sufferers from the new pestilence, was lodged in an outbuilding separated from the hospital proper by a stretch of waste land. A porter, after some delay, led me through this miniature wilderness to the door of the isolation ward. The low building was dominated by a clump of pines.

A nursing sister admitted me, conducting me in silence along a narrow passage to Petrie's room.

As I entered, and the sister withdrew, I saw at a glance the cause of the suppressed feverish excitement which I had detected even in the bearing of the lodge porter.

Dr. Cartier was in tears. He was taking the pulse of the unconscious man. Nayland Smith, standing beside him, nodded to me reassuringly as I came in.

The purple shadow on Petrie's brow had encroached no farther—indeed, as I thought, was already dispersing!

Dr. Cartier replaced his watch and raised clasped hands.

"He is doing well," said Sir Denis. " '654' is the remedy . . . but what, exactly, is '654'?"

"We must know!" cried Dr. Cartier emotionally. "Thanks to the good God, he will revive from the coma and can tell us. We must know! There is no more that I or any man can do now. But Sister Thérèse is a treasure among nurses, and if there should be a development, she will call me immediately. I shall be here in three minutes. But to-morrow? What can we do? We must know!"

"I agree," said Sir Denis quietly. "Don't worry any more about it. I think you are about to win a great victory. I hope,

as I have told you, to recover a copy of the formula for
'654'—and as Dr. Petrie's safety is of such vital importance,
you have no objections to offer to my plan?"

"But none!" Cartier replied. "Except that this seems unnecessary."

"I never take needless risks," said Sir Denis drily.

But when Cartier was gone:

"I am going into Nice," Sir Denis said, "now, to put a
'phone call through to London."

"What!"

"There's a definite connexion, Sterling, between the appearance in Petrie's laboratory of a new species of tropical
fly at the same time as an unfamiliar tropical plant—the
latter bloodstained!"

"So much is obvious."

"The connecting link is the Burmese *dacoit* whom I heard,
and you and Mme. Dubonnet saw. He was the servant of a
dreadful master."

A question burned on my tongue, but:

"Sister Thérèse is all that Cartier claims for her—I have
interviewed the sister. She will attend to the patient from
time to time. But I'm going to ask you to do something,
Sterling, for me, and for Petrie."

"Anything you like. Just say the word."

"You see, Sterling, since Petrie left London and came here,
he had kept in close touch with Sir Manston Rorke, of the
School of Tropical Medicine—one of the three big names,
although I doubt if he knows more than Petrie. Some days
ago, Sir Manston called me up. He had formed a remarkable
opinion."

"What about?"

"About the French epidemic. Two cases, showing identical symptoms, occurred in the London dock area, and he
had had news of several in New York, and of one in Sydney,
Australia. Having personally examined the London cases
(both of which terminated fatally) he had come to the conclusion that this disease was not an ordinary plague. Briefly,
he believed that it was being induced artificially!"

"Good heavens, Sir Denis! I begin to believe he was right."

Nayland Smith nodded.

"I invited him to suggest a motive, and he wavered between a mad scientist and a Red plot to decimate unfriendly
nations! In my opinion, he wasn't far short of the truth; but
here's the big point: I have reason to believe that Petrie

submitted to Sir Manston the formula for '654'—and I'm going into Nice to call him up."

"God grant he has it," I said, glancing at the bed where the sick man lay.

"Amen to that. But in the meantime, Sterling—I may be away two hours or more—it's vitally important that Petrie should not be alone for one moment."

"I quite follow."

"So I want you to stand by here until I get back. What I mean is this—I want you to sit tight beside his bed."

"I understand. You may count on me."

He stared at me fixedly. There was something almost hypnotic in that penetrating look.

"Sterling," he said, "you are dealing with an enemy more cunning and more brilliant than any man you have ever met East or West. Until I return you are not to allow a soul to *touch* Petrie—except Sister Thérèse, or Cartier."

I was startled by his vehemence.

"It may be difficult," I suggested.

"I agree that it may be difficult; but it has to be done. Can I rely upon you?"

"Absolutely."

"I'm going to dash away now, to put a call through to Manston Rorke. I only pray that he is in London, and that I can locate him."

He raised his hand in a sort of salute to the insensible man, turned, and went out.

CHAPTER VII

## IVORY FINGERS

I THOUGHT of many things during the long vigil that followed. The isolation ward harboured six patients, but Petrie had been given accommodation in a tiny private room at one end. The corresponding room at the other end was the sanctum of Sister Thérèse.

It was a lonely spot, and very silent. I heard the Sister moving about in the adjoining ward, and presently she entered quietly, a fragile little woman, her pale face looking childishly small framed in the stiff white headdress of her order. Deftly and all but noiselessly she went about her duties; and, watching her, I wondered, as I had often wondered before, whence came the unquestioning faith which upheld such as Sister Thérèse and in which they found adequate reward for a life of service.

"You are not afraid of infection, M. Sterling?" she asked, her voice very low and gentle.

"Not at all, Sister. In *my* job I have to risk it."

"What do you do?"

"Hunt for new species of plants for the Botanical Society— and orchids for the market."

"But how fascinating! As a matter of fact, there is no danger of infection at this stage."

"So I am told by Dr. Cartier."

"It is new to us, this disease. But it is tragic that Dr. Petrie should fall a victim. However, as you see—"

She pointed.

"The *stigmata?*"

Sister Thérèse shuddered.

"It is so irreligious! But Dr. Cartier, I know, calls this mark the *black stigmata*. Yes—it does not increase. Dr. Petrie may conquer. He is a wonderful man. You will moisten his poor lips from time to time? I am praying that he may be spared to us. Good night, M. Sterling. Ring for me if he moves."

She withdrew in her gentle, silent way, leaving me to my thoughts. And by some queer mental alchemy these became transmuted into thoughts of Fleurette. I found myself contemplating in a sort of cold horror, the idea of Fleurette infected with this foul plague—her delicate beauty marred, her strong young body contorted by the work of some loathsome, unclassified bacillus.

And then, I fell to thinking about those who had contracted this thing, and to considering what Nayland Smith had told me. What association was there, to explain a common enmity, between London dock labourers and Dr. Petrie?

I stared at him as the thought crossed my mind. One of the strangest symptoms of this horror which threatened France was the period of complete coma preceding the end. Petrie looked like a dead man.

A searching wind, coming down from the Alps, had begun to blow at sunset. The pines, some of which almost overhung the lonely building, hushed and whispered insidiously.

I construed their whispering into a repetition of the words 'Fleurette—Derceto. . . .'

If dear old Petrie survived the crisis, I told myself, to-morrow should find me once more on the beach of Ste. Claire de la Roche. I might have misjudged Fleurette. Even if she were the mistress of Mahdi Bey, she was very young and so not past praying for.

I had just formed this resolution when a new sound intruded upon the silence of the sick room.

There was only one window—high in the wall which marked the end of the place. As I sat near the foot of Petrie's bed, this window was above, on my left.

And the sound, a faint scraping, seemed to come from there.

I listened to the hushing of the pines, thinking that the wind had grown higher and that some out-stretched branch must be touching the wall. But the wind seemed to have decreased, and the whisper, "Fleurette—Derceto" had become a sigh scarcely audible.

Raising my head, I looked up. . . .

A yellow hand, the fingers crooked in a clutching movement—a threat it seemed—showed for a moment, then disappeared, outside the window!

Springing to my feet, I stared wildly. How long had I been sitting there, dreaming, since Sister Thérèse had gone? I had no idea. My imagination pictured such an evil, mask-like face as I had seen at the Villa Jasmin—peering in at that high window.

One of the *dacoits* (the name was vaguely familiar, although I had never been in Burma) referred to by Nayland Smith, must be watching the place!

Was this what he had feared? Was this why I had been left on guard?

What did it mean?

I could not believe that Dr. Petrie had ever wronged any man. Who, then, was hounding him to death, and what was his motive?

Literally holding my breath, I listened. But there was no repetition of the scraping sound. The climber—the window was twelve feet above ground level—had dropped silently at the moment that I had sprung from my chair.

To rush out and search was obviously not in orders. My job was to sit tight. I was pledged to it.

But the incident had painted a new complexion on my duties.

I watched that high window keenly, and for a long time. Then, as I was on the point of sitting down, a slight sound brought me upright at a bound. I realized that my nerves were badly overtuned.

The door opened and Sister Thérèse came in, in her unobtrusive, almost apologetic way.

"A lady has called to see Dr. Petrie," she said.

"To see Dr. Petrie!"

"How could I refuse her, M. Sterling?" Sister Thérèse asked, gently. "She is his wife!" The little Sister glanced wistfully at the unconscious man. "And she is such a beautiful woman."

"Great heavens!" I groaned—"this is going to be almost unendurable. Is she very—disturbed, Sister?"

Sister Thérèse shook her head, smiling sadly.

"Not at all. She has great courage."

Just as poor Petrie had feared—his wife had come from Cairo—to find him . . . a doomed man.

"I suppose she must come in. But his appearance will be a frightful shock to her."

Anticipating a tragic interview, I presently turned to meet Mrs. Petrie, as Sister Thérèse showed her into the room. She was, I saw, tall and slender, having an indolent grace of bearing totally different from affectation. She was draped in a long wrap of some dark fur beneath which showed the edge of a green dress. Bare, ivory ankles peeped below its fringe, and she wore high-heeled green sandals with gold straps.

She had features of almost classic chiselling and perfectly moulded lips. But her eyes were truly remarkable. They were incredibly long, of the true almond shape and brilliant as jewels. By reason of the fact that Mrs. Petrie wore a little green beret-like hat set on one side of her glossy head, from which depended a figured gold veil, I could not determine the exact colour of those strange eyes: the veil just covered them.

Her complete self-posesssion reassured me. She glanced at Petrie, and then, as Sister Thérèse silently retired:

"It is very good of you, Mr. Sterling," she said—and her voice had an indolent, soothing quality in keeping with her personality—"to allow me to make this visit."

She seated herself in a chair which I placed for her beside Petrie's bed.

So this was "Kâramanèh"? I had not forgotten that strange name murmured by Nayland Smith as he had bent over

Petrie. "The most beautiful woman I have ever known. . . ."

And that Mrs. Petrie was beautiful none could deny; yet for some reason her appearance surprised me. I had not been prepared for a woman of this type. Truth to tell, although I didn't recognize the fact then, I had subconsciously given to Mrs. Petrie the attributes of Fleurette—a flower-like, tender loveliness wholly removed from the patrician yet exotic elegance of this woman who sat looking at the unconscious man.

Having heard of her passionate love for the doctor, I was surprised, too, by her studied self-possession. It was admirable, but, in a devoted wife, almost uncanny.

"I could do no less, Mrs. Petrie," I replied. "It is very brave of you to come."

She was bending forward, watching the sick man.

"Is there—any hope?" she asked.

"There is every hope, Mrs. Petrie. In other cases which the doctors have met with, the appearance of the purple shadow has meant the end—"

"But in this case?"

She looked at me, her wonderful eyes so bright that I thought she was suppressing tears.

"In Petrie's case, the progress of the disease has been checked—temporarily at any rate."

"How wonderful," she whispered—"and how strange."

She bent over him again. Her movements were feline in their indolent grace. One slender ivory hand held the cloak in place; the long nails were varnished to a jewel-like brightness. I wondered how these two had met, and how such markedly different types had ever become lovers.

Mrs. Petrie raised her eyes to me again.

"Is Dr. Cartier following some different treatment in—my husband's case?"

The nearly imperceptible pause had not escaped me. I supposed that a wave of emotion had threatened to overcome her when she found that name upon her lips and realized that the man himself tottered on the brink of the Valley.

"Yes, Mrs. Petrie; a treatment of your husband's known as '654'."

"Prepared, I suppose, by Dr. Cartier?"

"No—prepared by Petrie himself just before he was seized with illness."

"But Dr. Cartier, of course, knows the formula?"

That caressing voice possessed some odd quality of final-

ity; it was like listening to Fate speaking. Not to reply to
any question so put to one would have been a task akin to
closing one's ears to the song of the Sirens. And the darkly
fringed eyes, which, now, owing to some accident of reflected light, I thought were golden, emphasized the soft
command.

Indeed, I was on the point of answering truthfully, that
no one but Petrie knew the formula, when an instinct of
compassion gave me strength to defy that powerful urge.
Why should I admit so cruel a truth?

"I cannot say," I replied, and knew that I spoke the words
unnaturally.

"But of course it will be somewhere in my husband's possession? No doubt in his laboratory?"

Her anxiety—although there was no trace of tremor in her
velvety tones—was nevertheless unmistakable.

"No doubt, Mrs. Petrie," I said reassuringly—and spoke
now with greater conviction since I really believed that the
formula must be somewhere among Petrie's papers.

She murmured something in a low voice—and standing
up, moved to the head of the bed.

Whereupon, my difficulties began. For, as Mrs. Petrie
bent over the pillow, I remembered the charge which had
been put upon me, remembered Nayland Smith's words:
"You are not to allow a soul to *touch* him—"

I got up swiftly, stepped around the foot of the bed, and
joined Mrs. Petrie where she stood.

"Whatever you do," I said, "don't touch him!"

Slowly, she stood upright; infinitely slowly and gracefully.
She turned, and looked into my eyes.

"Why?" she asked.

"Because—" I hesitated: what could I say? "Because of
the possibility of infection."

"Please don't worry about that, Mr. Sterling. There is no
possibility of infection, at this stage. Sister Thérèse told me
so."

"But she may be wrong." I urged. "Really, I can't allow
you to take the risk."

Perhaps my principles ride me to death; I have been told
that they do. But I had pledged my word that no one
should touch Petrie, and I meant to stick to it. Logically, I
could think of no reason why this woman who loved him
should not stroke his hair, as I thought she had been about
to do. It was almost inhuman to forbid it. Yet by virtue of
Sir Denis's trust in me, forbid it I must.

"It may be difficult," I remembered saying to him. *How* difficult it was to be, I had not foreseen!

"Surely," she said—and her soft voice held no note of anger—"the risk is mine?"

Mrs. Petrie bent again over the pillow. She was on the point of resting those slender, indolent hands on Petrie's shoulders.

She intended, I surmised, to kiss his parched lips. . . .

## CHAPTER VIII

## "BEWARE—"

As those languorous ivory hands almost rested on Petrie's shoulders, and full red lips were but inches removed from the parched, blue lips of the unconscious man, I threw my arms around Mrs. Petrie and dragged her away!

She was light and resilient as a professional dancer. I had been forced to exert considerable strength because of her nearness to the doctor. She was swept back, lying against my left arm and looking up at me in a startled, yet imperious way, which prepared me to expect an uncomfortable sequel.

During one long moment she remained motionless, our glances meeting. Her cloak had slipped, exposing a bare arm and shoulder. I was partly supporting her, and trying frenziedly to find words to excuse my apparent violence. When, still looking up at me, she turned slightly.

"Why did you do that?" she asked. "Was it . . . to save me from contagion?"

The cue was a welcome one; I seized it gladly.

"Of course!" I replied, but knew that my assurance rang false; "I warned you that I should not allow you to touch him."

She continued to watch me, resting in the crook of my arm; and I had never experienced such vile impulses as those which goaded me during those few seconds. The most singular promptings were dancing in my brain. I thought she was offering me her lips, or rather, challenging me to reject the offer. With a movement so slight that it might have been accidental, she seemed to invite me to caress her.

Yes, the most utterly damnable thing. I, in whose blood there runs a marked streak of Puritanism, I, with poor Petrie lying there in the grip of a dread disease, suddenly wanted to crush this woman—his wife—in my arms!

It was only a matter of hours since I had met Fleurette on the beach of Ste. Clare de la Roche, and had become so infatuated with her beauty and charm that I had been thinking about her almost continuously ever since. Yet here I stood fighting against a sudden lawless desire for the wife of my best friend—a desire so wild that it threatened to swamp everything—friendship, tradition, honour!

Perhaps I might have conquered—unaided; I am not prepared to say. But aid came to me, and came in the form of what I thought at the time to be a miracle. As I looked down into those enigmatical, mocking eyes, in a silence only broken by the hushing of the pines outside the window—a voice—a groaning hollow voice, a voice that might have issued from a tomb—spoke.

"Beware . . . *of her*," it said.

Mrs. Petrie sprang back. A fleeting glimpse I had of stark horror in the long, narrow eyes. My heart, which had been beating madly, seemed to stop for a moment.

I twisted my head aside, staring down at Petrie.

Was it imagination—or did I detect a faint quivering of those swollen eyelids? Could it be *he* had spoken? That slight movement, if it had ever been, had ceased. He lay still as the dead.

"Who was it?" Mrs. Petrie whispered, her patrician calm ruffled at last—"whose voice was that?"

I stared at her. The spell was broken. The glamour of those bewitched moments had faded—dismissed by that sepulchral voice. Mrs. Perie's lashes now veiled her long, brilliant eyes. One hand was clenched, the other hidden beneath her cloak. My ideas performed a complete about-turn. Some hidden, inexplicable madness had possessed me; from the consequences of which I had been saved by an act of God!

"I don't know," I said hoarsely. "I don't know. . . ."

CHAPTER IX

# FAH LO SUEE

THE end of that interview is hazy in my memory. Concerning one detail, however, I have no doubt: Mrs. Petrie did not again approach the sick man's bed. Despite her wonderful self-discipline, she could not entirely hide her apprehension. I detected her casting swift glances at Petrie and—once—upward towards the solitary window.

That awful warning, so mysteriously spoken—could have related only to *her*. . . .

I rang for Sister Thérèse and arranged that the night concierge should conduct the visitor to her car. I suspected that the neighbourhood was none too safe.

Mrs. Petrie gave me the address of an hotel in Cannes, asking that she be kept in touch. She would return, she said, unless summoned earlier, at eight in the morning. She had fully regained her graceful composure by this time, and I found myself wondering what her true nationality could be. Her languid calm was hard to reconcile with wifely devotion: indeed I had expected her to insist upon remaining.

And when, with a final glance at Petrie and an enigmatical smile at me, she went out with Sister Thérèse, I turned and stared at the doctor. I could detect no change whatever, except that it seemed to me that the purple shadow on his brow was not so dark.

Could it be he who had spoken?

His face was dreadfully haggard, looking almost emaciated, and his lips, dry and cracked, were slightly parted so as to expose his teeth. In that unnatural smile I thought I saw the beginning of the death grin which characterized this ghastly pestilence.

He did not move, nor could I detect him breathing. I glanced at the window, high above my head, where not so long before I had seen those crooked yellow fingers. But it showed as a black patch in the dull white mass of the wall.

The pines began whispering softly again: "Fleurette—Derceto. . . ."

40

If Petrie had not spoken—and I found it hard to believe that he had—whose was the voice which had uttered the words "Beware . . . of her?"

I had ample time to consider the problem and many others as well which had arisen in the course of that eventful day. Dr. Cartier looked in at about eleven o'clock, and Sister Thérèse made regular visits.

There was no change to be noted in Petrie's condition.

It was a dreary vigil, in fact an eerie one. For company I had an apparently dead man, and some of the most horrible memories which one could very well conjure up as a background for that whispering silence.

At some time shortly after midnight I heard swift footsteps coming along the passage which led to Petrie's room. The door opened and Nayland Smith walked in.

One glance warned me that something was amiss.

He crossed and stared down at Petrie in silence, then, turning to Sister Thérèse, who had entered close behind him:

"I wonder, sister," he said rapidly, "if I might ask you to remain here until Dr. Cartier arrives, and allow Mr. Sterling and myself the use of your room?"

"But of course, with the greatest pleasure," she replied, and smiled in her sweet, patient way.

Together we went along the narrow corridor and presently came to that little room used by the nurse on duty. It was very simple and very characteristic.

There was a glass-fronted cabinet containing medicines, dressings and surgical appliances. Beside a little white table was placed a very hard, white enamelled chair. An open book lay on the table; and the only decoration was a crucifix on the distempered wall.

Sir Denis did not speak for a moment, but paced restlessly to and fro in that confined space, twitching at the lob of his ear—a habit which I later came to recognize as indicative of deep thought.

Suddenly he turned and faced me.

"Sir Manston Rorke died early yesterday morning," he said, "from an overdose of heroin or something of the kind!"

"What!"

I had been seated on the edge of the little table, but at that I sprang up. Sir Denis nodded grimly.

"But was he—addicted to drugs?"

"Apparently. He was a widower who lived alone in a flat in Curzon Street. There was only one resident servant—a man who had been with him for many years."

41

"It's Fate," I groaned. "What a ghastly coincidence!"

"Coincidence!" Sir Denis snapped. "There's no coincidence! Sir Manston's consulting rooms in Wimpole Street, where he kept all his records and pursued his studies, were burgled during the night. I assume that they found what they had come for. A large volume containing prescriptions is missing."

"But, if they found what they came for—"

"That was good enough," he interrupted. "Hence my assumption that they did. Sir Manston had a remarkable memory. Having destroyed the prescription book, the next thing was to destroy . . . that inconvenient memory!"

"You mean—he was *murdered?*"

"I have little doubts on that point," Sir Denis replied harshly. "The butler has been detained—but there's small hope of learning anything from him, even if he knows. But I gather, Sterling"—he fixed a penetrating stare upon me—"that a similar attempt was made here, to-night."

"*Here?* Whatever do you mean, Sir Denis?"

But even as I spoke the words, I thought I knew, and:

"Why, of course!" I cried—"the *dacoit!*"

"*Dacoit,*" he rapped. "What *dacoit?*"

"You don't know? But, on second thoughts, how could you know! It was shortly after you left. Someone looked in at the window of Petrie's room—"

"Looked in?" He glanced up at the corresponding window of Sister Thérèse's room. "It's twelve feet above ground level."

"I know. Nevertheless, someone looked in. I heard a faint scuffling—and I was just in time to catch a glimpse of a yellow hand as the man dropped back."

"Yellow hand?" Sir Denis laughed shortly. "Our cross-eyed friend from the Villa Jasmin, Sterling! He was spying out the land. Shortly after this, I suggest, the *lady* arrived?"

I stared at him in surprise.

"You are quite right. I suppose Sister Thérèse told you? Mrs. Petrie came a few minutes afterwards."

"Describe her," he directed tersely.

Startled by his manner, I did my best to comply when:

"She has green eyes," he broke in.

"I couldn't swear to it. Her veil obscured her eyes."

"They are green," he affirmed confidently. "Her skin is the colour of ivory and she has slender indolent hands. She is as graceful as a leopardess, of the purring of which treacherous creature her voice surely reminded you?"

Sir Denis's sardonic humour completed my bewilderment. Recalling the almost tender way in which he had spoken the words, "Poor Kâramanèh," I found it impossible to reconcile those tones with the savagery of his present manner.

"I'm afraid you puzzle me," I confessed. "I quite understood that you held Mrs. Petrie in the highest esteem."

"So I do," he snapped. "But we are not talking about Mrs. Petrie!"

"Not talking about Mrs. Petrie! But—"

"The lady who favoured you with a visit to-night, Sterling, is known as Fah Lo Suee (I don't know why). She is the daughter of the most dangerous man living to-day, East or West—Dr. Fu Manchu!"

"But, Sir Denis!"

He suddenly grasped my shoulders, staring into my eyes.

"No one can blame you if you have been duped, Sterling. You thought you were dealing with Petrie's wife: it was a stroke of daring genius on the part of the enemy—"

He paused; but his look asked the question.

"I refused to permit her to touch him, nevertheless," I said.

Sir Denis's expression changed. His brown, eager face lighted up.

"Good man!" he said, in a low voice, and squeezed my shoulders, then dropped his hands. "Good man."

It was mild enough as appreciation goes, yet somehow I valued those words more highly than a decoration.

"Did she mention my name?"

"No."

"Did you?"

I thought awhile, and then:

"No," I replied. "I am positive on the point."

"Good!" he muttered, and began to pace up and down again. "There's just a chance—just a chance *he* has overlooked me. Tell me, omitting no detail that you recall, exactly what took place."

To the best of my ability, I did as he directed.

He interrupted me once only: when I spoke of that sepulchral warning—

"Where was the woman when you heard it?" he rapped.

"Practically in my arms. I had just dragged her back."

"The voice was impossible to identify?"

"Quite."

"And you could not swear to the fact that Petrie's lips moved?"

"No. It was a fleeting impression, no more."

"It was after this episode that she subjected you to her hypnotic tricks?"

"Hypnotic tricks!"

"Yes—you have narrowly escaped, Sterling."

"You refer," I said with some embarrassment, for I had been perfectly frank—"to my strange impulses?"

He nodded.

"No. It was the voice which broke the spell."

He twitched his ear for some moments, then:

"Go on!" he rapped.

And when I had come to the end.

"You got off lightly," he said, "She is as dangerous as a poised cobra! And now, I have another job for you."

"I'm ready."

"Hurry back to Villa Jasmin—and call me up here if all's well there. Have you a gun?"

"No. I lent mine to the chauffeur."

"Take this." He drew an automatic from his topcoat pocket.

"Drive like hell and shoot if necessary. You are a marked man."

As I hurried out, Dr. Cartier hurried in.

"Ah!" Nayland Smith exclaimed. "I regret troubling you, doctor; but I want you to examine Petrie very carefully—"

"What! there is some change?"

"I don't know. That's what I want you to find out."

## CHAPTER X

## GREEN EYES

THE two-seater which had been placed at Petrie's disposal was no beauty, but the engine was fairly reliable, and I set out along the Corniche about as fast as it is safe to travel along such a tortuous road.

I suppose it had taken me a ridiculously long time to grasp the crowning horror which lay behind this black business. As I swung around the dangerous curves of that route, the parapet broken in many places and the mirror of the Mediterranean lying far below on the right, my brain grew very active.

The discovery of a fly-catching plant near the place where a man had been seized by this frightful infection, coupled with our finding later a similar specimen in Petrie's laboratory, had suggested pretty pointedly that human agency was at work. Yet, somehow, in spite of the apparition of that grinning, yellow face in the kitchen-garden of the villa, I had not been able to realize, or not been able to believe, that human agency was actually *directing* the pestilence.

Sir Denis Nayland Smith had adjusted my perspective. Someone, apparently a shadowy being known as Fu Manchu, was responsible for these outbreaks!

And the woman who had posed as Petrie's wife, the woman who had tried, and all but succeeded in her attempt, to bewitch me, was of the flesh and blood of this fiend. She was Chinese; and her mission had been—what?

To poison Petrie—as Sir Manston Rorke had been poisoned?

As I swung into the lighted tunnel cut through the rock, I laughed aloud when that seeming absurdity presented itself to my mind.

A new disease had appeared in the world. Yes; of this, I had had painful evidence. It was possibly due, according to Sir Denis, to the presence in France of an unfamiliar fly—what he had called a genus-hybrid.

So much I was prepared to admit.

But how could any man be responsible for the appearance of such an insect, anywhere and at any time; much less in such widely separated places as those which had been visited by the epidemic?

The Purple Shadow. . . .

I had nearly reached the end of the rock cutting. There was a dangerous corner just ahead; and I had allowed my thoughts to wander rather wide of the job in hand. A big car, a Rolls-Royce, appeared suddenly. The driver—some kind of African as I saw—was taking so much of the road on the bend that no room was left for me.

Jamming on the brakes, I had pulled close in against the wall of the tunnel . . . and I acted only just in time.

The driver of the Rolls checked slightly and swept right—missing me by six inches or less!

I had a clear, momentary view of the occupants of the car which had so nearly terminated my immediate interest in affairs. . . .

How long I stayed there after the beautiful black and silver thing had purred away into the darkness, I don't know. But I remember turning round and staring over the folded, dusty hood in a vain attempt to read the number.

The car had two occupants.

In regard to one of these occupants I wondered if the wild driving of the negro chauffeur and my preoccupation with the other had led me to form a false impression. Because, when the Rolls had swept on its lordly way, I realized that my memory retained an image of something not entirely human.

A yellow face buried in the wings of an upturned fur collar I had certainly seen: a keen wind from the Alps made the night bitingly cold. The man wore a fur cap pulled down nearly to his brows, creating a curiously mediaeval effect. But this face had a placid, almost god-like immobility, gaunt, dreadful, yet sealed with power like the features of a dead Pharaoh.

Some chance trick of lighting might have produced the illusion (its reality I could not admit); but about the second traveller I had no doubts whatever.

Her charming head framed—as that other skull-like head was framed—in the upturned collar of a fur coat . . . I saw Fleurette!

And I thought of a moss-rose. . . .

I turned to the wheel again.

Fleurette!

She had not seen me, had not suspected that I was there. Probably, I reflected, it would not have interested her to know.

But her companion? I tested the starter, wondering if it would function after the shock. I was relieved to find that it did. The Rolls was miles away, now, unless the furious driving of the African chauffeur had led to disaster. . . . That yellow face and those glittering green eyes—I asked myself the question: Could this be Mahdi Bey?

Somehow I could not believe the man with Fleurette to be an Egyptian. Yet, I reflected, driving on, there had been that about him which had conjured an image to my mind. . . . The image of Seti The First—that King of Egypt whose majesty had survived three thousand years. . . .

CHAPTER XI

# AT THE VILLA JASMIN

THE car in which Nayland Smith had come from Cannes was standing just where the steep descent to the little garage made a hairpin bend. I supposed that the man had decided to park there for the night. But I was compelled to pull in behind, as it was impossible to pass.

I walked on beyond the bend to the back of the bungalow. A path to the left led around the building to the little veranda; one to the right fell away in stepped terraces, skirting the garden and terminating at the laboratory.

My mind, from the time of that near crash with the Rolls up to this present moment had been preoccupied. The mystery of Fleurette had usurped my thoughts. Fleurette—her charming little bronzed face enveloped in fur; a wave of her hair gleaming like polished mahogany. Now, as I started down the slope, a warning instinct spoke to me. I found myself snatched back to dangerous reality.

I pulled up, listening; but I could not detect the Kohler engine.

Some nocturnal flying thing hovered near me; I could hear the humming of its wings. Vividly, horribly, I visualized that hairy insect, with its glossy back, and almost involuntarily, victim of a swift, overmastering and sickly terror, I began striking out right and left in the darkness. . . .

Self-contempt came to my aid. I stood still again. The insect, probably some sort of small beetle, was no longer audible. I thought of the fly-haunted swamps I had known, and grew hot with embarrassment. The Purple Shadow was a ghastly death; but Petrie had faced it unflinchingly. . . .

Natural courage returned. A too vivid imagination had betrayed me.

I reached the laboratory and found it dark and silent. This was not unexpected. I supposed that the man had turned in on the couch. He was a tough type who had served in the French mercantile marine; I doubted if he were ever troubled by imagination. He had been given to understand, since this was the story we had told to Mme. Dubonnet, that

47

Petrie was suffering from influenza. He had accepted without demur Dr. Cartier's assurance that there was no danger of infection.

Walking around to the door, I rapped sharply.

There was no reply.

Far below, I could see red roofs peeping out of purplish shadow, and, beyond, the sea gleaming under the moon; but by reason of its position, the laboratory lay in darkness.

Having rapped several times without result, I began to wish that I had brought a torch, for I thought that then I could have looked in at the window. But even as the idea crossed my mind, I remembered that the iron shutters were drawn.

Thus far, stupidly, I had taken it for granted that the door was locked. But failing to get a response from the man inside, I now tried the handle and found, to my great surprise, that the door was unlcoked.

I opened it. The laboratory was pitch black and reeked of the smell of mimosa.

"Hullo, there!" I cried, "are you asleep?"

There was no reply, but I detected a sound of heavy breathing as I groped for the switch. When I found it the lamps came up very brightly, dipped, and then settled down.

"My God!" I groaned.

The man from Cannes lay face downward on the couch!

I ran across and tried to move him. He was a big, heavy fellow, and one limply down-stretched arm, the fingers touching the floor, told me that this was no natural repose. Indeed, the state of the place had prepared me.

It was not merely in disorder—it had been stripped. Petrie's specimen slides, and all the documents which were kept in the laboratory had been removed!

The smell of mimosa was everywhere; it was getting me by the throat.

I rolled the man over on his back. My first impression, that he had been drinking heavily, was immediately dispelled. He was insensible, but breathing stertorously. I shouted and shook him, but without avail. My Colt automatic, which I had lent him, lay upon the floor some distance away.

"Good heavens!" I whispered, and stood there, listening.

Except for the hum of the engine in its shed near by and the thick breathing of the man on the couch, I could hear nothing. I stared at the chauffeur's flushed features.

Was it . . . the Purple Shadow?

My medical knowledge was not great enough to tell me.

The man might have been stunned by a blow or be suffering from the effects of an anaesthetic. Certainly, I could find no evidence of injury.

It was only reasonable to suppose that whatever the marauders had come to look for, they had found. I decided to raise the metal shutters and open a window. That stifling perfume, for which I was wholly at a loss to account, threatened to overpower me. I wondered if the searchers had upset a jar of some queer preparation of Petrie's.

How little I appreciated at that moment the monumental horror which lay behind these opening episodes in a drama destined to divert the whole course of my life.

I came out of the laboratory. Some kind of human contact, sympathy, assistance, was what I most desired. Leaving the lights on, and the door and window open, I began to make my way up the steep path bordering the kitchen-garden, towards the villa. I had slipped my own automatic into my pocket and so was now doubly armed.

In my own defence I think I may say that blackwater fever leaves one very low, and, as Petrie had warned me, I had been rather overdoing it for a convalescent. This is my apologia for the fact that as I climbed up that narrow path to the Villa Jasmin, I was conscious of the darkest apprehension. I became convinced, suddenly but quite definitely, that I was being watched.

I had just stepped on to the veranda and was fumbling with the door-key, when I heard a sound which confirmed my intuition.

From somewhere behind me, near the laboratory which I had just left, came the call, soft but unmistakable, on three minor notes, of a *dacoit!*

I flung the door open and turned up the light in the small, square lobby. Then, I reclosed the door. What to do was the problem. I thought of the man lying down there helpless—at the mercy of unguessed dangers. But he was too heavy to carry, and at all costs I must get to the 'phone—which was here in the villa.

I threw open the sitting-room door, and entered the room in which, that evening, I had quested through works in several languages for a clue to the strange plant discovered by Petrie. I switched on the lamps.

What I saw brought me up sharply with a muttered exclamation.

The room had been ransacked!

Two cabinets and the drawers of a writing-table had

been emptied of their contents. The floor was littered with papers. Even the bookshelves had not escaped scrutiny. A glance showed me that every book had been taken from its place. They were not in their right order.

Something, I assumed, had disturbed the searchers.

What?

Upon this point there was very little room for doubt. That cry in the garden had given warning of my approach. To whom?

To someone who must actually be in the villa, now!

My hand on the butt of an automatic, I stood still, listening. I was unlikely ever to forget the face I had glimpsed at the end of the kitchen-garden. It was possible that such a horror was stealthily creeping upon me at the present moment. But I could hear no sound.

I thought of Petrie—and the thought made me icily, and murderously, cool. Petrie—struck down by the dread disease he had risked his life to conquer; a victim, not of fate, but of a man—

A man? A fiend! A devil incarnate he must be who had conceived a thing so loathsome.

Dr. Fu Manchu!

Who was this Dr. Fu Manchu of whom even Nayland Smith seemed to stand in awe? A demon—or a myth? Indeed, at the opening stage of my encounter with the most evil and the most wonderful man who, I firmly believe, has ever been incarnated, I sometimes toyed with the idea that the Chinese doctor had no existence outside the imagination of Sir Denis.

All these reflections, more or less as I have recorded them, flashed through my mind as I stood there listening for evidence of another presence in the villa.

And although I heard not the faintest sound, I *knew*, now, that someone was there—someone who was searching for the formula of "654," and, therefore, not a Burmese body-guard or other underling, but one cultured enough to recognize the formula if it should be found!

Possibly . . . Dr. Fu Manchu!

I stepped up to the writing-desk, upon which the telephone stood—and in doing so noticed that the shutters outside the window had been closed. First and foremost, I must establish contact with Sir Denis. I thought I should be justified in reporting that the enemy had not yet found the formula.

The automatic in my right hand, I took up the receiver

in the left. Because of the position of the instrument, I was compelled to turn half away from the open door.

I could get no reply. I depressed the lever. There was no answering ring. . . .

A slight sound, and a change in the illumination of the room brought me about in a flash.

The door was closed!

And the telephone line was dead—cut.

I leapt to the door, grasped the handle, and turned it fiercely. I remained perfectly cool—which is my way of seeing red. The door was locked.

At which moment the lights went out.

## CHAPTER XII

# MIMOSA

I LISTENED intently, not knowing what to expect. That this was a prelude to an attack on my life, I did not doubt.

The room was now in complete darkness, for, as I had already noted, the outside shutters had been closed. There were two points from which this attack was to be apprehended: the door or the window. There was no chimney, heat being provided by a stove, the pipe of which was carried out through an aperture in the wall high up near the ceiling.

At first, I could not hear a sound.

Very cautiously I bent and pressed my ear to the thin panelling of the door. Now, I detected movement—and, furthermore, sibilant whispering. I could hear my own heart beating, too.

After a lapse of fully a minute, I became certain that *someone else* was standing on the other side of the door, as I was listening.

A murderous rage possessed me.

It was unnecessary to recall Sir Denis's instructions: "Don't hesitate to shoot." I didn't intend to hesitate . . . I was anxious for an opportunity. Petrie's haggard face was always before my mind's eye. And if Nayland Smith were correct, Sir Manston Rorke also had been foully done to death by this callous, foul group surrounding the creature called Fu Manchu.

A very slight movement upon the woodwork now enabled me to locate the exact position of the one who listened.

I hesitated no longer.

Standing upright, I clapped the nose of my automatic against the panel at a point about waist high, and fired through the door. . . .

The report in that tiny, enclosed space was deafening, but the accuracy of my judgment was immediately confirmed. A smothered, choking cry and a groan, followed by the sound of a heavy fall immediately outside, told me that my shot had not gone astray.

Braced tensely, I stood awaiting what should follow. I anticipated an attempt to rush the room, and I meant to give an account of myself.

What actually happened was utterly unexpected.

Someone was opening the outer door of the villa; then I heard a low voice—and it was a woman's voice!

I had stepped aside, anticipating that my own method might be imitated, but now, heedless of risk, I bent and listened again. A faint smell of burning was perceptible where I had fired through the woodwork.

That low, musical voice was speaking rapidly—but not in English, nor in any language with which I was familiar. It was some tongue containing strange gutterals. But even these could not disguise the haunting music of the speaker's voice.

The woman called Fah Lo Suee was outside in the lobby.

Then, I heard a man's voice, a snarling, hideous voice, replying to her; and, I thought, a second. But of this I could not be sure.

They were dragging a heavy body out on to the veranda. There came a choking cough. Such was my mood, that I could have cheered aloud. One of the skulking rats had had his medicine!

As these movements proceeded in accordance with rapidly spoken orders in that unforgettable voice, I turned to considerations of my own safety. Tip-toeing across the room and endeavouring to avoid those obstacles the position of which I could remember, I mounted on to the writing table.

Slipping the automatic into my pocket, I felt for the catch of the window, found it, and threw the window open: the shutters, I knew, I could burst with a blow, for they were old, and the fastener was insecure.

I moved farther forward, resting upon one knee, and raised my hands.

As I did so, a ghastly thing happened—a thing unforeseen. I was faced by a weapon against which I had no defence.

Pouring down through the slats of the shutters came a stifling cloud of vapour. I was drenched, saturated, blinded by *mimosa!* A faint hissing sound accompanied the discharge; and as I threw one arm across my face in a vain attempt to shield myself from that deadly vapour, this hissing sound was repeated.

I fell on to both knees, rolled sideways, and tried to throw myself back.

But the impalpable abomination seemed to follow me. I was enveloped in a cloud of it. I tried to cry out—I couldn't breath—I was choking.

A third time I heard the hissing sound, and then I think I must have rolled from the table on to the floor. My impression at the time was of falling—falling into dense, yellow banks of cloud, reeking of mimosa. . . .

## CHAPTER XIII

## THE FORMULA

"STERLING, Sterling! wake up, man! You're all right, now."

I opened my eyes as directed, and apart from a feeling of pressure on the temples, I experienced no discomfort.

I was in my own bed at the Villa Jasmin!

Nayland Smith was standing beside me, and a bespectacled, bearded young man whom I recognized for one of Dr. Cartier's juniors, was bending down and watching me anxiously.

Without any of that mental chaos which usually follows unconsciousness, I remembered instantly all that had happened, up to the moment that I had rolled from the table.

"They drugged me, Sir Denis," I said, "but I can tell you all that happened."

"The details, Sterling. I have already reconstructed the

outline." He turned to the doctor. "You see, this drug apparently has no after-effects."

The medical man felt my pulse, then turned in amazement to Sir Denis.

"It is truly astounding," he admitted. "I know of no property in any species of mimosa which could explain this."

"Nevertheless," rapped Sir Denis, "the smell of mimosa is still perceptible in the sitting-room."

The French doctor nodded in grave agreement. Then, as I sat up—for I felt as well as I had ever felt in my life—

"No, please," he insisted, and laid his hand upon my shoulder: "I should prefer that you lie quiet for the present."

"Yes, take it easy, Sterling," said Nayland Smith. "There was another victim here, last night."

"The man in the laboratory?"

"Yes; but he's none the worse for it. He dozed off on the couch, he tells me, and they operated in his case, I have discovered, by inserting a tube through the ventilator in the wall above. He sprang up at the first whiff, but never succeeded in getting to his feet."

"Please tell me," I interrupted, excitedly, "is there any blood in the lobby?"

Sir Denis shook his head grimly.

"I take it that *you* are responsible for the shot-hole through the door?"

"Yes, and I scored a bull!"

"The lobby is tiled. They probably took the trouble to remove any stains. Apart from several objects and documents which they have taken away, they have left everything in perfect order. And now, Sterling—the details."

Sir Denis looked very tired: his manner was unusually grave; and:

"Before I begin," I said, rapidly—"Petrie? Is there any change?"

The Frenchman shook his head.

"I am very sorry to have to tell you, Mr. Sterling," he replied, "that Dr. Petrie is sinking rapidly."

"No? Good God! Don't say so!"

"It's true!" snapped Nayland Smith. "But tell me what I want to know—I haven't a minute to waste."

Filled with a helpless anger, and with such a venomous hatred growing in my heart for the cruel, cunning devil directing these horrors, I outlined very rapidly the events of the night.

"Even now," said Nayland Smith savagely, "we don't know if they have it."

"The formula for '654'?"

He nodded.

"It may have been in Rorke's study in Wimpole Street, or it may not; and it may have been here. In the meantime, Petrie's case is getting desperate, and no one knows what treatment to pursue. Fah Lo Suee's kindness towards yourself, following a murderous assault upon one of her servants, suggests success. But it's merely a surmise. I must be off!"

"But where are you going, Sir Denis?" I asked, for he had already started towards the door. "What are *my* orders?"

He turned.

"Your orders," he replied, "are to stay in bed until Dr. Brisson gives you permission to get up. I am going to Berlin."

"To Berlin?"

He nodded impatiently.

"I spent some time with the late Sir Manston Rorke," he went on rapidly, "at the School of Tropical Medicine, as I have already told you. And I formed the impression that Rorke's big reputation was largely based upon his friendship with Professor Emil Krus, of Berlin, the greatest living authority upon Tropical Medicine.

"I suspected that Rorke almost invariably submitted proposed treatments to the celebrated German, and I hope—I *only* hope—that Petrie's formula '654' may have been sent on to the Professor for his comments. I have already been in touch by telephone with Berlin, but Dr. Emil Krus proved to be inaccessible.

"The French authorities have placed a fast plane and an experienced pilot at my service, and I leave in twenty minutes for the Tempelhof aerodrome."

I was astounded—I could think of no words; but:

"It is Dr. Petrie's only chance," the Frenchman interrupted. "His condition is growing hourly worse and we have no idea what to do. It is possible that the great Krus"—there was professional as well as national jealousy in his pronounciation of the name—"may be able to help us. Otherwise—"

He shrugged his shoulders.

"You see, Sterling?" said Nayland Smith. "Take care of yourself."

He ran out.

I looked up helplessly into the bespectacled face of Dr.

Brisson. Dawn was breaking, and I realized that I must have been insensible for many hours.

"Such friendship is a wonderful thing, doctor," I said.

"Yes. Sir Denis Nayland Smith is a staunch friend," Brisson replied; "but in this—there is more than friendship. The South of France, the whole of France, Europe, perhaps the world, is threatened by a plague for which we know of no remedy. The English doctor Petrie has found means to check it. If we knew what treatment should follow the injection of his preparation '654', we could save his life, yet."

"Is it, then, desperate?"

"It is desperate. But as surely you can appreciate, we could also save other lives. If a wide-spread epidemic should threaten to develop, we could inoculate. I do not understand, but it seems that there is *some one* who opposes science and favours the plague. This is beyond my comprehension, but one thing is clear to me. Only Dr. Petrie, who is dying, and Professor Krus—perhaps—know how to fight this thing. You see? It may be that the fate of the world is at stake."

Indeed I saw, and all too plainly.

"Have the police been informed of the outrages here last night?" I asked.

The Frenchman shrugged his shoulders and his bearded face registered despair.

"In this matter I am distracted," he declared, "and I have ceased even to think about it. Sir Denis Nayland Smith, it seems, has powers from Paris which override the authorities of Nice. The Department is in his hands."

"You mean that no inquiry will be made?"

"Nothing—as I understand. But as I confessed to you, I do not understand—at all."

I sprang up in bed—my brain was super-active.

"This is awful!" I exclaimed. "I must do something—I must *do* something!"

Dr. Brisson rested his hands upon my shoulders.

"Mr. Sterling," he said, and his eyes, magnified by the powerful lenses of his spectacles, were kindly, yet compelling: "what you should do—if you care to take my advice—is this: you should rest."

"How can I rest?"

I sank back on the pillows whilst he continued to watch me.

"It is difficult, I know," he went on. "But what I tell you, Dr. Cartier would tell you, and your friend Dr. Petrie, also. You are a very strong man, full of vigour, but you have recently recovered from some severe illness. This I can see. The Germans are very clever—but we in France are not without knowledge. For at least four hours you should sleep."

"How can I sleep?"

"There is nothing you can do to help your friend. All that experience has taught us, we are doing. I offer you my advice. An orderly from the hospital is in the lobby, and will remain there until he is relieved. Your housekeeper, Mme. Dubonnet, will be here at eight o'clock. Please take a small cachet which I have in my bag, and resign yourself to sleep."

I don't know to what extent the doctor's kindly and deliberate purpose influenced me, but as he spoke I recognized how weary I was.

The hiatus induced by that damnable mimosa drug had rested me not at all: my brain was active as from the moment that I had succumbed to it. My body was equally weary.

"I agree with you, doctor," I said, and grasped his hand. "I don't think I need your cachet. I can sleep without any assistance."

He nodded, and smiled.

"Better still," he declared. "Nature is always right. I shall close the shutters and leave you. Ring for your coffee when you awake. By then, if Sir Denis's instructions have been carried out, the telephone will have been repaired, and you can learn the latest news about Dr. Petrie."

I remember seeing him close the shutters and walk quietly out of the room. I must have been very tired . . . for I remember no more.

## CHAPTER XIV

# IN MONTE CARLO

I WOKE late in the afternoon.

Body, brain and nerves had been thoroughly exhausted; but now I realized that my long sleep had restored me.

Mme. Dubonnet was in the kitchen, looking very unhappy. The telephone had been repaired that morning, she told me, but it was all so mysterious. The house had been disturbed, and there were many things missing. And the poor, dear doctor! They had told her, only two hours before, that there was no change in his condition.

I turned on the bath taps and then went to the telephone.

Dr. Brisson was at the hospital. In answer to my anxious inquiry, he said in a strained, tired voice that there was nothing to report. He could not conceal his anxiety, however.

Something told me that dear old Petrie's hours were numbered. Sir Denis Nayland Smith had not been in touch.

"I trust that he arrived safely," he concluded, "and succeeded in finding Dr. Emil Krus."

"I shall be along in about an hour."

"Nothing of the kind, my dear Mr. Sterling, I beg of you. It would only add to our embarrassment. You can do nothing. If you would consent to take my advice again, it would be this: drive out somewhere to dinner. Try to forget this shadow, which unfortunately you can do nothing to dispel. Tell the housekeeper where you intend to go, so that we can trace you, should there be news—good or bad."

"It's impossible," I replied: "I feel I must stand by."

But the tired, soothing voice at the other end of the line persisted. A man would relieve Mme. Dubonnet at the villa just before dusk; "and," Brisson conclued, "it is far better that you should seek a change of scene if only for a few hours. Dr. Petrie would wish it. In a sense, you know, you are his patient."

In my bath, I considered his words. Yes, I supposed he was right. Petrie had been insistent that I should not overdo things—mentally or physically. I would dine in Monte Carlo, amid the stimulating gaiety of the strangest capital in the world.

I wanted to be at my best in this battle with an invisible army. I owed it to Petrie—and I owed it to Nayland Smith.

In spite of my determination, it was late before I started out. The orderly from the hospital had arrived. He had nothing to report. Sir Denis was of the opinion, I learned, that there was just a possibility of a further raid upon the Villa Jasmin being attempted, and the man showed me that he was armed.

He seemed to welcome this strange break in his normal duties. I told him that I proposed to dine at Quinto's Restaurant. I was known there, and he could get in touch, or leave a message at any time.

Then, heavy-hearted, but glad in a way to escape if only

for a few hours, from the spot where Petrie had been stricken down by his remorseless, hidden enemy, I set out for Monaco.

Some new and strange elements had crashed into my life. It was good to get away to a place dissociated from these things and endeavour to see them in their true perspective. The route was pathetically familiar.

It had been Petrie's custom on two or three evenings in the week, to drive into Monte Carlo, dine, and spend an hour or so in the Casino. He was no gambler—nor am I—but he was a very keen mathematician and he got quite a kick out of pitting his wits against the invulnerable bank.

I could never follow the principle of his system. But whilst, admittedly, we had never lost anything, on the other hand, we had not gained.

My somewhat morbid reflections seemed to curtail the journey. I observed little of the route, until I found myself on the long curve above Monte Carlo. Dusk had fallen, and that theatrical illumination which is a feature of the place had sprung into life.

I pulled up for a moment, looking down at the unique spectacle—wonderful, for all its theatricality. The blazing colour of the flower-beds, flood-lighted and set amid palms; the emerald green of terraced lawns falling away to that ornate frontage of the great Casino.

It is Monte Carlo's one and only "view", but in its garish way it is unforgettable.

I pushed on down the sharp descent to the town, presently halting before the little terrace of an unpretentious restaurant. Tables were laid under the awning, and already there were many diners.

This was Quinto's, where, without running up a ruinous bill, one may enjoy a perfect dinner and the really choice wines of France.

The genial maitre d'hôtel met me at the top of the steps, extending that cosmopolitan welcome which lends a good meal an additional savour. Your true *restaurateur* is not only an epicure; he is also a polished man of the world.

Yes, there was a small table in the corner. But I was alone to-night! Was Dr. Petrie busy?

I shook my head.

"I am afraid he is very ill," I replied cautiously.

Hitherto the authorities had succeeded in suppressing the truth of this ghastly outbreak so near to two great pleasure resorts. I had to guard my tongue, for an indiscreet word might undo all their plans of secrecy.

"Something serious?" he asked, with what I thought was real concern: everybody loved Petrie.

"A serious chill. The doctors are afraid of pneumonia."

Quinto raised his hands in an eloquent southern gesture.

"Oh, these chilly nights!" he exclaimed. "They will ruin us! So many people forget to wrap themselves up warmly in the Riviera evenings. And then—" he shrugged— "they say it is a treacherous climate!"

He conducted me to a table in an angle of the wall, and pointed out, as was his custom, notabilities present that evening.

These included an ex-Crown Prince, Fritz Kreisler, and an internationally popular English novelist residing on the Côte d'Azur.

The question of what I should eat and what I should drink was discussed as between artists; for the hall-mark of a great maitre d'hôtel is the insidious compliment which he conveys to his patron in conceding the latter's opinions to be worthy of the master's consideration.

When the matter was arranged and the wine-waiter had brought me a cocktail I settled down to survey my fellow-guests.

My survey stopped short at a table in the opposite corner.

A man who evidently distrusted the chill of the southern evenings sat there, his back towards me. He wore a heavy coat, having an astrakhan collar: and, what was more peculiar at dinner, he wore an astrakhan cap. From my present point of view, he resembled pictures I had seen of Russian noblemen of the old régime.

Facing him across the small, square table was *Fleurette!*

Over one astrakhan-covered shoulder of her companion our glances met. Dim light may have created the illusion, but I thought that the flower-like face turned pale, that the blue eyes opened very widely for a moment.

I was about to stand up, when a slight, almost imperceptible movement of Fleurette's head warned me unmistakably not to claim the acquaintance.

## CHAPTER XV

# FAIRY TRUMPET

I ASKED myself the question: had the gesture been real or had I merely imagined it?

Fleurette wore a light wrap over a very plain black evening frock. Her hair smouldered under the shaded lights so that it seemed to contain sparks of fire. She had instantly glanced aside. I could not be wrong.

At first I had experienced intense humiliation, but now my courage returned. True, she had conveyed the message: "Don't speak to me." But it had been in the nature of a warning, an admission of a mutual secret understanding, and in no sense a snub.

She was, then, not inaccessible. She was hedged around, guarded, by the jealous suspicions of her Oriental master.

I could doubt no longer.

The man seated with his back to me was the same whom I had seen in the car driven by the negro chauffeur. Despite his non-conformity to type, this was Mahdi Bey. And Fleurette, for all her glorious, virgin-like beauty, must be his mistress.

She deliberately avoided looking in my direction again. Her companion never moved: his immobility was extraordinary. And presently, through the leaves of the shrubs growing in wooden boxes, I saw the black and silver Rolls, almost directly opposite the restaurant.

My glance moved upward to the parapet guarding a higher road which here dips down and forms a hairpin bend.

A man stood there watching.

Difficult though it was from where I sat to form a clear impression of his appearance, I became convinced, nevertheless, that he was one of the tribe of the *dacoits* . . . either the same, or an opposite number, of the yellow-faced horror I had seen in the garden of the Villa Jasmin!

And at that moment, as my waiter approached, changing the plates in readiness for the first course, I found myself swept back mentally into the ghastly business I had come there to forget. I experienced a sudden chill of foreboding.

If, as I strongly suspected, one of the murderous Burmans was watching the restaurant—did this mean that I had been followed there? If so, with what purpose? I no longer stood between Petrie's enemies and their objective; but—

I had wounded, probably killed, one of their number. I had heard much of the implacable blood feuds of the Indian thugs; it was no more than reasonable to suppose that something of the same kind might prevail amongst the *dacoits* of Burma.

I glanced furtively upward again. And there was the motionless figure leaning against the parapet.

In dress there was nothing to distinguish the man from the ordinary Monaco workman, but my present survey confirmed my first impression.

This was one of the yellow men attached to the service of Dr. Fu Manchu.

I cast my memory back over the route I had so recently traversed. Had any car followed me? I could not recollect that it was so. But, on the other hand, I had been much abstracted, driving mechanically. Dusk had fallen before I had reached Monaco. If an attempt were contemplated, why had it not taken place upon the road?

The problem was beyond me. . . . But there stood the watcher, motionless by the parapet.

And at this very moment, and just as the wine-waiter placed a decanter of my favourite Pommard before me, I had a remarkable experience—an experience so disturbing that I sat quite still for several seconds, my outstretched hand poised in the act of taking up the decanter.

Close beside my ear—as it seemed, out of space, out of nowhere—that same high, indescribable note became audible; that sound which I believe I have already attempted to describe as the call of a fairy trumpet. . . .

Once before, and once only, I had heard it—on the beach of Ste. Claire de la Roche.

Some eerie quality in the sound affected me now, as it had affected me then. It was profoundly mysterious; but one thing was certain. Unless the sound were purely a product of my own imagination, or the result of some trouble of the inner ear—possibly an aftermath of illness—it could not be coincidence that on the two occasions that I had heard it Fleurette had been present.

My hand dropped down to the couvert—and I looked across at her.

Her eyes were fixed on the face of her companion who

sat with his back to me, in that dreamy, faraway regard which I remembered.

Then, her delicate lips moved, and I thought, although I could not hear her words, that she was replying to some question which he had addressed to her.

And, as I looked and realized that she was speaking, that strange sound ceased as abruptly as it had commenced.

I saw Fleurette glance aside; her expression changed swiftly. But her eyes never once turned in my direction. I stared beyond her, up through the leaves of the shrubs and towards the parapet on the other side of the street.

The Burman had disappeared. . . .

## CHAPTER XVI

# THE DACOIT

"You are wanted on the telephone, Mr. Sterling."

I started as wildly as a man suddenly aroused from sleep. A dreadful premonition gripped me icily. I stood up.

"Do you know who it is?"

"I believe the name was Dr. Cartier, sir—"

In that moment, Fleurette and her mysterious companion were forgotten; the lurking yellow man faded from my mind as completely as he had faded from my view. This was news of Petrie; and something told me it could only be bad news.

I hurried through the restaurant to the telephone booth, and snatched up the receiver.

"Hullo, hullo!" I called. "Alan Sterling here. Is that Dr. Cartier?"

Brisson's voice answered me: his tone prepared me for what was to come.

"I mentioned Dr. Cartier's name in case you should not be familiar with my own, Mr. Sterling. I would not have disturbed you—for you can scarcely have begun your dinner yet—had I not promised to report any news at once."

"What is it?" I asked eagerly.

"Prepare yourself to know that it is bad."

"Not . . . ?"

"Alas—yes!"

63

"My God!"

"There was no final convulsion—no change. '654' might have saved him—if we had known what treatment to pursue after the first injection. But the coma passed slowly into . . . death."

As I listened to those words, a change came over my entire outlook on the future. A cold rage, and what I knew to be an abiding rage, took possession of me. The merciless fiends, for no reason that I could possibly hope to imagine, had ended an honourable and supremely useful life; that kindly personality which had lived only to serve, had been snatched away, remorselessly.

Very well. . . . It was murder, calculated, callous murder. This was a game that two could play. What I had done once, I could do again, and again—and every time that I got within reach of any one of the foul gang!

Dr. Fu Manchu!

If such a person existed I asked only to be set face to face with him. That moment, I vowed, should be his last—little knowing the stupendous task to which I vowed myself.

Fah Lo Suee—a woman; but one of them. The French had not hesitated to shoot female spies during the World War. Nor should I, now.

I had reached the head of the steps when Victor Quinto touched my shoulder. Details were indefinite, but my immediate objective was plain. One of the Burmans was covering my movements. I planned to find that Burman; and—taking every possible precaution to insure my own get-away—I planned to kill him. . . .

"You have had bad news, M. Sterling?"

"Dr. Petrie is dead," I said, and ran down the steps.

I suppose many curious glances followed; perhaps Fleurette had seen me. I didn't care. I crossed the street and walked up the opposite slope. A man was lounging there, smoking a cigarette—a typical working-class Frenchman; and I remembered that he had stood there for part of the time during which the *dacoit* had watched the restaurant.

"Excuse me," I said.

The man started, and turned.

"Did you chance to see an Oriental who stood near you a few minutes ago?"

"But yes, m'sieur. Some one, I suppose, off one of the foreign yachts in the harbour? He has gone only this last two minutes."

"Which way?"

He pointed downward.

"Towards the Jardin des Suicides," he replied, smiling.

"Suitable spot if I catch him there," I muttered; then, aloud: "Drink my health," I said, thrusting a note into his hand. "I shall need your kind wishes—"

"Thank you, m'sieur—and good night. . . ."

I remember starting the car and driving slowly down the slope to the corner by the Café de Paris. I had had no glimpse of the Burman. Here, viewing the activity which surges around the Casino, seeing familiar figures at the more sheltered café tables, noticing a gendarme in an Offenbach uniform, a hotel 'bus—I pulled up.

My determination remained adamant as ever; but I suddenly recognized the hopelessness of this present quest. I must cast my hook wisely; uesless to pursue one furtive shark. My place was beside Cartier, beside dear old Petrie—in the centre of the murderous school. . . .

I set out. I had not dined; nor had I tasted my wine. But I was animated by a vigorous purpose more stimulating than meat and drink.

That purpose, as I view it now, was vengeance. Some part of me, the Highland, had seen the Fiery Cross. I was out for blood. I had consecrated myself to a holy cause: the utter destruction of Dr. Fu Manchu and of all he stood for.

Petrie dead!

It was all but impossible to accept the fact—yet. I dreaded my next meeting with Sir Denis: his hurt would be deeper even than my own. And throughout the time that these bitter reflections occupied my mind, I was driving on, headlong, my steering controlled by a guiding Providence.

Without having noted one landmark on the way, I found myself high up on the Corniche Road. Beyond a piece of broken parapet outlining a sharp bend, I could see twinkling lights far ahead and below. They were, I thought, the lights of Ste. Claire de la Roche. I slowed up to load my pipe.

The night was very still. No sound of traffic reached my ears.

I remembered having stuck a spare box of matches in a fold of the canvas hood. I turned to get it. . . .

A malignant yellow face, the eyes close-set and slightly oblique, stared into mine!

The *dacoit* was perched on the baggage-rack!

What that hideous expression meant—in what degree it was compounded of animosity and of fear caused by sudden discovery—I didn't pause to consider. But that my cold purpose was to be read in my face, the Burman's next move clearly indicated.

Springing to the ground he began to run.

He ran *back*: I had no chance to turn the car, but I was out and after him in less time than it takes me to record the fact. This was a murder game: no quarter given or expected!

The man ran like Mercury. He was already twenty yards away. I put up a tremendous sprint and slightly decreased his lead. He glanced back. I saw the moonlight on his snarling teeth.

Pulling up, I took careful aim with the automatic—and fired. He ran on. I fired again.

Still he ran. I set out in pursuit; but the *dacoit* had thirty yards start. If he had ever doubted, he knew, now, that he ran for his life.

In a hundred yards I had gained nothing. My wind was not good for more than another hundred yards at that speed. Then—and if I had had enough breath, I should have cheered—he stumbled, tottered, and fell forward on to hands and knees!

I bore down upon him with grim determination. I was not ten feet off when he turned, swung his arm, and something went humming past my bent head!

A knife!

I checked and fired again at close range.

The Burman threw his hands up and fell prone in the road.

"Another one for Petrie!" I said breathlessly.

Stooping, I was about to turn him over, when an amazing thing happened.

The man whipped around with a movement which reminded me horribly of a snake. He threw his legs around my thighs and buried fingers like steel hooks in my throat!

Dragging me down—down—remorselessly down—he grinned like a savage animal cornered but unconquerable. . . . The world began to swim about me; there was a murmur in my ears like that of the sea.

I thought a car approached in the distance. . . . I saw bloody foam dripping from the *dacoit's* clenched teeth. . . .

CHAPTER XVII

# THE ROOM OF GLASS

WHEN I opened my eyes my first impression was that the *dacoit* had killed me—that I was dead—and that the Beyond was even more strange and inconsequential than the wildest flights of Spiritualism had depicted.

I lay on a couch, my head on a pillow. The cushions of the couch were of a sort of neutral grey colour; so was the pillow. They were composed, I saw, of some kind of soft rubber, and were inflated. I experienced considerable difficulty in swallowing, and raising a hand to my throat found it to be swollen and painful.

Perhaps, after all, I was not dead; but if alive, where in the known world could I be?

The couch upon which I lay—and I noted now that I was dressed in white overalls and wore rubber-soled shoes!—was at one end of an enormously large room. The entire floor, or that part of it which I could see, was covered with this same neutral grey substance which may have been rubber. The ceiling looked like opaque glass, and so did the walls.

Quite near to me was a complicated piece of apparatus, not unlike, I thought, a large cinematograph camera, and mounted on a moveable platform. It displayed a number of huge lenses, and there were tiny lamps here and there in the amazing mechanism, some of them lighted.

A most intricate switchboard was not the least curious feature of this baffling machine. Farther beyond, suspended from the glass ceiling, hung what I took to be the largest arc lamp I had ever seen in my life. But although it was alight, it suffused only a dim, purple glow, contributing little to the general illumination.

Half hidden from my point of view stood a long glass table (or a table composed of the same material as the ceiling and the walls) upon which was grouped the most singular collection of instruments and appliances I had ever seen, or even imagined.

67

Huge glass vessels containing fluids of diverse colours, masses of twisted tubing, little points of fire, and a thing like an Egyptian harp, the strings of which seemed to be composed of streaks of light which wavered and constantly changed colour, emitting a ceaseless crackling sound. . . .

I closed my eyes for a moment. My head was aching furiously, and my mouth so parched that it caused me constantly to cough, every cough producing excruciating pain.

Then I opened my eyes again. But the insane apartment remained. I sat up and swung my feet to the floor.

The covering had the feeling of rubber as its appearance indicated. My new view-point brought other objects within focus. In a white metal rack was ranged a series of vessels resembling test-tubes. The smallest was perhaps a foot high, and from this the others graduated like the pipes of an organ, creating an impression in my mind of something seen through a powerful lens.

Each tube was about half filled with some sort of thick fluid, and this from vessel to vessel, passed through shades from deepest ruby to delicate rose pink.

I stood up.

And now I could see the whole of that fabulous room. I perceived that it was a kind of laboratry—containing not one instrument nor one system of lighting with which I was acquainted!

Other items of its equipment now became visible, and I relized that a continuous throbbing characterized the place. Some powerful plant was at work. This throbbing, which was more felt than heard, and the crackling of those changing rays, alone disturbed the silence.

Still doubting if I really lived, if I had been rescued from the *thug,* I asked myself—assuming it to be so—who was my rescuer, and to what strange sanctuary had he brought me?

No human figure was visible.

And now I observed a minor, but a curious point: the rubber couch upon which I had been lying was placed in a corner. And upon the floor-covering were two black lines forming a right angle. Its ends, touching the walls, made a perfect square—in which I stood.

I looked about that cavernous place, pervaded by a sort of violet light, and I realized that certain pieces of apparatus, and certain tables, were surrounded by similar black marks upon the floor.

Apparently there was no door, nor could I find anything

resembling a bell. If this were not mirage—or death—what was this place in which I found myself; and why was I there alone?

I set out to explore.

One step forward I made, and had essayed a second, when I recall uttering a loud cry.

As my foot crossed the black mark on the floor, a shock ran through my body which numbed my muscles! I dropped to my knees, looking about me—perhaps, had there been any to see, as caged animals glare from their cages.

What did it mean? That some impassable barrier hedged me in!

The shock had served a double purpose: it had frightened me intensely—this I confess without hesitation; but as I got to my feet again, I knew that also it had revived that cold, murderous rage which had governed my mind up to the moment that the *dacoit* had buried his fingers in my throat.

"Where the devil am I?" I said aloud; "and what am I doing here?"

I sprang forward . . . and fell back as though a cunning opponent had struck me a straight blow over the heart!

Collapsed on the rubber-covered floor I lay quivering—temporarily stunned. I experienced, now, not so much fear, as awe. I was a prisoner of the invisible.

But, looking about at the nameless things which surrounded me, I knew that the invisible must be controlled by an intelligence. If this were not death—I had fallen into a trap.

I rose up again, shaken, but master of myself. Then, I sat down on the couch. I felt in the pocket of my overalls—and found my cigarette case! A box of Monaco matches (which rarely light) was there also. I lighted a cigarette. My hands were fairly steady.

Some ghostly image of the truth—a mocking reply to those doubts which I had held hitherto—jazzed spectrally before me. I stared around, looking up at the dull, glassy roof, and at unimaginable instruments and paraphernalia which lent this place the appearance of a Martian factory, devoted to experiments of another age—another planet.

Then I sprang up.

A panel in one of the glass walls slid open. A man came in. The panel closed behind him. He stood, looking in my direction.

CHAPTER XVIII

# DR. FU MANCHU

HE wore a plain yellow robe and walked in silent, thick-soled slippers. Upon his head was set a little black cap surmounted by a coral bead. His hands concealed in the loose sleeves of his robe, he stood there, watching me.

And I knew that this man had the most wonderful face that I had ever looked upon.

It was aged, yet ageless. I thought that if Benvenuto Cellini had conceived the idea of executing a death-mask of Satan in gold, it must have resembled very closely this living-dead face upon which my gaze was riveted.

He was fully six feet in height and appeared even taller by reason of the thickly padded slippers which he wore. For the little cap (which I recognized from descriptions I had read to be that of a mandarin of high rank) I substituted mentally the ashtrakhan cap of the traveller glimpsed in the big car on the Corniche Road; for the yellow robe, the fur-collared coat.

I knew at the instant that he entered that I had seen him twice before; the second time, at Quinto's.

One memory provoked another.

Although in the restaurant he had sat with his back towards me, I remembered now, and must have noted it subconsciously at the time, that tortoiseshell loops had surrounded his yellow, pointed ears. He had been wearing spectacles.

Then, as he moved slowly and noiselessly in my direction, I captured the most elusive memory of all—

I had seen this man in a dream—riding a purple cloud which swept down upon a doomed city!

The veil was torn—no possibility of misunderstanding remained. Those brilliant green eyes fixed upon me in an unflinching regard, conveyed as though upon astral rays a sense of force unlike anything I had known.

*This was Dr. Fu Manchu!*

My gothic surroundings, the man's awesome personality, my attempt to cross the black line surrounding an invisible prison, these things had temporarily put me out of action. But now, as this definite conviction seized upon my mind, my hand plunged into my pocket.

Flesh and blood might fail to pass that mysterious zone; perhaps a bullet would succeed.

The man in the yellow robe now stood no more than ten feet away from me. And as I jerked my hand down, a sort of film passed instantaneously over the green eyes, conveying a momentary—but no more than momentary—impression of blindness. This phenomenon disappeared in the very instant that I came to my senses—in the very instant that I remembered I was wearing strange garments. . . .

How mad of me to have looked for a charged automatic in the pocket of these white overalls!

I set my foot upon the smouldering cigarette which I had dropped, and with clenched fists faced my gaoler; for I could no longer blink the facts of the situation.

"Ah! Mr. Sterling," he said, and approached me so closely that he stood but a pace beyond the black line. "Your attempt to explore the radio research-room caused a signal to appear in my study, and I knew that you had revived."

His voice had a guttural quality, the sibilants being very stressed. He spoke deliberately, giving every syllable its full value. I suppose, in a way, he spoke perfect English, yet many words so treated sounded wholly unfamiliar so that I knew I had never heard them pronounced in that manner before.

I could think of nothing to say. I was helpless and this man had come to mock me.

"You seem to have a disregard for the sanctity of human life," he continued, "unusual in Englishmen. You killed one of my servants at the Villa Jasmin—a small matter. But your zeal for murder did not end there. Fortunately, I was less than half a mile behind at the time, and I had you carried to a place of safety before some passing motorist should be attracted by the spectacle of two bodies in the Corniche road. You mortally wounded Gana Ghat, head of my Burmese bodyguard."

"I am glad to hear it," I replied.

Those green eyes watched me immutably.

"Rejoice not unduly," he said softly. "I wished you no harm, but you have thrust yourself upon me. As a result, you find yourself in China—"

"In *China!*"

I heard the note of horror in my own voice. My glance

strayed swiftly round that incredible room, and returned again to the tall, impassive yellow-robed figure.

Good heavens! it was a shattering idea—yet not wholly impossible. I had no means of knowing how long I had been unconscious. The dreadful theory flashed through my mind, that this brilliant madman—for I could not account him sane—had, by means of drugs, kept me in a comatose condition, and had had me transported in some private vessel from France to China.

I tried to challenge those glittering green eyes—but the task was one beyond my powers.

"You left me no choice," Dr. Fu Manchu went on. "I can permit no stranger to intrude upon my experiments. It was a matter of deciding between your death—which would not have profited me—and your services, which may do so."

He turned slowly and walked in the direction of the hidden glass door. He was within one step of it when it slid noiselessly open. He glanced at me over his shoulder.

"Follow," he directed.

Since at the moment I could see no alternative to obedience, I stepped cautiously forward.

There was no shock when I passed the black line, but I continued to move warily across that silent floor, in the direction of the opening in which the Chinaman stood, glancing back at me.

The idea of springing upon him the moment I found myself within reach, crossed my mind. But *China!* If I should actually be in China, what fate awaited me in the event of my attack being successful?

I knew something of the Chinese, having met and employed many of them. I had found them industrious, kindly and simple. My knowledge of the punishments inflicted by autocratic officials in the interior was confined entirely to hearsay. Certain stories came back to me now, counselling prudence. If Nayland Smith were correct, it would be a good deed to rid the world of this Chinese physician—even at the price of a horrible martyrdom.

But I might fail . . . and pay the price nevertheless.

These were my thoughts as I drew nearer and nearer to the glass door. I had almost reached it when Fu Manchu spoke again.

"Dismiss any idea of personal attack," he said in a soft voice, the sibilants more than usually pronounced. "Accept my assurance that it could not possibly succeed. Follow!"

He moved on, and I crossed the threshold into a small

room furnished as a library. Many of the volumes burdening the shelves were in strange bindings, and their letterings in characters even less familiar. There was a commodious table upon which a number of books lay open. Also, there was a smell in the room which I thought I identified as that of burning opium; and a little jade pipe lying in a bronze tray served to confirm my suspicion.

The library was lighted by one silk-shaded lantern suspended from the ceiling, and by a peculiar globular lamp set in an ebony pedestal on a corner of the table.

So much I observed as I crossed this queer apartment, richly carpeted, and out by means of a second doorway into the largest glass-house I had seen outside Kew Gardens. Its floor was covered with that same rubber-like material used in the "radio research-room."

The roof was impressively lofty, and the vast conservatory softly lighted by means of some system of hidden lamps. Tropical heat prevailed and a damp, miasmatic smell. There were palms there, and flowering creepers, rare shrubs in perfect condition and banks of rumorous orchids embedded mid steaming moss.

CHAPTER XIX

## THE SECRET JUNGLE

THE place was a bulb-hunter's paradise, a dream-jungle, in parts almost impenetrable, by reason of the fact that luxurious growths had overrun the sometimes narrow paths.

I discovered as we proceeded that it was divided into sections and that the temperature, in what was really a series of isolated forcing-houses, varied from tropical to subtropical. The doors were very ingenious. There was a space between them large enough to accommodate several persons, and a gauge set beside a thermometer which could be adjusted as one door was closed before the next was opened.

Let me confess that I, myself, had ceased to exist. I was submerged in the flowers, in the jungle, in the vital, intense personality of my guide. This was phantasy—yet it was not phantasy. It was mad reality: the dream of a super-scientist, a genius whose brilliance transcended anything normally recognized, expressed in rare foliage, in unique blooms.

Dr. Fu Manchu consented to enlighten me from point to point.

At an early stage he drew my attention to species which I had sought in vain in the forests of Brazil; to orchids which Borneo, during one long expedition, had failed to reveal to me: Indian varieties and specimens from the Burmese swamps. . . .

"This is mango-apple, a fruit which first appeared here two months ago. . . . Notice near its roots, the beautiful flowers which occasion the heavy perfume—*Cypripedium-Cycaste;* a hybrid cultivated in these houses successfully for the first time . . . the very large blooms are rose-peonies—scentless, of course, but interesting. . . ."

At one point in a very narrow path, overhung by a most peculiar type of hibiscus in full bloom, he paused and pointed.

I saw pitcher-plants of many species, and not far away *drosophyllum*—of that kind of which I had already met with two specimens.

"These insectivorous varieties," said Dr. Fu Manchu, "have proved useful in certain experiments. I have outlined several inquiries, upon which I shall request you to commence work shortly, relating to this interesting subject. We come now to the botanical research-room."

He opened a door, and with one long-nailed yellow hand beckoned me imperiously to follow.

I obeyed.

He closed the door and adjusted the gauge, continuing to speak as he did so.

"You will work under the direction of Companion Herman Trenck—"

"What!" His words aroused me from a sort of stupor. "Dr. Trenck? Trenck died five years ago in Sumatra!"

Dr. Fu Manchu opened the second door, and I saw a beautifully equipped laboratory, but much smaller than that in which I had first found myself.

A Chinaman wearing white overalls resembling my own bowed to my guide and stood aside as we entered.

Bending over a microscope was a grey-haired, bearded man. I had met him once; twice heard him lecture. He stood upright and confronted us.

No possibility of doubt remained. It was Herman Trenck . . . who had been dead for five years!

Dr. Fu Manchu glanced aside at me.

"It will be your privilege, Mr. Sterling," he said, "to meet under my roof many distinguished dead men."

He turned to the famous Dutch botanist.

"Companion Trenck," he continued, "allow me to introduce to you your new assistant, Companion Alan Sterling, of whose work I know you have heard."

"Indeed, yes," said the Dutchman cordially, and advanced with outstretched hand. "It is a great pleasure to meet you, Mr. Sterling, and a great privilege to enjoy such assistance. Your recent work in Brazil for the Botanical Society is well known to me."

I shook hands. I was a man in a dream. This was a dream meeting.

Of the bona fides of Dr. Trenck in life, there could never have been any question. His was one of the great names in Botany. But now, I thought, I had entered a spirit world, under the guidance of a master magician.

"If you will pardon me," said Trenck, "there is something here to which I must draw the Doctor's attention."

I made no reply. I stood stricken silent, now most horribly convinced that my first impression had been the true one—that definitely I was dead. And I watched, as that tall, gaunt figure in the yellow robe bent over the microscope. Herman Trenck studied his every movement with intense anxiety; and presently:

"Not yet," said the Chinaman, standing upright. "But you are very near."

"I agree," said the Dutch botanist earnestly.

"That I am still wrong?"

"It is more probable, Doctor, that *I* am wrong. . . ."

And it was at this moment, whilst I firmly believed that I had stepped into the other world, that a phrase flashed through my mind, spoken in a low, musical voice: "Think of me as Derceto. . . ."

Fleurette!

This thought was powerful enough to drag me away from that phantasmal laboratory—powerful enough to make me forget, for a moment, Dr. Fu Manchu, and the dead Dutch botanist who talked with him so earnestly.

Was Fleurette also a phantom?

Did Fleurette belong to the life of which until recently I had believed myself to form a unit, or was she one of the living-dead? In either case, she belonged to Dr. Fu Manchu; and every idea which I had formed respecting her was

75

scrapped, swept away by this inexorable tidal wave which had carried me into a ghost world. . . .

A new thought. Perhaps this was insanity!

In the course of my struggle with the *dacoit* I might have received a blow upon the skull, and all this be but a dream; delirium, feverish fancy.

Through all these chaotic speculations a guttural voice issued a command:

"Follow."

And, dumbly, blindly, I followed.

## CHAPTER XX

# DREAM CREATURES

I FOUND myself in a long, gloomily lighted corridor.

My frame of mind by this time was one which I cannot hope to convey in words. In a setting fantastic, chimerical— I had found myself face to face with that eerie monster whose existence I had seriously doubted—Dr. Fu Manchu. I had been made helpless by means of some electrical device outside my experience. I had seen botanical monstrosities which challenged sanity . . . and I had shaken the hand of a dead man!

Now, as I followed my tall, yellow-clad guide:

"The radio research-room," he said, "in which you recently found yourself, is in charge of Companion Henrick Ericksen."

This was too much; it broke through the cloud of apathy which had been descending upon me.

"Ericksen!" I exclaimed—"discoverer of the Ericksen Ray? He died during the World War—or soon after!"

"The most brilliant European brain in the sphere of what is loosely termed radio. Van Rembold, the mining engineer, also is with us. He 'died', as you term it, a few months before Ericksen. His work in the radium mines of Ho Nan has proved to be valuable."

Yet another door was opened, and I entered into half-light to find myself surrounded by glass cases, their windows set flush with the walls and illuminated from within.

"My mosquitoes and other winged insects," said Dr. Fu

Manchu. "I am the first student to have succeeded in producing true hybrids. The subject is one which possibly does not interest you, Mr. Sterling, but one or two of my specimens possess characteristics which must appeal even to the lay mind."

Yes; this was delirium. I recognized now that connecting link, which, if sought for, can usually be found between the most fantastic dream and some fact previously observed, seemingly forgotten, but stored in that queer cupboard which we call the subconscious.

The ghastly fly which had invaded Petrie's laboratory—this was the link!

I proceeded, now, as a man in a dream, convinced that ere long I should wake up.

"My principal collection," the guttural voice went on, "is elsewhere. But here, for instance, are some specimens which have spectacular interest."

He halted before the window of a small case, and resting one long, yellow hand upon the glass, tapped with talon-like nails.

Two gigantic wasps, their waisted bodies fully three inches long, their wing-span extraordinary, buzzed angrily against the glass pane. I saw that there was a big nest of some clay-like material built in one corner of the case.

"An interesting hybrid," said my guide, "possessing saw-fly characteristics, as an expert would observe, but with the pugnacity of the wasp unimpaired, and its stinging qualities greatly increased. Merely an ornamental experiment, and comparatively useless."

He moved on. I thought that such visions as these must mean that I was in high fever, for I ceased to believe in their reality.

"I have greatly improved the sand-fly," Dr. Fu Manchu continued; "a certain Soudanese variety has proved to be most amenable to treatment."

He paused before another case, the floor thickly sanded, and I saw flea-like, winged creatures nearly as large as common house-flies. . . .

"The spiders may interest you."

He had moved on a few steps. I closed my eyes, overcome by sudden nausea.

The dream, as is the way with such dreams, was becoming horrible, appalling. A black spider, having a body as large as a big grape fruit, and spiny legs which must have had a span of twenty-four inches, sat amidst a putrid looking litter in which I observed several small bones, watching us with eyes which gleamed in the subdued light like diamonds.

It moved slightly forward as we approached. Unmistakably, it was *watching* us; it had intelligence!

No horror I had ever imagined could have approximated to this frightful, gorged insect, this travesty of natural laws.

"The creature," said Dr. Fu Manchu, "has a definitely developed brain. It is capable of elementary reasoning. In regard to this I am at present engaged upon a number of experiments. I find that certain types of ant respond also to suitable suggestion. But the subject is in its infancy, and I fear I bore you. We will just glance at the bacteria, and you might care to meet Companion Frank Narcomb who is in charge of that department."

I made no comment—I was not even shocked.

Sir Frank Narcomb—for some time physician to English Royalty and one of the greatest bacteriologists in Europe, had been a friend of my father's!

I had been at Edinburgh at the time of his death, and had actually attended his funeral in London!

A door set between two cases slid open as my guide approached it. In one of these cases I saw an ant-hill inhabited by glittering black ants, and in the other, a number of red centipedes moving over the leaves of a species of cactus, which evidently grew in the case. . . .

In a small, but perfectly equipped laboratory, a man wearing a long, white coat was holding up a test-tube to a lamp and inspecting its contents critically. He was quite bald and his skull had a curious, shrivelled appearance.

But when, hearing us enter, he replaced the tube in a rack and turned, I recognized that this was indeed my father's old friend, aged incredibly and with the lines of suffering upon his gaunt face, but beyond any question Sir Frank Narcomb himself!

"Ah, doctor!" he exclaimed.

I saw an expression of something very like veneration spring into the tired eyes of this man, who, in life, had acknowledged none his master in that sphere which he had made his own.

"The explanation eludes me," he said. "Russia persistently remains immune!"

"Russia!"

I had never heard the word spoken as Dr. Fu Manchu spoke it. Those hissing sibilants were venomous.

"Russia! It is preposterous that those half-starved slaves of Stalin's should survive when stronger men succumb. *Russia!*"

With the third repetition of the name a sort of momentary frenzy posssesed the speaker. During one fleeting instant I looked upon this companion of my dream as a stark maniac. The madman discarded the gown of the scientist and revealed himself in his dreadful, naked reality.

Then, swiftly as it had come, the mood passed. He laid a long yellow hand upon the shoulder of Sir Frank Narcomb.

"Yours is the most difficult task of all, Companion," he said. "This I appreciate, and I am arranging that you shall have more suitable assistance." He glanced in my direction and I saw that queer film flicker across his brilliant eyes. "This is Mr. Alan Sterling, with whom, I am informed, you are already acquainted."

Sir Frank stared hard. As I remembered him he had been endowed with a mass of bushy, white hair; now, he was a much changed man, but the shrewd, wrinkled face remained the same. Came a light of recognition.

"Alan!" he said, and stretched out his hand. "It's good to meet you here. How is Andrew Sterling?"

Mechanically I shook the extended hand.

"My father was quite well, Sir Frank," I replied in a toneless voice, "when last I heard from him."

"Excellent! I wish he could join us."

In the circumstances, I could think of nothing further to say, but:

"Follow!" came the guttural order.

And once more, I followed.

## CHAPTER XXI

# THE HAIRLESS MAN

Our route up a flight of stairs, rubber-covered like every other place I had visited with the exception of that strange study pervaded with opium fumes.

"The physiological research-room," Dr. Fu Manchu said, "would not interest you It is very small in this establishment, although Companion Yamamata, who is at present in charge, is engaged upon a highly important experiment in synthetic genesis."

We entered a long, well-lighted corridor, with neat white doors right and left, each bearing a number like those in a hotel. These doors were perfectly plain and possessed neither handles nor keyholes.

"Some of the staff reside here," my guide explained.

He pressed a button in the wall beside a door numbered eleven, and the door slid noiselessly open. I saw a very neat sitting-room, with other rooms opening out of it.

"Temporarily," the guttural voice continued. . . .

There was a strange interruption.

A sort of quivering note sounded, a gong-like note, more a vibration of the atmosphere than an actual sound. But Dr. Fu Manchu stood rigidly upright, and his extraordinary eyes glanced swiftly left along the corridor.

"Quick!" he said harshly, "inside! And close the door— there is a corresponding button in the wall. One pressure closes the door; two open it. Remain there until you are called if you value your life."

His harsh imperious manner had its effect. Some of the secret of this strange man's power lay in the fact that he never questioned his own authority, or the obedience of those upon whom he laid his orders.

The force behind those orders was uncanny.

With no other glance in my direction he set off along the corridor, moving swiftly, yet with a sort of cat-like dignity.

With his withdrawal, some part of my real self began to clamour for recognition. I hesitated on the threshold of the little room, watching him as he went. And when the tall figure, with never a backward glance, disappeared where the corridor branched right, something like a cold wave of sanity came flooding back to my brain.

This was neither delirium nor death! It was mirage. This place was real enough—the long corridor and the white doors—but the rest was hypnotism; a trick played for what purpose I could not imagine, by a master of that dangerous art!

That the woman called Fah Lo Suee was an adept, Sir Denis had admitted. This was her father, and her master.

Those living-dead men were phantoms, conjured up by his brain and displayed before me as an illusionist displays the seemingly impossible. Those vast forcing-houses, the big laboratory, the horrible insects in their glass cases! It was perhaps his method of achieving conquest of my personality, submerging me and then using me.

Very well! I was not conquered yet. I could still fight!

That curious throbbing, as of a muted gong, continued incessantly.

What did it mean? What was the explanation of Dr. Fu Manchu's sudden change of manner and his hurried departure.

"Close the door . . . and remain there until you are called, if you value your life!"

These had been his words. He had spoken with apparent sincerity.

And now as I watched, I saw a strange thing. At the foot of the stairs which we had ascended, I saw a door dropping slowly from the roof. I could feel the slight vibration of the mechanism controlling it.

I glanced swiftly left, along the corridor.

A similar door was descending just where the passage branched off!

They were Stone doors, or something very like them, such as are used in sea-going ships. Was this the meaning of that constant vibrating note which now was beginning to tell upon my nerves?

What had happened? Had fire broken out? If so, I might well be trapped between the two doors, for I knew of no other exit. Further reflection assured me that these devices could not be intended for use in such an emergency as fire. What then was their purpose, and what was it that Dr. Fu Manchu had feared?

The answer came even as the question flashed into my mind.

Heralded by a hoarse, roaring sound, a *Thing*, neither animal nor human, a great, naked misshapen creature resembling an animated statue by Epstein, burst into view at the end of the corridor!

It had a huge head set upon huge shoulders. The head was hairless and the entire face, trunk and limbs glistened moistly like the skin of an earth-worm. The arms were equally massive; but I saw that the hands were misformed, the fingers webbed, and the thumbs scarcely present.

The legs were out of all proportion to that mighty trunk, being stumpy, dwarfed, and terminating in feet of a loathsome pink colour—feet much smaller than the great hands, but also webbed.

From the appalling, glistening, naked face, two tiny eyes set close together beside a flattened nose with distended nostrils, glared, redly, murderously, in my direction.

Uttering a sound which might have proceeded from a wounded buffalo, the creature hurled itself towards me. . . .

## CHAPTER XXII

# HALF-WORLD

I SPRANG back, looking wildly right and left for the button which controlled the door.

The worm-man was almost upon me, and, transcending all fear of a violent death was the horror of contact with those moistly glittering limbs. The control button proved to be on the right. I pressed it.

And the door began to close rapidly and smoothly.

In the very instant of its closing, a loathsome, moist mass appeared in the narrowing opening.

My heart leaped, and then seemed to stop. I thought that one of those great pink arms was about to be thrust through. Judging the door to be a frail one, I looked in those few instants upon a fate more horrible than any which had befallen man since prehistoric times.

The door closed.

And now came a hollow booming, and a perceptible vibration of the floor upon which I stood.

That unnameable thing was endeavouring to batter a way in! I inhaled deeply, and knew such a sense of relief as I could not have believed possible under the roof of Dr. Fu Manchu.

The door was of metal. Not even the unnatural strength of the monster could prevail against it.

All sounds were curiously muted here; but one harsh bellow of what I took to be frustrated rage reached me very dimly. Then silence fell.

I pressed my ear aginst the enamelled metal but could hear nothing save a vague murmuring, with which was mingled the rumble of those descending doors.

Thereupon, I stood upright; and as I did so, a stifled exclamation brought me sharply about.

Fleurette was in the room just behind me!

She wore a blue and white pyjama suit and blue sandals, Her beautiful eyes registered the nearest approach to fear which I had seen in them. She had told me, I remembered, that nothing frightened her, but to-day or to-night—for I had lost all count of time—something had definitely succeeded in doing so. Her face, which was so like a delicate flower, was pale.

"You!" she whispered: "what are *you* doing here?"

I swallowed; not without difficulty. I suffered from an intense thirst, and my throat remained very sore by reason of its maltreatment at the hands of the *dacoit*.

My heart began jumping in quite a ridiculous way.

Yet, I suppose the phenomenon was not so ridiculous, for Fleurette was more lovely than I had ever believed a woman could be. Oddly enough, her beauty swamped the last straw of reality upon which I had clutched in the corridor with its rows of white doors and which had remained with me up to the moment that the worm-man had appeared. I sank back again into a sea of doubt, from which, agonizingly, I had been fighting to escape.

Fleurette was dead! *I* was dead! This was a grim, a ghastly half-world, horribly reminiscent of that state which Spiritualists present to us as the after-life.

"I have joined you," I replied.

My words carried no conviction even to myself.

"What?"

Her expression changed; she watched me with a new, keen interest.

"I have joined you."

Fleurette moved towards me and laid one hand almost timidly upon my shoulder.

"Is it true?" she asked, in a low voice.

I had thought that her eyes were blue, but now I saw that they were violet. The life beyond, then, was a parody of that which we had lived on earth. I had seen travesties of my own studies in those monstrous houses; I had met with the fabulous Dr. Fu Manchu; I had watched men still pursuing the secrets they had sought in life—amid surroundings which were a caricature of those they had known during their earthly incarnation.

Horror there was, in this strange borderland, but, as I looked into those violet eyes, I told myself that death had its recompenses.

"I am glad you are here," said Fleurette.

"So am I."

She glanced aside, and went on rapidly:

"You see, I have been trained not to feel fear, but whenever I hear the alarm signal and know that the section doors are being closed—I feel something very like it! I don't suppose you know about all this yet?" she added.

Already normal colour was returning to those rose-petal cheeks, and she dropped into a little armchair, forcing a smile.

"No," I replied, watching her; "it's unpleasantly strange."

"It must be!" She nodded. "I have lived amongst this sort of thing on and off as long as I can remember."

"Do you mean *here?*"

"No; I have never been here before. But at the old palace in Ho Nan the same system is in use, and I have been there many times."

"You must travel a lot," I said, studying her fascinatedly, and thinking that she had the most musical voice in the world.

"Yes, I do."

"With Mahdi Bey?"

"He nearly always comes with me; he is my guardian, you see."

"Your guardian?"

"Yes." She looked up, a puzzled frown appearing upon her smooth forehead. "Mahdi Bey is an old Arab doctor, you know, who adopted me when I was quite tiny—long before I can remember. He is very, very clever; and no one in the world has ever been so kind to me."

"But my dear Fleurette, how did you come to be adopted by an Arab doctor?"

She laughed: she had exquisite little teeth.

"Because," she said, and at last that for which I had been waiting, the adorable dimple, appeared in her chin; "because I am half an Arab myself."

"What!"

"Don't I look like one? I am sunburned now, I know; but my skin is naturally not so many shades lighter."

"But an Arab, with violet eyes, and hair like . . . like an Egyptian sunset."

"Egyptian, yes!" She laughed again. "Evidently you detect the East even in my hair!"

"But," I said in amazement, "you have no trace of accent."

"Why should I have?" She looked at me mockingly. "I am a most perfect little prig. I speak French also without any foreign accent: Italian, Spanish, German, Arabic and Chinese."

"You are pulling my leg."

That maddening dimple reappeared, and she shook her head so that glittering curls danced and seemed to throw out sparks of light.

"I know such accomplishments are simply horrible for a girl—but I can't help it. This learning has been thrust upon me. You see, I have been trained for a purpose."

And as she spoke the words, dancing, vital youth dropped from her like a cloak. Those long-lashed eyes, which I had an insane desire to kiss, ceased to laugh. Again, that rapt, mystical expression claimed her face. She was looking through me at some very distant object. I had ceased to exist.

"But, Fleurette," I said desperately, "*what* purpose? There can be only one end to it. Sooner or later you will fall in love with—somebody or another. You will forget your accomplishments and everything. I mean it's a sort of law. What other purpose is there in life for a woman?"

In a far-away voice:

"There is no such thing as love," Fleurette murmured. "A woman can only *serve*."

"What ever do you mean?"

"You are new to it all. You will know to-morrow or perhaps even to-night."

I had taken a step in her direction when something arrested me—drew me up sharply.

Like a fairy trumpet it sounded, again, that unaccountable call which I had heard twice before—coming from nowhere; from everywhere; from inside my brain!

Fleurette stood up, giving me never another glance, and moved to that end of the room opposite to the door by which I had entered. She touched some control hidden in the wall. A section slid open. As she crossed the threshold, she turned: I could see a lighted corridor beyond.

"The danger is over now," she said. "Good-bye."

I stood staring stupidly at the blank expanse of wall where only a moment before Fleurette had been, when I heard a sound behind me. I turned sharply.

The white door was open! The woman whom Nayland Smith had called Fah Lo Suee stood there, looking at me.

With the opening of the door a faint vibration reached my ears. The "sections doors" (so Fleurette had described them) were being raised.

Fah Lo Suee wore what I took to be a Chinese dress, by

virtue of its style, only; for it was of a patternless, shimmering gold material. Her unveiled eyes were green as emeralds; their resemblance to those of the terrible doctor was unmistakable.

"Please come," she said; "my father is waiting for you."

## CHAPTER XXIII

# THE JADE PIPE

As I followed that slim, langurous figure, mentally I put myself in the witness box. And this was the question to which I demanded an answer:

Am I alive, or dead?

On the whole I was disposed now to believe that I was alive. Therefore, I put this second question:

Am I sane?

To which query I could find no answer.

If the occurrences of the past few hours were real, then I had stepped into a world, presumably in China, where natural laws were flouted; their place taken by laws created by the Chinese physician.

At the foot of the stairs, Fah Lo Suee turned sharply left, and opened one of the sliding doors which seemed to be common in the establishment. She beckoned me to follow, and I found myself in a carpeted, warmly lighted corridor. She bent across me to reclose the door.

"You must forget all that is past and all that is puzzling you," she whispered, urgently, speaking close to my ear. "My father knows that you and the little Rose-petal are acquainted. Don't speak—listen. He will question you, and you will have to answer. When you go to Yamamata's room, do not fear the injection. But all that you are told will happen when you have received the Blessing of the Celestial Vision, *see that you carry out*. . . . Pretend—it is your only chance. Pretend! I will see you again as soon as possible. Now follow me."

These strange words she had spoken with extraordinary rapidity, as she had bent over me, apparently fumbling with the button which controlled the door.

And now, with that slow, lithe, cat-like walk in which again I recognized her father, she moved ahead, leading me. My brain was working with feverish rapidity.

The little Rose-petal!

This must be the Chinese name of Fleurette. Our association, I gathered, did not meet with the approval of Dr. Fu Manchu. And what was the Blessing of the Celestial Vision? This I had yet to learn.

At the end of the corridor, I saw a small green lamp burning before an arched opening. Here, Fah Lo Suee paused, signalling me to be silent.

"Remember," she whispered.

The green light in the little lamp flickered, and a heavy door of panelled mahogany slid aside noiselessly.

"Go in," said Fah Lo Suee.

I obeyed. The door closed behind me and a whiff of air laden with fumes of opium told me that I was in that queer study which, presumably, was the sanctum of Dr. Fu Manchu.

One glance was enough. He was seated at the big table, his awful but majestic face resting upon one upraised palm. The long nails of his fingers touched his lips. His brilliant eyes fixed me so that I experienced almost a physical shock as I met their gaze.

"Sit down," he directed.

I discovered that a Chinese stool was set close beside me. I sat down.

Dr. Fu Manchu continued to watch me. I tried to turn my eyes aside, but failed. The steel-grey eyes of Sir Denis Nayland Smith were hard to evade, but I had never experienced such a thraldom as that cast upon me by the long, narrow, green eyes of Dr. Fu Manchu.

All my life I had doubted the reality of hypnotism. Sir Denis's assurance that Fah Lo Suee had nearly succeeded in hypnotizing me at the hospital had not fully registered; I had questioned it. But now, in that small, opiated room, the reality of the art was thrust upon me.

This man's eyes held a power potent as any drug. When he spoke, his voice reached me through a sort of mist, against which something deep within—my spirit, I suppose—was fighting madly.

"I have learned that you are acquainted with the little flower whose destiny is set upon the peak of a high mountain. Of this, I shall ask you more later. She is nature's rarest jewel: a perfect woman. . . . You have, unwittingly,

87

as I believe, thrust yourself into the cogs of the most delicate machine ever set in motion."

I closed my eyes. It was a definite physical effort, but I achieved it.

"Now, when you are about to devote your services to the triumph of the Si-Fan, consider the state of the world. The imprint of my hand is upon the nations. Mussolini so far has eluded me; but President Hoover, who stood in my path, makes way for Franklin Roosevelt. Mustapha Pasha is a regrettable nuisance, but my organization in Anatolia neutralizes his influence. Von Hindenburgh! the old marshal is a granite monument buried in weeds. . . ."

Persistently I kept my eyes closed. This dangerous madman was thinking aloud, communicating his insane ideas to a member of the outer world, and at the same time pronouncing my doom—as I realized: for the silence of the father confessor is taken for granted.

"Rumania, the oboe of the Balkan orchestra . . . I have tried to forget King Carol—but negligible quantities can upset the nicest equation by refusing to disappear. A man ruled by women is always dangerous—unless the women are under my orders. . . . Women are the lever for which Archimedes was searching, but they are a lever which a word can bend. You may have heard, Alan Sterling, that I have failed in my projects. But consider my partial successes. I have disturbed the currencies of the world. . . ."

That strange, guttural voice died away, and I ventured to open my eyes and to look at Dr. Fu Manchu.

He had lighted a little spirit-lamp which formed one of the items upon the littered table, and above the flame, on the end of a needle, he was twirling a bead of opium. He glanced up at me through half-closed eyes.

"Something upon which Science has not improved," he said softly. "Yes, I could hasten the crisis which I have brought about, if I wished to do so."

He dropped the bead into the jade bowl of a pipe which lay in a tray beside him.

"Here is a small brochure," he went on, and took a book from a table rack, thrusting it in my direction. *Apologia Alchymiae*—a re-statement of Alchemy. It is the work of a London physician—Mr. Watson Councell, whose recent death I regret, since otherwise I should have solicited his services. There are five hundred copies of this small handbook in circulation. Singular to reflect, Alan Sterling, that no one has attempted the primitive method of manufacturing synthetic

gold, as practised by the alchemists and clearly indicated in
these few pages. For fable is at least as true as fact. Gold"
. . . he placed the stem of the pipe between his yellow
teeth . . . "I could drown the human race in gold!"

"But Russia is starving, and the United States under-
nourished. The world is a cheese, consuming itself. Even
China—my China. . . ."

He fell silent—and I watched him until he replaced the
little pipe in its tray, and struck a gong which stood near
to his left hand.

A pair of Chinamen, identical in appearance, and wearing
identical white robes, entered behind me—I suddenly found
one at either elbow. Their faces resembled masks carved
in old ivory and mellowed by the smoke of incense.

Dr. Fu Manchu spoke a few rapid words in Chinese—then:

"Companion Yamamata will see you," he said, his voice
now very drowsy and that queer film creeping over the
brilliant eyes: "he will admit you to the Blessing of the
Celestial Vision, by which time I shall be ready to discuss
with you certain points in regard to the future, and to instruct you in your immediate duties."

One of the Chinese servants touched me upon the shoulder
and pointed to the open doorway. I turned and walked out.

## CHAPTER XXIV

# COMPANION YAMAMATA

I PRESENTLY found myself in a typical reception room of a
consulting surgeon. I was placed in a chair around which
were grouped powerful lights for examination purposes. Companion Yamamata, who was scrutinizing some notes, immediately stood up and introduced himself, peremptorily
dismissing the Chinamen.

He was young and good looking in the intellectual Japanese manner; wore a long white coat having the sleeves
rolled up; and as he rose from the table where he had been
reading the notes, he laid down a pair of tortoiseshell-rimmed
glasses and looked at me with humorous, penetrating eyes.
He spoke perfect English.

"I am glad that you are becoming a Companion, Mr. Sterling," he said. "Your province of science is not mine, but I am given to understand by Trenck that you are a botanist of distinction. Your medical history"—he tapped the pages before him—"is good, except for malarial trouble."

I stared at him perhaps somewhat stupidly. His manner was utterly disarming.

"How do you know that I have had malaria?" I asked. "I don't think I display any symptoms at the moment."

"No, no, not at all," he assured me. "But, you see, I have your history before me. And this malaria has to be taken into account, especially since it culminated in blackwater so recently as three months ago. Blackwater, you know, is the devil!"

"I do know," said I, grimly.

"However"—he displayed gleaming teeth in a really charming smile—"I am accustomed to these small complications, and I have prepared the dose accordingly. Will you please strip down to the waist. I always prefer to make the injection in the shoulder."

He stepped to a side-table and took up a hypodermic syringe, glancing back at me as he did so.

"Suppose I object?" I suggested.

"Object?" He wrinkled his brow comically. "Object to enthusiasm?—object to be admitted to knowledge conserved for hundreds of centuries?—to salvation physical as well as intellectual! Ha, ha! that is funny."

He went on with his preparations.

I reviewed the words of the woman Fah Lo Suee. To what extent could I rely upon them? Did they mean that for some reason of her own she was daring to cross the formidable mandarin, her father? If so, what was her reason? And supposing that she had lied or had failed, what was this Blessing of the Celestial Vision to which I should be admitted?

I suspected that it was the administration of some drug which would reduce me to a condition of abject mental slavery.

/That there was vast knowledge conserved in this place, that experiments ages ahead of any being carried out in the great cultural centres of the world were progressing here, I could not doubt; I had had the evidence of my own eyes. But to what end were these experiments directed?

Something of my thoughts must have been reflected upon my face, for:

"My dear Mr. Sterling," said the Japanese doctor, "it is so useless to challenge the why, and demand the wherefor. And you are about to be admitted to the Company of the Si-Fan. A new world which trembles in the throes of birth will be your orange, of which you shall have your share."

I made to stand up—to confront him. I could not move! And Dr. Yamamata laughed in the most good-humoured manner.

"Many jib at the last fence," he assured me, "but what is to be, will be, you know. Allow me to assist you, Mr. Sterling."

He stepped behind me, and with the adroit movement of a master of ju-jitsu, peeled my overalls down over my shoulders, pinioning my arms. He unbuttoned my shirt collar.

"Injections are always beastly," he admitted. "For myself, they induce a feeling of nausea; but sometimes they are necessary."

I experienced a sharp stab in the shoulder and knew that the needle point of the syringe had been thrust into my flesh. I clenched my teeth; but I was helpless. . . .

He was cleaning the syringe at a wash-basin on the other side of the room. His manner was that of a dental surgeon who has deftly made a difficult extraction.

"A pleasant glow pervades your body, no doubt?" he suggested, "You see, I am accustomed to these small operations. It will be succeeded, I assure you, by a consciousness of new power. No task which may be set—and the tasks set by the Doctor are not simple ones—will prove too difficult."

He replaced the parts of the syringe upon a glass rack and began to wash his hands.

"When you are rested I shall prescribe a whisky and soda, which I know is your national beverage, and then you will be ready for your second interview with the Doctor."

He glanced back at me smilingly.

"Is my diagnosis correct?"

"Perfectly," I replied, conscious of the fact that no change whatever had taken place in my condition, and mindful of the words of that strange, evil woman.

I had a part to play. Not only my own life, but other lives—thousands, perhaps millions—depended upon my playing it successfully!

"Ah!" he beamed delightedly, and began to dry his hands. "Sometimes novitiates shout with joy—but blackwater has somewhat lowered your normal vitality."

"Nevertheless," I replied, grinning artificially, "I feel that I want to shout."

"Then, shout!" he cried, revealing those gleaming teeth in a happy smile. "Shout! the chair is disconnected. Jump about! Let yourself go! Life is just beginning!"

I moved. It was true . . . I could stand up.

"Ah!" I cried, and stretched my hands above my head. It was a cry and a gesture of relief. Fah Lo Suee had tricked the Japanese doctor! And I was free—free in mind and body . . . but in China, and under the roof of Dr. Fu Manchu!

"Splendid!" Yamamata exclaimed, his small, bright eyes registered pure happiness. "My congratulations, Companion Sterling. We will drink to the Master who perfected this super-drug—which makes men giants with the hearts of lions."

He took up a decanter and poured out two liberal pegs of whisky.

"There was a slight faux-paus earlier this evening," he went on. "A nearly perfected *homonculus*—not in your province, Companion, but I am an enthusiast in my own—escaped from the incubator. The formula is, of course, the Doctor's. I had contributed some small items to its perfection, and the specimen who disturbed the household had points of great interest."

He added soda to the whisky and handed a glass to me. I resigned myself to this gruesome conversation and merely nodded. Yamamata raised his glass.

"Comrade Alan Sterling—we drink to the Mandarin Fu Manchu, master of the world!"

It was a badly-needed drink, and I did not challenge his toast; then:

"The specimen had enormous physical strength," he went on, "and that blind elemental fury which characterizes these products—a fact recognized even by Paracelsus. The section doors had to be closed. And I felt dreadfully guilty."

I drank down half the contents of my tumbler; and:

"What became of . . . the thing?" I asked.

"Most regrettably," Yamamamata replied, shaking his head, "the vital spark expired. You see, the temperature of the corridors was unsuitable."

"I see—"

I stopped short.

That clear, indefinable sound or vibration which I had first heard upon the beach of Ste. Claire de la Roche, came to me again, I saw Yamamata raise one hand and press it against his ear. The sound ceased.

"Dr. Fu Manchu is waiting for you," he said.

He extended both hands cordially, and I grasped them.

For a moment I had all but forgotten my part; in the horror of the story of that *life* which was not human, which had been bred, I gathered, in an incubator. . . .

But now, in time—I remembered.

"I am going to kneel at his feet," I said, endeavouring to impart a quality of exaltation to my voice.

And as I spoke, the smile vanished from the face of Dr. Yamamata as writing sponged from a slate.

"We *all* kneel at his feet," he said solemnly.


## CHAPTER XXV

# THE LIFE PRINCIPLE


DRENCHED in the opium fumes of that stygian room, I stood again before Dr. Fu Manchu. His eyes were brilliant as emeralds, the pupils mere pin-points; and he lay back in a padded chair, watching me. I had thought out the words which I would speak, and I spoke them now.

"I salute the Master of the World," I said, and bowed deeply before him.

That the Blessing of the Celestial Vision produced some kind of mental exaltation was clear to me. This I must enact; but it was a mighty task which rested upon my shoulders. That cold hatred which had possessed me at the moment that the news of Petrie's death had come, now again held absolute sway. I knew that Sir Denis Nayland Smith had not romanced when he had said that this man was Satan's own—apparently eternal.

At whatever cost—my life was nothing in such a contest!— I would help to throw him down. *I* would be the feeble instrument which should prove that he was *not* eternal.

He was monstrous—titanic—dreadful—Hell's chosen emissary. But if I could live, if I could hope to trick this gigantic evil brain, I would find means to crush him; to stamp him out; to eradicate this super-enemy of all that was clean and wholesome.

I could not forget the dead men in his workshops. This monster clearly possessed knowledge transcending natural laws. He laughed at God. No matter! he was still human— or so I must continue to believe.

The price of doubt was insanity. . . .

He watched me awhile in silence, and then:

"In two hours, Companion Sterling," he said, "you will be called for duty. This is your private telephone."

He handed to me what looked like a signet ring, made of some dull, white metal. I had to clench my teeth at the moment of contact with those long, talon-like nails; but I took the ring and stared at it curiously.

"It is adjustable," Dr. Fu Manchu continued. "Place it upon that finger which you consider most suitable. It is an adaptation—much simplified by Ericksen—of the portable radio now in use amongst the French police. It does not convey the spoken word. Morse code is used. You know it?"

"I regret to say that I do not."

"It is simple. You will find a copy of the code in your room. The call-note used by Ericksen is highly individual, but inaudible a short distance away from the receiver. Companion Trenck will call you to-night for duty, and give you further particulars."

As he spoke, I started—suppressing an exclamation.

A queer, whistling note had sounded, almost in my ear, and some vague grey shape streaked past me, alighted upon the big table with its litter of strange books and implements, and with a final spring settled upon the yellow-robed shoulder of Dr. Fu Manchu!

Out from a ball of grey fur, a tiny, wizened face peered at me. One of those taloned hands reached upward and caressed the little creature.

"Probably the oldest marmoset in the world," said the guttural voice. "You would not believe me if I told you Peko's age."

And as the Chinaman spoke, the wizened little creature perched upon his shoulder, looked down into that majestic, evil face, made a mocking, whistling sound, and clutched with tiny fingers at the little skullcap which Dr. Fu Manchu wore.

"I shall not detain you now. Urgent matters call me. You may possibly have noticed that Professor Ascheim and Dr. Hohlwag of Berlin have found *hormone*—the life principle—

in coal deposits. It will prove to be *female*. The *male* I had already found. It is expressed in a rare orchid which possesses the property of extracting this essence of life from certain Burmese swamps which have absorbed it during untold centuries.

"It flowers at regrettably long intervals. Companion Trenck is endeavouring to force some specimens forward under special conditions."

He struck the little gong beside him upon the table.

Almost instantaneously, as though he had arisen from the floor like an Arab genii, one of the white-clad Chinese servants appeared, in the doorway to the right of, and behind, Dr. Fu Manchu's chair.

A guttural order was spoken; the servant bowed to me and stood aside.

I bowed deeply to that strange figure in the padded chair, the tiny, wrinkled-faced monkey crouched upon his shoulder—and went out.

I was conducted back to the long corridor with its rows of white-painted doors. That numbered eleven was opened by the Chinese servant, and I found myself in the small, comfortably appointed sitting-room. My silent guide indicated an adjoining bedroom with a bathroom opening out of it; whereupon I dismissed him.

As the sliding door closed and I found myself alone, I examined more particularly these apartments which had been allotted to me. They were beautifully appointed. Silk pyjamas lay upon the temptingly turned-down bed; and although I had never felt in greater danger in the whole of my life, the lure was one I could not resist.

I recognized a weariness of brain and body which demanded sleep. I made a brief survey of the three rooms before turning in, but although I failed to find any means of entrance or exit other than that opening upon the corridor, that such another exit existed, I knew.

Nevertheless, nature triumphed. . . .

I cannot remember undressing, but I vaguely recall tucking my head into the cool pillow. I was asleep instantly.

The sleep that came to me was not dreamless.

I stood again, a spectator unseen, in the opium-laden atmosphere of Dr. Fu Manchu's study. Fleurette sat in a high-backed chair, her eyes staring straightly before her. The long yellow hand of Fu Manchu was extended in her direction, and a large disc which appeared to be composed of some kind of black meteoric stone was suspended from the ceiling of the room, and was slowly revolving.

As I watched, its movements became more and more rapid, until presently it resembled a globe throwing out ever-changing sparks of light.

The room, Fleurette, the Chinese doctor disappeared. I found myself fascinatedly watching those sparks, their ever-changing colour.

As I watched, a picture formed, mistily, and then very clearly, so that presently it resembled a miniature and very sharp cinematograph projection.

I saw the Tempelhof aerodrome at Berlin. I had been there several times and knew it well. I saw Nayland Smith descend from a plane and hurry across the ground to where a long, low, powerful police car awaited him.

The car drove off. And as in a moving picture, I followed it.

It skirted Berlin and then headed out into a suburb with which I was not acquainted. Before a large house set back beyond a thick shrubbery, the car pulled up, and Sir Denis, springing out, opened the gate and ran up a path over-arched by trees.

A crowd of people was assembled before the house. I saw fire engines and men uncoiling a hose. Through all these, angrily checking their protests, Nayland Smith forced his way, and began to run towards the house. . . .

Something touched me, coldly.

In an instant I was awake—in utter darkness—my heart thumping.

Where was I?

In the house of Dr. Fu Manchu! . . . and someone, or something, was close beside me.

## CHAPTER XXVI

# THE ORCHID

"Do not speak—nor turn on the light!"

Fah Lo Suee! Fah Lo Suee was somewhere in the room near me.

"Listen—for there are some things you must know to-night. First, look upon yourself as in China. For although this is France—"

"France! I am still in France?"

"You are in Ste. Claire de la Roche. . . . It makes no difference; you are in China. No one can leave here day or night without my father's consent—or mine. Very soon now he opens his war upon the world. He will almost certainly succeed; he has with him some of the finest brains in science, military strategy and politics which Europe, Asia and America have ever produced."

I resigned myself to the magic of her voice.

But if I was indeed in Ste. Claire, it remained to be seen if no one could leave.

This house, she told me, was a mere outpost, used chiefly as a base for certain experiments. Elsewhere she had allies of her own, but in Ste. Claire, none.

"For you see I do not agree with all that my father plans—especially his plans concerning Fleurette—"

"Fleurette! What are those plans?"

"Ssh!" Cool fingers were laid upon my arm. "Not so loudly. It is about her I came to tell you. She was chosen—before her birth—for this purpose. She has Eastern and Western blood; her pedigree on both sides is of the kind my father seeks. I am his only child. It will be Fleurette's duty to give him a son—"

"What! Good God! You mean he *loves* her?"

Fah Lo Suee laughed softly.

"How little you know him! She is part of an experiment—the success of which is of political importance. But listen," she lowered her voice, "I do not wish this experiment to take place. . . . Soon, very soon, we shall be leaving France. Fleurette—I think—has found *love*. She is of a race, on her mother's side, to whom love comes swiftly. . . ."

"Do you mean. . . ."

"I mean that if you want Fleurette I will help you. Is that direct enough? It was for this reason I emptied the syringe and recharged it with a harmless fluid. I had seen—once, in the bay; again, in this room. . . ."

She had seen me on the beach! Hoping—doubting—trying to think, to plan, I listened. . . .

Fah Lo Suee had gone.

That voice which seemed to caress the spirit, in which there was a fluttering quality like the touch of butterfly wings and sometimes a hard, inexorable purpose which made me think of the glittering beauty of a serpent, had ceased. The presence of the sorceress was withdrawn.

The room remained in utter darkness; yet I seemed to see her gliding towards the door, and I envisioned her as a slender ivory statue created by some long-dead Greek, and endowed with life, synthetic but potent, by a black magician whose power knew no bounds.

I waited, as I had promised to wait, until I thought that fully a minute had elapsed; then I groped for the switch, found it, and flooded the room with light.

The door, visible from where I lay, I saw to be closed, nor had I heard it open. The location of the other door I did not know.

But I was the sole occupant of the place.

I had still half an hour before I should be summoned to the strange duties which awaited me—half an hour in which to think, to try to plan.

Going into the bathroom, I turned on the taps. Shaving materials and every other toilet necessity were provided in lavish form. I remembered that I had to memorize the Morse Code, and leaving the taps running, I returned to the little sitting-room and took up a chart of Morse which lay there on the table.

A brief inspection satisfied me that I could learn it in a few hours. I have the kind of brain which can assimilate exact information very rapidly.

I returned to the bathroom and mechanically proceeded. . . .

To what extent could I rely upon the dream, or what had seemed to be a dream, which had preceded the visit of Fah Lo Suee? There was no evidence, so far as I could see, to indicate that one episode was more real than the other.

Perhaps the woman's visit had been part of the same dream—or perhaps I had dreamed neither! That almost miraculous experiments in radio and television were being carried out in these secret laboratories, I could not doubt. It might be that that queer scene, resembling one in the cave of some mediaeval astrologer, had actually taken place; that for some reason accidentally or purposefully I had become a witness of it.

"There is as much truth in fable as in fact," Dr. Fu Manchu had said, when he had drawn my attention to the handbook of the modern alchemist.

Perhaps the lost Sybilline books upon which much of the policy of ancient Rome was based, were not mere guesses, but scientific prophecy. Perhaps Fu Manchu had discovered Fleurette to possess the fabulous powers one attributed to the Cumaean oracle. . . .

I considered the strange things which Fah Lo Suee had told me, but greater significance lay, I thought, in the facts which she had withheld. Nevertheless, some glimmering of an enormity about to be loosed upon the world, was penetrating even to my dull mind.

For good or evil, I must now work in concert with this treacherous woman. Her purpose was revealed and it was one which I understood. In her alone lay safety, not only for myself, but for Western civilization.

I had just completed dressing when that tiny penetrating sound seemed to vibrate throughout my frame. It sustained one long note and then ceased; no attempt was made to send me a message other than the signal which told me that my six hours' watch had commenced.

The door slid open and one of the white-robed Chinamen appeared in the opening, inclining his head slightly and indicating that I should follow him. I slipped the code book into a pocket of my overall. . . .

Exit without leave (which only Fu Manchu had power to give) was out of the question, Fah Lo Suee had assured me. Failing outside assistance, there was no means of leaving save by the main gate.

This was the problem exercising my mind as I followed my silent guard downstairs and along to the botanical research room.

I found the famous Dutch botanist in a state of great scientific excitement. Already I was partly reconciled to the indisputable fact that he had died some years earlier in Sumatra. He led me to a small house where artificial sunlight prevailed.

About the mummy-like roots of some kind of dwarf mangrove which grew there, a bank of muddy soil steamed malariously. The place stank like an Amazon forest in the rainy season.

"Look!" said Trenck, with emotion.

He pointed; and, creeping up from the steaming mud, I saw tender flesh-coloured tendrils clasping the swampy roots.

"The orchid of life!" Trenck cried. "The Doctor so terms. But imagine! watch this thermometer—watch it as though your life depended, Mr. Sterling! Here is a culture of *fourteen days!* In its natural state in Burma, flowering occurs

99

at intervals of rarely less than eighty years! Do you realize what this means?"

I shook my head rather blankly.

"Come, Companion! It means that if we can produce flowers, and I expect these buds to break within the next few hours, no one of us, no member of the Si-Fan, shall ever die except by violence!"

Probably my expression had grown even more blank, for:

"The Doctor has not told you?" he went on excitedly. "Very well! The knowledge which we accumulate is common to us all, and it is my privilege to explain to you that from this orchid the Doctor has obtained a certain oil. It is the missing ingredient for which the old alchemists sought. It is the Oil of Life!"

As he spoke, mentally I conjured up the face of Dr. Fu Manchu, recalling the image which had occurred to me—that of Seti the First, the Egyptian Pharaoh. Could it be possible that this Chinese wizard had solved a problem which had taunted the ages?

"He spoke of it," I said, "but gave me no details. How old then is Dr. Fu Manchu?"

Trenck burst out laughing.

"Do you think," he cried, his voice rising to a note almost hysterical, "that a man could know what *he* knows in one short span of life? How can I tell you? It is only necessary to prevent the veins from clogging as in vegetable life. The formula which first came into his possession demanded an ingredient no longer obtainable. For this, after nearly thirty years' inquiry, he found a substitute in the oil expressed from this Burmese orchid. Ah! I must go, It is tantalizing to leave at such a moment, but regulations must be obeyed. But I forget; you are a novice. I will show you how to call me if a bud breaks."

He hurried back to the laboratory and pointed to a dial set upon the wall. He illustrated its simple mechanism and it was not unlike that of a dial telephone.

"You see," he said, "my number is ninety-five."

He twisted the mechanism until the number ninety-five appeared in a small, illuminated oval.

At which moment I heard again that strange vibrating note, which had so intrigued me on the beach at Ste. Claire.

Trenck pressed a button and the number ninety-five disappeared from the illuminuated space, and that incredibly high sound which was almost like the note of a bat, ceased.

"At the moment that a bud begins to break," he said,

Moreover, recognizing the imminence of his danger, Fu Manchu might open his war on the world!

Yet, now that I knew myself to be not in China, but in Ste. Claire de la Roche, my determination to endeavour to get in touch with Nayland Smith was firmly established: the route alone remained doubtful.

And upon this point I formed a sudden resolution.

I had noted that in one of the houses—the first which I had entered with Dr. Fu Manchu, and the loftiest; that in which many fantastic species of palms grew—there was a spiral staircase leading to a series of gangways. By means of these presumably the upper foliage of the trees could be inspected.

From up there, I thought, I might obtain a view of whatever lay outside, and thus get my bearings. Otherwise, I was just as likely to penetrate farther and farther into this maze of laboratories and workshops, as to find a way out of it.

I had one chance, and I didn't know what it was worth. But given anything like decent luck, I proposed to risk it.

For a minute or more I looked in through the observation window to the small house flooded with synthetic sunshine, where those queer, flesh-like orchids were clambering up from steaming mud around the contorted mongo roots. They seemed to be moving slightly, as is the way with such plants, in a manner suggesting the breathing of a sleeping animal.

I moved on to the door which communicated with the first of the range of forcing-houses, or the last in the order in which I had inspected them. It was the one containing the pitcher-plants and other fly-catching varieties.

It was dimly lighted within and the door slid open as I pressed the control button. I closed it, adjusted the gauge, then opened the inner door and went in.

The steamy heat of the place attacked me at once. It was like stepping out of a temperate clime into the heart of a jungle. The air was laden with perfumes—pleasant and otherwise; the predominant smell being that of an ineffable rottenness which characterizes swampy vegetation.

I threaded my way along a narrow path. So far, I had met with success—probably all the doors were unfastened.

It proved to be so, nor did I meet a soul on the way.

And when at last I stood in the most imposing house of all, palms towering high above my head. I became conscious of an apprehension against which I knew I must fight . . . that the note of recall would suddenly sound in my brain.

Yet to have discarded the metal ring would have been folly.

There was an odd whispering amongst the dim palm-tops, for the place was but half lighted. It felt and smelled like a tropical forest. Much of the glass composing the walls was semi-opaque. What lay beyond, I had no means of finding out.

I moved cautiously along until I came to that spiral stair-case I had noted. It was situated at no great distance from the doorway through which I had originally entered.

Cautiously I began to ascend, my rubber-soled shoes creating a vague thrumming sound upon the metal steps. I reached the top of the first staircase and saw before me a narrow gangway with a single handrail—not unlike those found in engine-rooms.

Palm boles towered above me and fronds of lower foliage extended across the platform. I advanced, sometimes ducking under them, to where vaguely I had seen a second stair leading higher.

I mounted this until I found myself amongst the tops of wildly unfamiliar trees; narrow galleries branched off in several directions. I selected one which seemed to lead to the glass wall. I saw queer fruit glowing in the crowns of trees unknown. Normally I could not have resisted inspect-ing it more closely; but to-night my professional enthusiasms must be subdued: a task of intense urgency claimed me.

Then, I had almost come to where one gangway joined another running flat against the glass wall, up very near to the arching roof, when I pulled up, inhaled deeply, and clutched at the handrail. . . .

Uttering a shrill whistling sound, *something* swung from a golden crest on my right, perched for a moment on the rail, not a yard from where I stood, chattered up at me and sprang into bright green foliage of an overhanging palm!

My heart was beating rapidly—but I tried to laugh at myself.

It was Fu Manchu's marmoset!

I had begun to move on again when once more I pulled up.

Surely it was not the Doctor's custom to allow his pet to roam at large in these houses? It had presumably escaped from its usual quarters, and sooner or later the Doctor, or someone else, would seek it?

I stood still, listening. I could hear nothing save the faint whispering of the leaves.

Moving on to the side gallery I saw ahead of me through glass windows a rugged slope topped by a ruined wall and

dragon chair-arms; he might have been carved from old ivory.

My rubber-soled shoes making no sound, I stepped into the room, and stood watching him closely. His eyes were closed. He was asleep, or—

I glanced at the jade-bowled pipe which lay upon the table before him. I sniffed the fumes with which the room was laden.

Here was the explanation which I had been slow to grasp.

Dr. Fu Manchu was in an opium trance—possibly the only sleep which that restless, super-normal brain ever knew!

I glanced rapidly about the room, wondering if any other man, not enthralled by the Blessing of the Celestial Vision, had ever viewed its strange treasures and lived to tell the world of them.

And now, as I stood there in the presence of that insensible enemy of Western civilization, I asked myself a question: What should I do?

If I could find a way out of this maze I believed I had a fighting chance to escape from Ste. Claire. I was in China only in the sense that this place was under the domination of the Chinese doctor. Actually, I was in France; my friends were within easy reach if I could get in touch with them.

Why should I not kill him?

He had killed Petrie—dear old Petrie, one of the best friends I had ever had in life: he had killed, for no conceivable reason, those other poor workers in vineyards and gardens. And, according to Sir Denis, this was but the beginning of the sum of his assassinations.

I stood quite close to him; only the big table divided us. And I studied the majestic, evil mask which was the face of Dr. Fu Manchu.

He was helpless, and I was a young, vigorous man. Would it be a worthy, or an unworthy deed. It is an ethical point which to this day I have never settled satisfactorily.

All I can say in defence of my inaction is, that confronting Dr. Fu Manchu, helpless and insensible, I knew, although my reason and my Celtic blood rose in revolt against me, that something deep down in my consciousness bade me not to touch him!

Supreme Evil sat enthroned before me, at my mercy—perhaps the nearest approach to Satan incarnate which this troubled world has ever known. And perhaps, for that reason, inviolable.

I dared not to lay a finger upon him—and I knew it!

No, I must pursue my original plan—gain my freedom.

The mahogany arched recess communicated I knew with a corridor at the end of which was a stair leading to the rooms with white doors. The door which faced the table opened into the big laboratory called the radio research-room.

Which of these should I attempt?

I had decided upon that leading to the laboratory when something occurred to me which produced a chill at my heart.

The opened doors into the palm-house!

*Who* had opened them, since, obviously, Dr. Fu Manchu had not done so?

I stood quite still for a moment; then turned slowly, and looked out into that misty jungle beyond.

Someone had come out of this room during the time that I had been creeping about upon those gangways in the palm-tops. A patrol? A patrol who, having heard me, would now be waiting for me.

I listened; but no sound came from that tropical jungle. And now dawned a second thought. One acquainted with the iron routine of that place would never have left both doors open!

What did it mean?

An urge to escape from this drug-laden room, from the still figure in the carven chair, seized me.

I stepped softly towards the archway—only to realize that the control was hidden. I could see no trace of one of those familiar glass buttons, resembling bell-pushes, which took the place of door-knobs in this singular household. Perforce, then, I must try my luck in the radio research-room.

Beside the door facing Dr. Fu Manchu I could see the control-button which opened it. I turned, pressed that button . . . and the door slid silently open.

I stepped out into the violet-lighted laboratory.

Looking swiftly right and left I could see no one. The place was empty as when I had first discovered myself in its vastness. Almost directly at my feet a black line was marked upon the rubber floor.

I inhaled deeply. Could I cross it?

Clenching my teeth, I stepped forward. Nothing happened. I was free of the radio research-room.

But now my case was growing desperate. I could not believe myself to be the only person awake in that human ant-hill. Sooner or later I must be detected and challenged. My only chance was to find another way out of the radio

might be others yet to be negotiated. I determined to experiment.

The door had slid open to the right. I remembered that my hand had rested at a point about three feet from the floor. I pressed now right of the door, but there was no response. I pressed to the left. The door remained open. Baffled, I stepped back—and the door closed, swiftly and silently!

The principle was obscure, but the method I had solved.

I opened it again and stepped in to the foot of the stairs. How did I close it now?

The solution of this problem evaded me. I began to mount the stairs—and as my foot touched the first step, the door closed behind me!

I mounted, silent in my rubber-soled shoes, reached the landing, and looked about me, wondering what I should do next.

A short, dark passage opened to the right, and another, longer one, to the left. At the end of the latter I saw a green light burning. I could hear no sound. I determined to explore the shorter passage first. I began to tip-toe along it; then I paused, and stood stock-still.

The door at the foot of the stairs had opened and someone had come through.

I was being followed!

A momentary panic touched me. Had the opium sleep of Dr. Fu Manchu been an elaborate pretence? Could it be that he, after all, had been watching me throughout?—that it was this dreadful being himself who was upon my track?

I hurried to the end of that narrow passage; but there were doors neither right nor left, nor at its terminus.

It was wood-panelled, and I looked about desperately for one of the control buttons. Suddenly, I saw one, pressed it and the door slid open.

I filled my breath with sharp night air, and I looked upon the stars. I stood on a paved terrace bordered by a low parapet. Below me lay a rocky gorge cloaked in vegetation. Beyond was the sea and, instinct told me, the beach of Ste. Claire.

Steps descended on the left. I made no attempt to close the door, but began hurrying down.

Rock plants, ferns, cacti, grew upon the wall. Moonlight painted a sharp angle of shadow upon the steps. I came to a bend and turned. The steps below were completely in shadow. I began to grope my way down.

And at the third step, I pulled up sharply and listened.

Someone had come out on to the terrace above; he was following me!

I had yet to find my way to the sea; but having won freedom from the house of Dr. Fu Manchu and gained the clean free air, it would be a dead man that this tracker carried back again. And unless he shot me down before coming to close quarters, there would be a classic struggle at some point between this and the beach.

The insidious atmosphere of that secret place, as I realized now, had taken its toll of my spirit. But under the stars—free—free from that ghastly thraldom, my cold hatred of the Chinese doctor and of all his works and his creatures, surged back upon me chokingly.

Fleurette!

The dark schemes of Fah Lo Suee could never save her. One hope only I had and I included Fleurette in it optimistically, for no word of love had ever passed between us.

I must find Nayland Smith—surround this scorpion's nest—and put an end to the menace which threatened the peace of the world.

Courage came to me: I felt capable of facing even Dr. Fu Manchu himself.

And throughout this time I had been groping my way down dark steps; and now I came to yet another bend. Thus far I had made no sound. I stood still, listening; and clearly I heard it . . . footsteps following me.

It was eerie—uncanny.

Whomever it might be, the Chinese doctor or one of his creatures, why had he not challenged me—why this silent pursuit? I could only suppose that a trap awaited me.

Someone was on guard at the foot of the stairs, and the one who followed was content to make sure that I did not double back.

Some impassable obstacle lay between me and the beach. It might be—and the thought turned my heart cold—such an obstacle as I had once met with in the radio research-room!

In that event, I should be trapped.

I pulled up, groping upon the wall beside the steps. Some kind of creeping plant grew there in profusion, indeterminable in the darkness. I pulled it aside and craned over, looking down.

Below, as I dimly saw, was a sheer descent of a hundred feet or more. These steps were built around the face of the gorge. Lacking ropes, there was no other means of reaching the beach.

This discovery determined my course.

Unknown dangers were ahead, but a definite enemy was on my trail. Even now, as I stood there listening, I could hear him cautiously descending, step by step.

He exercised great precaution, but in the silence of the night, nevertheless, I could detect his movements. I must deal with him first. Moreover, as I recognized, I must deal with him speedily. This stealthy pursuit was taking toll of my nerves.

I pictured to myself Dr. Fu Manchu, some strange death in his hand, stalking me—the man who had presumed to trick him—cat-like, cruel, and awaiting his own movement to spring.

I looked about me: my eyes were becoming used to semi-darkness. I taxed my brain for some scheme of dealing with the tracker.

And as I began again to grope my way down the steps and came to another bend, a possible plan presented itself. The next flight, branching away at a sharp angle, was palely lighted by the moon. A sharp shadow-belt cut anglewise across the first three steps.

Making as little noise as possible, I hauled myself up upon the parapet; not without injury, for a spiny kind of cactus grew there. But I finally reached the desired position, squatting in dense shadow.

With the advantage which this take-off gave me, I aimed to wait until my follower reached the bend, and then to spring upon his back and hurl him down the steps, trusting to break his neck and to save my own. . . .

I had no more than poised myself for the spring, when I heard him on the last step of the shadowy stairs.

He paused for a long time—I could hear him breathing. I clenched my fists and prepared to spring. . . . He took a pace forward.

For one instant I saw his silhouette against the light.

"My God!" I cried. *"You!"*

It was *Nayland Smith!*

CHAPTER XXX

# NAYLAND SMITH

"THANK God I found you, Sterling," said Nayland Smith when the first shock of that meeting was over. "It's a break-neck job in the dark, but I think we should be wise to put a greater distance between ourselves and the house. Do you know the way?"

"No."

"I do, from here. I discovered it to-night. There are five flights of stone steps and then a narrow path—a mere goat track on the edge of a precipice. It ultimately leads one down to the beach. There may be another way; but I don't know it."

"But," said I, as we began to grope our way downward—"when we get to the beach?"

"I have a boat lying off, waiting for me. We have a lot to tell each other, but let's make some headway before we talk."

And so in silence we pursued our way, presently coming to the track of which Nayland Smith had spoken, truly perilous navigation in the darkness; a false step would have precipitated one into an apparently bottomless gorge.

Willy-nilly I began listening again for that eerie recall note which I was always expecting to hear, wondering what would happen if it came and I did not obey—and what steps would be taken in the awful house of Dr. Fu Manchu.

Some parts of the path were touched by moonlight, and here we proceeded with greater confidence. But when it lay, as it often did, in impenetrable shadow overhung by great outjutting masses of rock, it was necessary to test every foot of the way before trusting one's weight to it.

At a very easy gradient the path sloped downward, until at the end of twenty minutes' stumbling and scrambling it ended in a narrow cutting between two huge boulders.

Far ahead, framed in their giant blackness, I saw the moon glittering on the sea and white-fringed waves gently lapping the shore.

Clear of the cutting—which Nayland Smith appeared to distrust—he dropped down upon a pebbly slope.

112

"Phew!" he exclaimed. "One of the strangest experiences of a not uneventful life!"

I dropped down beside him; nervous excitement and physical exertion had temporarily exhausted me.

"There's definitely no time to waste," he went on, speaking very rapidly. "It might be wiser to return to the boat. But a few minutes' rest is acceptable, and I doubt if they could overtake us now. Bring me up to date, Sterling, from the time you left Quinto's restaurant. I have interviewed the people there, and your movements as reported, prior to the moment when you drove away in Petrie's car, struck me as curious. You crossed and spoke to a man who was standing on the opposite side of the street. Why?"

"I had seen one of the *dacoits* watching me, and I wanted to find out which way he had gone."

"Ah! and did you find out?"

"Yes."

"Good. Go ahead, Sterling, and be as concise as you can."

Whereupon I told him, endeavouring to omit nothing, all that had taken place. Frankly, I did not expect to be believed, but Nayland Smith, who in the darkness was busily loading his pipe, never once interrupted me until I came to the incident where, escaping from the worm-man, I had turned to find Fleurette in the room.

"Who is this girl?" he rapped; "and where did you meet her?"

"Perhaps I should have mentioned the incident before, Sir Denis," I replied, "but naturally I did not believe it to have any connexion with this ghastly business. I met her on the beach, out there."

And I told him as shortly as possible of my first meeting with Fleurette.

"Describe her very carefully," he directed tersely.

I did so in loving detail.

"You say she has violet eyes?"

"They appear sometimes very dark violet; sometimes I have thought they were blue."

"Good. Go on with the story."

I went on; telling him of Fah Lo Suee's intervention, and of how she had tricked the Japanese surgeon; of my second interview with Dr. Fu Manchu, and even of the dream which I had had. Then, of Fah Lo Suee's midnight visit, outlining what she had told me. Finally, I described my escape, and the opium-sleep of Dr. Fu Manchu. Sir Denis had lighted his pipe and now was smoking furiously.

"Amazing, Sterling," he commented. "You seem actually to have seen what took place in Berlin. You have correctly described my movements up to the time that I reached the house of Professor Krus. This can have been no ordinary dream. It is possible that this girl possesses a gift of clairvoyance which Dr. Fu Manchu uses. And it rather appears that, given suitable circumstances, her visions or whatever we should term them are communicated to your own brain. Have you ever dreamed of her before?"

"Yes," I replied, my heart giving a sudden leap. "I fell asleep at the Villa Jasmin shortly after our first meeting, and dreamed that I saw her and Dr. Fu Manchu—whom I had never met at the time—riding in a puple cloud which was swooping down upon a city . . . I thought, New York—"

"Ah!" rapped Nayland Smith, "my theory was right. There was once another woman, Sterling, who, under hypnotic direction from Dr. Fu Manchu, possessed somewhat similar gifts. The Doctor is probably the most accomplished hypnotist in the world. Many of his discoveries are undoubtedly due to his employment of these powers. And it would seem that there is some affinity between this girl's brain and your own."

My heart beat faster as he spoke the words.

"But as to what happened in Berlin: I arrived to find the Professor's laboratory in flames!"

"What!"

"The origin of the fire could not be traced. Incendiarism was suspected by the police. Briefly, the place was burned to a shell, in spite of the efforts of the fire brigade. It is feared that the Professor was trapped in the flames."

"Dead?"

"At the time of my hurried departure, the heat remained too great for any examination of the ruins. But from the moment that Dr. Krus was seen to enter his laboratory, no one attached to his household ever saw him again."

"Good heavens!" I groaned, "the very gods seem to have been fighting against poor Petrie."

"The gods?" Nayland Smith echoed grimly. "The gods of China—Fu Manchu's China. . . ."

"Whatever do you mean, Sir Denis?"

"The burglary at Sir Manston Rorke's," he said, "Sir Manston's sudden death—the fire at Professor Krus's laboratory, and his disappearance: these things are no more coincidences than Fah Lo Suee's visit to the hospital where Petrie lay. Then—something else, which I am going to tell you."

He rested his hand upon my knee and went on rapidly:

"I dashed back to the aerodrome: there was nothing more I could do in Berlin. There came a series of unaccountable delays—none of which I could trace to its source. But they were deliberate, Sterling, they were deliberate. Someone was interested in hindering my return. However, ultimately I got away. It was late in the afternoon before I reached the hospital. I had had the news—about Petrie—when I landed, of course."

He stopped for a moment, and I could tell he was clenching his pipe very tightly between his teeth; then:

"As is the custom," he went on, "in cases of pestilence in a hot climate, they had . . . buried him."

I reached out and squeezed his shoulder.

"It hit *me* very hard, too," I said.

"I know it did. There is a long bill against Dr. Fu Manchu, but you don't know all, yet. You see, the history of this brilliant Chinese horror is known to me in considerable detail. Although I didn't doubt your word when you assured me that Fah Lo Suee had not touched Petrie in the hospital, you may recall that I questioned you very closely as to where she was sitting during the greater part of her visit?"

"I do."

"Well!" He paused, taking his pipe from between his teeth and staring at me in the darkness. "She had brought something—probably hidden in a pocket inside her fur cloak—"

"You mean—"

"I mean that she *succeeded* in the purpose of her visit. Yes, Sterling! Oh, no blame attaches to you. The hellcat is nearly as brilliant an illusionist as her illustrious father. Briefly, when Cartier and Brisson gave me a detailed account of the symptoms which had succeeded the end—I was not satisfied."

"Not satisfied of what?"

"You shall hear."

He paused for a moment and grasped my arm.

"Listen!"

We sat there, both listening intently.

"What did you think you heard?" I whispered.

"I am not certain that I heard anything; but it may have been a vague movement on the path. Are you armed?"

"No."

"I am. If I give the word—run for it. I'll bring up the rear. The boat is hidden just under the headland. They will pull in and we can wade out to them."

## CHAPTER XXXI

# FU MANCHU'S ARMY

"Your disappearance on the road from Monte Carlo," Nayland Smith went on, "puzzled me extraordinarily. The guiding hand behind this business had ceased to be a matter of speculation: I knew that we were dealing with Dr. Fu Manchu. But where you belonged in the scheme was not clear to me. I had urgent personal work to do, necessitating the bringing of pressure to bear on the French authorities. Therefore, I delegated to a local chief of police the task of tracing your movements step by step on the night of your disappearance.

"This was undertaken with that admirable thoroughness which characterizes police work here, and involved a house to house inquiry along many miles of the Corniche Road. In the meantime, working unremittingly, I had secured the powers which I sought. Petrie's grave—a very hurried one—was reopened. . . ."

"What!"

"Yes; it was a pretty ghastly task. In order to perform it in secrecy, we had to close the place and post police upon the roads approaching it. However, it was accomplished at last, and the common coffin in which the interment had taken place was hauled up and laid upon the earth."

"My God!" I groaned.

"I have undertaken some unpleasant duties, Sterling, but the sound of the screws being extracted and the thought that presently—"

He broke off, and sat silent for a while.

"It was done at last," he went on, "and I think I came nearer to fainting than I have ever been in my life. Not from horror, not from sorrow; but because my theory—my eleventh-hour hope—had proved to have a substratum of fact.

"What do you mean, Sir Denis?"

116

"I mean that Petrie was not in the coffin!"

"Not in the coffin! . . . It was empty?"

"Not at all." He laughed grimly. "It contained a body right enough. The body of a Burman. The mark of Kali was on his brow—and he had died from a shot wound in the stomach."

"Good heavens! The *dacoit* who—"

"Exactly, Sterling! Your late friend of the Villa Jasmin, beyond doubt. You will observe that Dr. Fu Manchu finds uses for his servants—dead, as well as living!"

"But this is astounding! What does it mean?"

Quite a long time elapsed before Sir Denis replied:

"I don't dare to hope that it means what I wish it to mean," he said; "but—Petrie was not buried."

I was literally breathless with astonishment, but at last:

"Whenever can so amazing a substitution have taken place?" I asked.

"The very question to which I next applied myself," Nayland Smith replied. "Half an hour's inquiry established the facts. The little mortuary which, I believe, you have visited, is not guarded. And his body, hastily encased as I have indicated, lay there throughout the night. The mortuary is a lonely building, as you may remember. For Dr. Fu Manchu's agents such a substitution was a simple matter."

"What do you think?" I broke in.

"I don't dare to tell you what I think—or hope. But Dr. Fu Manchu is the greatest physician the world has ever known. Come on! Let's establish contact with the police boat."

He stood up and began to walk rapidly down to the beach. We had about reached the spot where first I had set eyes upon Fleurette, when a boat with two rowers and two men in the stern shot out from shadow into moonlight and was pulled in towards us.

Sir Denis suddenly raised his arm, signalling that they should go about.

I watched the boat swing round, and saw it melt again into the shadows from which it had come. I met the glance of eyes steely in the moonlight.

"An idea has occurred to me," said Sir Denis.

I thought that he watched me strangely.

"If it concerns myself," I replied, "count on me for anything."

"Good man!"

He clapped his hand on my shoulder.

117

"Before I mention it, I must bring you up to date. Move back into the shadow."

We walked up the beach and then:

"I checked up on the police reports," he went on. "That dealing with Ste. Claire was the only one which I regarded as unsatisfactory. Ste. Claire, as you probably know, was formerly an extensive monastery; in fact, many of the vineyards in this neighbourhoood formerly yielded their produce to the Father Abbot. When the community dispersed, it came into the possession of some noble family whose name I have forgotten. The point of interest and the point which attracted me, was this:

"The place is built on a steep hillside, opening into a deep cleft which we have just negotiated, rather less than a mile in length. The chief building, now known as a villa, but a reconstruction of the former monastery, is surrounded by one or two other buildings—and there is a little straggling street. It has been the property for the past fifteen years of a certain wealthy Argentine gentleman, regarding whose history I have set inquiries on foot.

"More recently, the lease was taken over by one, Mahdi Bey, of whom I have been able to learn very little—except that he practiced as a physician in Alexandria at one time, and is evidently a man of great wealth. He it was who closed Ste. Claire to the public. However, the police in the course of their inquiries paid a domiciliary visit some time during yesterday afternoon. They were received by a major domo who apologized for the absence of his master, who is apparently in Paris.

"They were shown over the villa and the adjoining houses, occupied now, I gather, by dependants of the Bey. No information was obtained upon the subject of your disappearance.

"But, in glancing through the police report, bearing in mind that I was definitely looking for a place occupied by Dr. Fu Manchu, a process of elimination showed me that of all the establishments visited, Ste. Claire alone remained suspect.

"The Argentine owner had built a number of remarkable forcing-houses. The police, under my directions and unaware of the reasons for them, were ostensibly searching for an escaped criminal, which enabled them tactfully to explore the various villas en route. I noted in their report that they had merely glanced into these houses, nor did I come upon any account of the enormous wine-cellars, enlargements of natural caves, which I was informed, lay below the former monastery.

"The character and extent of Dr. Fu Manchu's new campaign dawned upon me suddenly, Sterling. I wonder if it has dawned upon you?"

"I'm afraid it hasn't," I confessed. "I have alternated between the belief that I was dead and the belief that I was delirious, almost throughout the time that I have been in that house. But, knowing now that what I saw was not phantasy, I am still in doubt, I must confess, as to the nature of this 'war' which threatens."

"Its nature is painfully clear," Nayland Smith rapped. "Somewhere in this place there are thousands—perhaps millions—of these damnable flies! The deaths of which we know were merely experimental. The cases were watched secretly, with great interest by Dr. Fu Manchu or his immediate agents. It was the duty of one of his servants—probably a Burman—to release one of these flies in the neighbourhood of the selected victim. I have learnt that they seek shadow during the day time, and operate at dusk and in artificial light. Directly there was presumptive evidence that the fly had bitten the selected subject, it was the duty of Fu Manchu's servant to place a spray of this fly-catching plant—the name of which I don't know—where it would attract the fly.

"To make assurance doubly sure, the seductive leaves were sprayed with human blood! Vegetable fly-papers, Sterling—nothing less!"

"My God! It's plain enough to me now."

"Such experiments have apparently been carried out all over the world.

"That Dr. Fu Manchu—or the Si-Fan, which is the same thing—has international agents I know for a fact. This means that collections of these flies, which have been specially bred to carry the new plague and to spread it, exist at unknown centres in various parts of Europe, Asia, Africa and Australia—also, doubtless in the Continent of America.

"Of all those seeking it, Petrie, alone, discovered a treatment which promised to be successful! Dr. Fu Manchu's allies would, of course, be inoculated against the plague. But do you see, Sterling, do you see what Petrie did, and why he stood in the Chinaman's way?"

I hesitated. I was beginning to grasp the truth, but before I could reply:

"The formula for '654' would have been broadcast to the medical authorities of the world, in the event of a general outbreak. This would have shattered Fu Manchu's army."

"Fu Manchu's army?"

"An army, Sterling, bred and trained to depopulate the white world! An army of *flies*—carrying the germ of a new plague; a plague for which medical science knows no remedy!"

I was awed, silenced.

"Police manned a boat in the neighbouring bay," Nayland Smith went on; "I distrusted the sound of a motor. They told me that there was a little beach attached to Ste. Claire. And in this again, I recognized such a spot as Fu Manchu would have chosen.

"At dusk, I waded ashore, ordering the boat to lie off in the shadow of the cliff. I was acting unofficially; I was outside the law if I should be wrong; but I had left a sealed envelope with the Chief of Police, telling him upon what evidence I had acted—if I should not return.

"I walked up the strip of sand, reached the pebbles and had just come to the big boulders, when I saw a speed-boat heading in! I took cover behind one of the boulders, and waited.

"It came right in. The police had orders not to show themselves unless they received a prearranged signal. A man waded ashore through the shallow water, and the boat immediately set out again, and soon had disappeared around the headland.

"I watched him come through the gap between the boulders. He was wearing gum-boots and went very silently. But I was rubber-shod, and could go silently, too. I followed him. It was a difficult business, because of the fact that part of the path, more then than now, was bathed in moonlight. But it evidently never occurred to the man to look back.

"In this way, unconsciously, he led me to the foot of the steps, and I followed him, flight by flight, to the top. I was craning over the parapet when he opened the door; but, nevertheless, it took me nearly ten minutes to find how it worked."

"Do you mean to say that you broke into that house, alone?"

"Yes. It was a one-man job: two would have bungled it."

I could find no words with which to reply. It was a

privilege merely to listen to a man at once so clear-headed and so fearless.

"I was first attracted," he went on, "by the long corridor at the end of which a green light burned. There was not a sound in the place and so I explored this corridor first. I discovered a sliding door operated by one of the button controls, and I opened it."

He paused—laughing shortly.

"I asked you to describe Fleurette particularly," he went on, "because my first investigation led me to Fleurette's bedroom!

"Yes, Sterling, the palace of The Sleeping Beauty. I could see her in the reflected moonlight, one arm thrown over her head, and her face turned towards the window. Your description was that of an artist. I agree with you; she is beautiful. Yet it wasn't her beauty which pulled me up, nor even the knowledge that I had made a mistake: it was something else."

"What?" I asked, eagerly.

"I knew her, Sterling! Yes! I know who she is, this mystery girl who has taken such a hold upon you."

"But, Sir Denis, do you mean . . ."

"I understand your eagerness, and you shall hear everything later. I was anxious to learn the colour of her eyes. You see, they were closed; she was alseep. I retired without disturbing her. I next descended the stairs."

"Good God! I wish I had your nerve!"

"Really, I had very little to fear."

"You may think so—but please go on, Sir Denis."

"My guide, of course, had disappeared, but I found a square space, with corridors opening right and left. The trail of wet rubber-boots gave me a clue. The imprint of fingers on a panel three feet from the floor enabled me to open the door. I found myself in that insane laboratory—"

"Insane is the word," I murmured.

"It was empty. It was permeated by a dim, violet light. And as I entered—the door closed! I was particularly intrigued by a piece of mechanism resembling an ancient Egyptian harp."

"I noticed it, also."

"I determined to investigate more closely, but there was a black mark on the floor surrounding the table on which this piece of mechanism stood—"

"Say no more, Sir Denis! I have had the same experience."

"Oh! Is that so? This rather checked me. I observed that

such a mark ran entirely around the laboratory close to the wall: you may have failed to notice this? And I can only suppose that this system of checking intruders had been disconnected in relation to the doors because the unknown man, who had unwittingly acted as my guide, was expected.

"As the idea flashed across my mind I had no more than time to duck, when the man in question came out!

"A panel slid open on the left-hand wall, and a Chinaman, still wearing wet gum-boots, closed the door behind him, crossed the laboratory, opened another door on the farther side, and disappeared.

"I waited for a while, listening to a sort of throbbing which alone disturbed the silence, and then, I too, ventured to open that door. Do you know what I found?"

"I can guess."

"I found myself face to face with Dr. Fu Manchu. . . ."

## CHAPTER XXXII

## RECALL

"FOR the past twenty years, Sterling, I have prayed for an opportunity to rid the world of this monster. My automatic was raised; I could have shot him where he sat. He hadn't a chance in a million. You know the room? I saw you come out of it.

"He was seated in that throne-like chair behind the big table, and his marmoset, that wizened little creature which I haven't seen for fifteen years, was asleep on his shoulder. The reek told me the story—Dr. Fu Manchu has always been addicted to opium. He was asleep."

"I know!" I groaned.

"You evidently conquered the same temptation. But I am still wondering if we are right. When I decided that I couldn't shoot him as he slept, I cursed my own ridiculous prejudices. A hundred, perhaps a thousand, deaths lay at this man's door—yet, it was impossible.

"I looked at him, seated there, and his crimes made a sort of bloody mountain behind him. I have never known so keen a temptation in my life, and I have never felt so deep a self-contempt in resisting one.

"Suddenly, I observed a door on the right of his chair, and I knew that Dr. Fu Manchu as an adversary might be disregarded for the moment. There was a button beside this door. I opened it, and saw a second a pace beyond. I opened this also.

"And I found myself looking into a tropical jungle! At which moment, the marmoset awakened, uttered its shrill, whistling cry, and whirled past me, disappearing among the trees in that misty place.

"I turned, my automatic raised, watching Fu Manchu. He didn't move. I ventured to take a step into that huge glasshouse. I looked all about me, at the banks of flowers, and up into the palm-tops. Further exploration would be madness, I thought. I had achieved my purpose.

"My next step was to get out, undetected, as I had got in. I had just turned, intent upon the idea of creeping back into the room of Fu Manchu, when I heard a sound of soft footsteps up amongst the palm-tops.

"This hastened my action. Without attempting to close the communicating doors, I crept back across the carpet of the study, and out into the big laboratory. I hesitated there for a moment; but finally I closed the door. I stood still, listening.

"But, apart from the throbbing, which apparently never ceased, there was no movement to be perceived.

"Avoiding the black marks, I set out, moving rapidly to the right. As I neared the wall at the end of that huge place, which as you have probably realized, is built entirely underground, an unpleasant fact dawned upon me.

"I could not remember at which point I had entered! And the blank spaces on the wall offered no clue.

"I was making tentative experiments when I heard someone come out from Dr. Fu Manchu's study . . . I dived to cover.

"The black marks upon the floor I knew I must avoid, and I had just found a hiding-place when someone began to walk along the laboratory towards me! Beyond the fact that he wore white overalls I had no means, from the position which I occupied, of identifying him.

"I saw this figure go up to a recess between two tall cases. The walls being divided into panels by a sort of metal beading, I was determined to make no mistake, and I crept forward in order to watch more closely.

"In my eagerness, I allowed one foot to intrude upon a

black mark surrounding an instrument resembling a search-light. The shock which ran up my leg brought me flatly to the floor. I cursed under my breath and lay there prone.

"When I ventured to look up, the man in the white over-alls had disappeared.

"The wall displayed its former even surface. But I knew where the door was, and I knew that I could open it by pressing hard three feet from the floor.

"Evidently, I had not been detected. I allowed fifty or sixty seconds to elapse, and then, in turn, I opened the door. I saw a flight of stairs ahead of me, and recognized them for those which I had descended. As I crept cautiously on to the first step, the door closed behind me.

"I waited, listening.

"Very faintly, for these mechanisms are beautifully ad-justed, I heard a door above being opened. I remembered it; it was the door by which I had come in.

"The rest, Sterling, you know. An unknown man, for I had never had a glimpse of your face, and your attire was un-familiar, was moving somewhere between me and the shore which I desired to reach."

He stopped, and:

"What's that?" he whispered.

An elfin note, audible above the faint sound of the sea, had reached my ears, as it had reached his.

"Someone is calling me," I said; "my absence has been noted."

## CHAPTER XXXIII

### I OBEY

I OFTEN remember the silence which fell between us at that moment. I thought I knew what Nayland Smith was think-ing—perhaps because I was thinking the same, myself.

"It's asking a lot, Sterling," he said at last. "I have a good old-fashioned police whistle in my pocket, and there's a police boat standing by. But I told you a while ago that an idea had occurred to me."

Remembering what Sir Denis had done that night, how,

alone, he had penetrated to this secret stronghold of Dr.
Fu Manchu, I set my course, and when next he spoke, I
was glad I had done so. His idea was mine!

"What's the mechanism?" he asked, sharply. "You said,
I think, it was a ring?"

I slipped the ring from my finger and handed it to him.
Already I saw his plan, and my part in it. But I was full out
for the rôle he had allotted to me, although I doubted
seriously if I should live to see it through.

He stood up, and silhouetted against the skyline I saw
him tugging at the lobe of his ear; then:

"I have no right to ask what I am going to ask, Sterling,"
he began—

"I had thought of it already," I interrupted. "I am game.
This is a fight to a finish and you are in charge, Sir Denis.
Just give me my orders."

He nodded shortly.

"Unless my calculations are wildly at fault, Sterling, Petrie
is up there, in that house—dead or alive—I don't know
which. But I *want* to know, before I make my next move."

Dimly I saw him slip the adjustable ring upon his finger,
and then:

"I will come back to the door," he said. "The whistle will
be audible to the men in the boat from that point. Make
straight for the dial—the one Herman Trenck explained to
you. The curse is, you don't know Morse."

"I have the code in my pocket."

"It isn't easy to work from printed instructions," he rapped
back. "What I have in mind is this: If you are not suspected, just call your number. What is it?"

"103," I replied. "It's on the ring."

"Good enough. Failing such a message within a period
of ten minutes, I shall raid the house at once: I have it
covered."

"That's quite clear, Sir Denis."

"In the event of your giving me the O.K., I shall wait for
the Morse message—but I shall wait only half an hour. The
plain call again will tell me. Try to find out if Petrie is there—
and if he is alive, or dead. One sustained note to mean he is
there, but dead: two short ones, that he is there, but alive."

And as he spoke, he was urging me forward, up the path,
grasping my arm and firing me with vital enthusiasm of
which he had such an abundant store.

"There may be difficulties about the missing ring," I suggested.

"A point I had been considering," he returned. "Have you any suggestions? You know the place better than I do. Where might you have lost it?—where would it be difficult to find?"

"Amongst the aquatic plants," I replied eagerly; "some of them grow in deep water."

"Good!" he snapped. "Let it be the aquatic plants. Do your damnedest in the next half hour to find old Petrie; then run for it. I shall be waiting for you. . . ."

We proceeded now in silence, groping our way along that perilous path. Once again, I found myself listening for that high, strange call-note; but it never came.

We mounted the many stone steps and reached the terrace. I saw a dim light shining out upon the pavement. The door was open.

"I left it open," said Nayland Smith, in a low voice. "I'll stay here. Send me the signal as soon as you are assured of your own safety." He grasped my hand hard. "Good luck! In half an hour. . . ."

As I reached the open door, and realized that I was about to enter again the house of Dr. Fu Manchu, a qualm touched me, for which I hope I may be forgiven.

It passed as swiftly as it came. It was succeeded by a feeling of shame, by a memory of what Sir Denis had done that night.

I stepped inside, looking swiftly right and left. The green lamp still burned at the end of the long corridor. And remembering who was sleeping there, I watched it lingeringly. Then I looked down the stairs, and I stood still, listening.

No one was in sight and there was not a sound audible. I pressed my finger upon the control button twice; the door closed. Then I began to descend the stairs.

Reaching the foot, I groped with my hand upon the panel which I knew concealed the door. Presently it responded, and bathed in that dim violet light, I saw the great laboratory ahead of me.

It was empty.

I stepped forward—and the door closed behind me. I began to cross the rubber-covered floor, heading for Dr. Fu Manchu's study.

This was the supreme moment.

I was disposed to think that it was he, awakening, who had summoned me. I lost count of time as I stood before that blank wall, charging myself with cowardice, flogging my failing courage.

At last I took the plunge . . . and the door opened.

He sat there like the mummy of Seti The First, upright in his throne. Opium still held him in its grasp. A jungle smell was mingling now with the poppy fumes, for the doors leading into the great palm-house remained open. The marmoset was crouching on that yellow shoulder, nor did he stir as I went tip-toe across the carpet.

So far, I was safe.

I closed the first door, hurried to the second, and closed that also. I hadn't the courage to pause to adjust the gauge. I ran through the place, ducking to avoid overhanging branches, many of them flower-laden. And coming to the next door, I pulled up and listened.

There was no pursuit.

From thence onward, I adjusted all the gauges, until, opening the final door, I stepped into the botanical research room, from which I had set out upon that memorable pilgrimage. . . .

Stock-still I pulled up on the threshold.

Fleurette stood there watching me!

## CHAPTER XXXIV

## DERCETO

"FLEURETTE!" I exclaimed.

She wore a silk wrap over night attire; sandals on her slim brown feet. She watched me gravely.

"Fleurette! Who called me?"

"I called you."

"But"—I was astounded—"how did you know—"

"I know most of the things that go on here," she returned calmly.

I moved nearer to her and looked at the dial close to which she was standing. My number—103—was registered upon it; and:

"How often did you call me?" I asked.

"Twice."

Her unmoving regard, in which there was an unpleasant question, began to disturb me.

My conception of her as a victim of the powerful and evil man who sought to destroy white civilization was entirely self-created. I remembered that she had been reared in this atmosphere from birth; and conscious of an unpleasant chill I realized that she, whom I regarded as a partner in misfortune, an ally, might prove to be the means of my unmasking. I decided to be diplomatic.

"Yes—of course you called me twice," I replied.

The second call would have been taken by Nayland Smith! How would he have read it?

"Why didn't you come?" she asked. "Where were you?"

Her beautiful eyes were fixed upon me with a regard which I found almost terrifying. An hour before, an instant before, I would have met her gaze gladly, happily; but now—I wondered.

After all, the romance between this girl and myself existed only in my own imagination. It was built upon nothing but a stairs of sand—her remarkable beauty. She was, as Dr. Fu Manchu had said, the most rare jewel—a perfect woman.

But I—I was far removed from a perfect man. Vanity had blinded me. She belonged body and soul to the group surrounding the Chinese doctor. And perhaps it was no more than poetic justice that she and none of the others should expose me.

"I was in the palm-house. I had never seen such trees. And, as you know, I am a botanist."

"But you were a long time coming," she insisted. "You are sure you were alone?"

As if a black cloud had lifted, I saw—or dared to hope that I saw—the truth in the regard of those sunset violet eyes. Or was it vanity, self-delusion, again? But, moving nearer to her:

"Alone!" I echoed. "Who could be with me at this hour of the night?"

And now at last, unfalteringly, I looked into her eyes.

"The Princess is very beautiful," she said in a low voice.

"The Princess?"

I had no idea at the moment to whom she referred; but chaotically, delightfully, it was as I had dared to hope!

My sudden, wild passion for this exquisite, unattainable girl had not failed utterly of its objective. She was sufficiently interested to be jealous! And now, watching her, it dawned upon me to whom she referred.

"Do you mean Fah Lo Suee?"

She made a little grimace, and turned aside.

"I wondered why you had joined us," she murmured. "If she is Fah Lo Suee to you—I know. I was merely curious. Good night."

She turned and walked away.

"Fleurette!" I cried. "Fleurette!"

She did not look back.

I sprang forward, threw my arms around her and held her. Even so, she did not look back; she merely stood still. But my doubts, my diffidence were gone: my heart was singing. . . .

She had given me that age-old sign which is woman's prerogative. The next move was mine. Revelation was so sudden, so wholly unexpected, that it swept me out of myself. To my shame I confess, that although vast issues hung in the balance, establishment of an understanding with Fleurette was the only thing in life at which at that moment I aimed.

I had fallen irrevocably in love with her, at first sight. Recognition of the fact that she was interested, produced a state of mind little short of delirium.

"Fleurette!" I said, holding her tightly and bending close to her averted head, "that woman you call the Princess, I call Fah Lo Suee, because I was told that that was her name: I know her by no other. She means nothing more to me than I thought I meant to you. I had seen her once only in my life before I came here. . . ."

I checked my words: I had been on the point of saying too much. Fah Lo Suee had told me, "she has Eastern blood in her, and to Eastern women love comes suddenly." Of all that Fu Manchu's daughter had revealed, this alone I was disposed to believe.

Fleurette turned quickly, and looked up at me.

Nothing, I think, short of sudden death, could have checked me then.

Raising my left hand to her shoulder, I twisted her about, so that I had her clasped in my arms. And stooping to those delicious, tremulous lips, I kissed her until we both were breathless.

One instantaneous moment there was of rebellion, and then such exquisite surrender that when presently she buried her lovely little head in my shoulder, so that I could feel her heart beating, I think there was in the whole world no happier man than I.

There was an old tradition in my family of which my mother had told me—that we were slow to hate, but quick to love. Fleurette and I were well met. I doubted if mutual love had ever been unmasked under circumstances more peculiar.

What she told me did not fully register at the time, nor, perhaps, were my questions those which Nayland Smith would have selected. Nevertheless, I learned much respecting this queer household of Dr. Fu Manchu.

I began to realize the greatness of the menace which he represented; because, through Fleurette, the knowledge came to me that many who served him, loved him.

Perhaps, among the lower orders of his strange entourage, fear was his sceptre. But, as I gathered—and I dared not speak a word to shatter that ideal—Fleurette's sentiments were those of profound respect.

Mahdi Bey, her guardian, had taught her to look upon the Chinese doctor as upon a man supreme among men. It was an honourable fate to be chosen by the Prince who one day would rule the world—be its Emperor. . . .

Fleurette had received a remarkable education, embracing the icy peaks of sexless philosophy, to which she had been taught to look up in a Buddhist monastery in the North of China, to the material feminism of a famous English school. Yet she remained completely human; for she lay in my arms whispering those replies to my eager questions.

She had not been denied the companionship of men, but always, in which ever part of the world she had chanced to find herself, had been constantly accompanied and never left alone in the society of others for more than those few minutes which Western social custom demands. There were girls of good family and of her own age in some of the larger establishments. But as to how they came to be there I was unable to form any idea: apparently they had been selected purely as companions for Fleurette. . . .

Fah Lo Suee, to whom she referred as "the Princess", she distrusted, but evidently feared. Fah Lo Suee, it seemed, had partisans of her own amongst the many leaders of this mysterious movement which Fleurette called the Si-Fan. Regarding the political side of the organization, she clearly knew next to nothing. That a great war was pending, in which Dr. Fu Manchu expected to overthrow all opposition, she was aware: the character of this war she did not seem even to suspect.

Without recourse to the Ericksen telephone, Dr. Fu Manchu was able to call her, she told me—and she was compelled to go to him.

He sometimes made her look into a disk in which strange images appeared. . . .

There were times—of which to-night was an instance—when his influence dropped from her—unaccountably: when she questioned the meaning of her life—and followed her own impulses. Those times, beyond doubt, although I did not tell her so, corresponded to the Doctor's bouts of opium-smoking.

"Why did you tell me to think of you as Derceto?"

Fleurette laughed, but not happily.

"Because you found me on the shore—and to love me meant destruction. . . ."

During the greater part of the telling of her strange story, she had lain in my arms—and there had been silent intervals. But at last, I seemed to hear the crisp voice of Sir Denis demanding that I should put duty first. . . .

CHAPTER XXXV

# THE SECTION DOORS

"He is here," said Fleurette. "Leave the door open, I will call if anyone comes."

At that moment, as I crossed the threshold into a small white bedroom, even Fleurette was forgotten. Petrie, pale as I had ever seen him, his hair blanched as by the brushes of ten years, lay there, watching me!

There was a dull flush on his forehead, where the purple shadow had been.

"Petrie, old man!" I whispered—"Petrie! . . . Thank God!"

Had I not met other dead men in the house of Dr. Fu Manchu, this must have been a moment of stupefaction.

He nodded weakly and smiled—the same patient smile which I knew, even extending his hand, which I grasped between both my own.

"This," I said, "is a miracle."

"I agree." His voice was very low. "I must have the constitution of a rattlesnake, Sterling. For I have not only sur-

131

vived the new plague—but an injection of the preparation known as 'Fu Manchu *Katalepsis*' or briefly—'F. *Katalepsis*.' "

"You *know* all this?"

"Yes; I even knew that you were here. But this is no time—"

He stopped, breathlessly, and I realized how weak he was.

"Don't tire yourself," I urged, grasping his shoulder. "Sir Denis is waiting for the news."

"Nayland Smith!" His eyes lighted up. "*He* is here?"

"Yes—standing by, outside."

Petrie clenched his teeth; closed his eyes. I recognized all that this news had meant to him; then:

"There is only one thing you must wait for," he said. "Give me that scribbling block from the table, Sterling, and a pencil."

I did as he directed—I could see that it would be useless to object.

"Lift me up," he went on. "It's going to be a struggle to write, but it has to be done—in case—of—accidents."

"What, Petrie? Why is all this necessary?"

He shook his head and began very slowly to write. Bending over him, I saw that he was writing a prescription.

The truth dawned upon me!

" '654'?"

He nodded, and went on writing. For a moment he paused, and:

"This must be circulated throughout the world," he whispered weakly—"without delay."

He glanced over what he had written, and nodded his wish to be laid back upon the pillows.

This accomplished, I tore the sheet off the block, folded it, and slipped it into a pocket of my overall.

"Now, bolt!" he whispered, "Bolt for your life while there's a chance. Everything depends upon your success."

I had turned to go—when, unaided, he suddenly sat upright in bed, his eyes fixed upon the open door.

"Alan!" I heard softly.

I turned in time to see Fleurette's head hurriedly withdrawn. Someone was coming!

"Sterling! Sterling!" Petrie clutched my shoulder: his eyes were suddenly wild. "*Who* was that at the door?"

"A friend . . . you need not be afraid . . . Fleurette."

"Fleurette? My God! Am I growing delirious?"

I assisted him back on to his pillows. His manner was alarmingly strange.

"Who is she?"

"She is a victim of Dr. Fu Manchu—but we are going to get her away."

"Great heaven!" He closed his eyes. "Can it be true? Is it possible? . . . Don't wait, Sterling—go . . . go!"

Indeed I knew that I had no alternative; and squeezing his hand hard, I ran out of the room.

Fleurette was standing just beyond the door, which she closed instantly upon my appearance.

"Someone is coming!" she said, in a low voice. "I think it is Companion Yamamata. Quick!—this way!"

She led me along a short passage to the head of a descending stair.

"Don't make a noise," she warned.

We crept to the bottom, my arm about her waist.

"Who is Dr. Petrie?" she whispered; "he stared at me as though he knew me; yet I have never seen him in my life before."

"He is one of my oldest friends," I replied, "and unfortunately I hadn't time to ask him. But I saw how he looked at you. Yes! he thinks he knows you—"

And now, I wondered what knowledge was common to Dr. Petrie and Sir Denis but not shared by me. . . .

*Both* had recognized Fleurette!

We turned a corner and I saw that we stood directly under a little green lamp.

"There is your way," said Fleurette—"straight ahead. It is the door on to the terrace."

At which moment I realized that we were standing directly outside her room.

"Darling, at last!" I exclaimed, and felt my heart leap. "Come on! hurry! There isn't a moment to waste!"

She slipped by me and opened the door of her room. I stared at her in blank amazement—and her expression baffled me. She took my hand, pulled me gently forward . . . and then closed the door.

"Someone might see or hear us in the corridor," she said. "We are safe here. Please say good-bye to me."

"What!"

She watched me, and in the dim light of that room which Nayland Smith had described as the Palace of the Sleeping Beauty, her eyes looked like violets wet with dew.

"What did you think I meant to do?" she asked softly. "I have never cared for anyone before. I suppose I am to blame because I cared for you? But although you have not told me—I know what you think of Dr. Fu Manchu . . . of all of us. You belong to the poor ignorant world. You are not really one of us. You are a spy."

I tried to take her in my arms, but she eluded me.

"Fleurette! This is madness!"

"The world is mad—Alan." The moment of hesitation before my name was a rainbow. "But you belong to it and you must go back. I should hate to believe that you could think me capable of deserting those who have never denied me anything as long as I can remember. No, dear, I sink or swim with my friends! I am betraying them, now, by letting you go. But the moment you have reached safety—I shall warn them."

"Fleurette!"

"If I could love you without wronging them, I would—but I can't." She rested her hands on my shoulders. "Please say good-bye to me. You must hurry—you must hurry!"

Then she was in my arms, and as her lips met mine I knew that the greatest decision of my life was being asked of me.

The philosophy of a young girl, crazy though it may be, is intensely difficult to upset—and beyond doubt there was fatalism in Fleurette's blood. Yet—how could I let her go?

My heart seemed to me to be beating like a steam hammer. I wanted to pick her up, to carry her from that accursed house. She began to plead.

"If you force me to go," I said, "I shall get you back—follow you if necessary all around the world."

"It would be useless. I can never belong to you—I belong to *him*."

I wanted to curse the name of Fu Manchu and to curse all his works. Knowing as I knew that he was a devil incarnate, a monster, an evil super-human, the monument which he stood for in the mind of this beautiful child—for she was little more—was a shrine I yearned to shatter.

Yet, for all the frenzy of passion which burned me up, enough of common sense remained to warn me that this was not the time; that such an attempt must be worse than futile.

I held her tightly, cruelly, kissing her eyes, her hair, her neck, her shoulders. I found myself on the verge of something resembling hysteria.

"I can't leave you here!" I said hoarsely: "I won't—I daren't. . . ."

A dim throbbing sound had become perceptible. This, at first, I had believed to be a product of excitement. But now Fleurette seemed to grow suddenly rigid in my arms.

"Oh, God!" she whispered—"quick, *quick!* Someone has found out! Listen!"

A cold chill succeeded fever.

"They are closing the section-doors! Quick, for your life . . . and for *my* sake!"

It was inevitable. For *her* sake?—yes! If I should be found there. . . .

She sprang to the control button.

The door remained closed.

She twisted about, her back pressed against the door, her arms outstretched—such terror in her eyes as I had hoped never to see there.

"All the doors have been locked as well," she whispered. "It is impossible to get out!"

"But, Fleurette!" I began—

"It's useless! It's hopeless!"

"But if I am found here?"

"It's unavoidable, now."

"I could hide."

"No one can hide from him. He could force me to tell him."

Her lips began to tremble, and I groaned impotently, knowing well that I could do nothing to comfort her—that I, and I alone, was the cause of this disaster about to fall.

And throughout those dreadful moments, the vibration of the descending doors might faintly be detected, together with that muted gong-note which I had learned to dread.

"There must be something we can do!"

"There is nothing."

Silence.

The sections-doors were closed.

And in that stillness I seemed to live again through years of life. I had in my pocket the means of saving the world. Useless, now! Within call, perhaps within sight from the terrace, eagerly awaiting me, was Sir Denis—freedom—sanity! And here was I, helpless as a mouse in a trap, awaiting . . . what?

My heart, which had been beating so rapidly, seemed to check, to grow cold; my brain jibbed at the task.

What would be Fleurette's fate if I were discovered there, in her room, by Dr. Fu Manchu?

CHAPTER XXXVI

# THE UNSULLIED MIRROR

MANY minutes elapsed, every one laden with menace. Then—came that eerie note which I knew.

Fleurette stood quite still. Used now to its significance and purpose, I could detect the dots and dashes of the Morse alphabet, given at a speed which only an adept could have followed.

The sound ceased.

Fleurette dropped into an armchair, looking up at me, hopelessly.

"They are searching for you," she said, in a dull tone. "*He* doesn't know yet."

I stood there dumb of tongue and dumb of brain for long moments; then, ideas began to come. Someone had called me—possibly Trenck—and I had not replied. Nayland Smith had received those messages.

What had they been and how had he construed them?

This uncertainty only added to the madness of the situation. I had an idea born of experience.

"Fleurette," I said, dropping upon my knees beside her, "why could I not have come in here as you came into my room when the alarm sounded?"

She looked at me; her face was like a beautiful mask: immutable, expressionless.

"It would be useless," she replied. "No one can lie to Dr. Fu Manchu."

And I accepted the finality of those words, for I believed it. I sprang upright. I had become aware of a faint distant vibration.

"Can the doors be raised separately?"

"Yes; any one of them can be raised alone."

I stepped across the room and pressed the control button. There was no response. I bent close to the metal, listening intently. I formed the impression, and it was a horrible impression, that the control-doors were being raised, one by one . . . that someone was slowly approaching this room in which I was trapped with Fleurette.

Beyond doubt, that ominous sound was growing nearer—growing in volume. And finally the vibration grew so great that I could feel it upon the metal against which my head rested.

I stepped back—my fists automatically clenched.

The door slid open—and Dr. Fu Manchu stood there watching me!

His majestic calm was terrible. Those long, brilliant eyes glanced aside and I knew that he was studying Fleurette.

"Woman—the lever which a word can bend," he said softly.

He made a signal with his long-nailed hand and two of his Chinese servants sprang in.

I stepped back, debating my course—

"Heroics are uncalled for," he added; "and could profit no one."

For an instant I glanced aside at Fleurette.

Her beautiful eyes were raised to Dr. Fu Manchu, and her expression was that of a saint who sees the Holy Vision!

He spoke rapidly in Chinese and entered the room, giving me not another glance. My arms were grasped and I found myself propelled forcibly out into the corridor. The strength of these little immobile men was amazing.

The section-door at the corner where those stairs terminated which led down to the radio research-room, was not yet fully raised: two feet or more still protruded from the slot in the ceiling which accommodated it.

Our human brains possess very definite limitations: mine had reached the edge of endurance.

My memory registers a blank from the moment that I left Fleurette's room to that when I found myself seated in a hard high-backed chair in the memorable study of Dr. Fu Manchu. Beside me Yamamata was seated, and at the moment at which I suppose my brain began to function again—suddenly that door which I knew led into the palm-house, opened, and Fah Lo Suee came in.

She wore a bright green pyjama suit, and was smoking a cigarette in a jade holder. One glance I received from her unfathomable eyes—but if it had conveyed a message, the message failed to reach me.

She closed the door by which she had entered and dropped on to a little settee close beside it.

I glanced at Yamamata. His yellow skin was clammy with perspiration. In doing so, I noticed that the door in the archway was open—and now through the opening came Dr. Fu Manchu; silent—with cat-like dignity.

The door closed behind him.

Yamamata stood up, and so did Fah Lo Suee. It was farcically like a court of law. I wrenched my head aside, clenching my teeth. My passion for Fleurette had thrown true perspective out of focus.

This man who assumed the airs of an emperor, was, in fact, a common criminal: the hangman awaited him. And then I heard his guttural voice:

"Stand up!"

All that was *me*, all that I had proudly been wont to regard as my personality, fought against this command—for a command it was. Yet—the plain fact must be recorded—I stood up. . . .

He took his seat in the dragon-carved chair behind the big table. I had kept my eyes deliberately averted, but now, in the silence which followed, I stole a glance at him. He was staring intently at Fah Lo Suee.

Suddenly he spoke:

"Companion Yamamata," he said softly—"you may go."

Yamamata sprang up; I saw his lips move, but no sound issued from them. He bowed, and opening the door which led into the big laboratory, went out, closing it behind him.

Dr. Fu Manchu began to speak rapidly in Chinese; and at the end of the first sentence, Fah Lo Suee, dropping her jade cigarette-holder into a bronze tray upon the floor, came down to her knees on the carpet and buried that evilly beautiful face in upraised hands—delicate ivory hands —patrician hands—shadows, etherealized, of those of her formidable father.

He continued to speak and she shrank lower and lower, but spoke no word—uttered no sound. Then:

"Alan Sterling," he said, suddenly expressing himself in English; "the ill-directed cunning of one woman and the frailty of another have taken your fate out of my control. There are men to whom women are dangerous—you, unhappily, would seem to be one of them."

And as he spoke, the remarkable fact disclosed itself to me that although Fah Lo Suee had spoken no word, already he *knew* her part in the conspiracy!

Good heavens! A suspicion sprang to my mind—Had Fah Lo Suee been watching? Was it *she* who had trapped me with Fleurette? Was this the end to which she had preserved my life: Fleurette's swift ruin, my own speedy death?

In its classic simplicity the scheme was Chinese, I thought. I looked at her where she crouched, abject.

The voice—the strange, haunting voice—spoke on:

"Millions of useless lives cumber the world to-day. Amongst them I must now include your own. The ideal state of the great Greek philosopher took no count of these. There can be no human progress without selection; and already I have chosen the nucleus of my new state. The East has grown in spirit, whilst the West has been building machinery. . . .

"My new state will embody the soul of the East.

"I am not ready yet for my warfare against the numerous, but helpless, army of the rejected. The Plagues of Egypt I hold in my hands, but I cannot control the course of the sun. . . .

"It may be that you, a gnat on the fly-wheel, have checked the machinery of the gods. Alone, you could never have cast a shadow upon my path: one of my own blood is the culprit."

He struck a little gong which hung close to his hand upon the table, and the door facing me as I sat, opened instantaneously and silently. One of those white-robed, image-like Chinamen entered, to whom Fu Manchu spoke briefly, rapidly.

The man bowed and went out. Fah Lo Suee's slender body seemed to diminish. She sank down until her head touched the carpet.

Dr. Fu Manchu tapped with a long nail upon the table, glancing aside at her where she crouched.

"Your Western progress, Alan Sterling," he said, "has resulted in the folly of women finding a place in the Councils of State. The myth you call Chivalry has tied your hands and stricken you mute. In the China to which I belong—a China which is not dead but only sleeping—we use older, simpler methods. . . . We have *whips*. . . ."

The door suddenly opened again, and two powerfully built negresses entered. Their attire consisted of red and white striped skirts fastened by girdles about their waists.

Dr. Fu Manchu addressed them rapidly, but now, I knew, he was not speaking Chinese.

He ceased, and pointed.

One of the negresses stooped; but even as she did so, Fah Lo Suee sprang to her feet with an elastic movement, turned flaming eyes upon that dreadful figure in the high-backed chair, and then, a negress at either elbow, walked out into the palm-house beyond.

139

I glanced at Dr. Fu Manchu, and he caught and held that glance. I realized that I was incapable of turning my eyes away.

"Alan Sterling," he said, "it is my purpose to save the world from itself. And to this end there must be a great purging. To-day or to-morrow, my dream will be fulfilled. One of those bunglers acting for what is sometimes termed Western civilization, may bring about my death by violence. There is none to succeed me. . . . My daughter—trained for a great purpose, as few women have been trained, and endowed with the physical perfections of a carefully selected mother, inherits the taint of some traitor ancestor. . . .

"I desire that a son shall succeed to what I shall build. The mother of that son I have chosen. Sex determination is a problem which at last I have conquered. Neither love nor passion will enter the union. But if you, Alan Sterling, have cast the shadow of either upon the unsullied mirror which I had patiently burnished to reflect my will . . . then the work of eighteen years is undone."

His guttural voice sank lower and lower, and the last few words sounded like a sibilant whisper. . . .

He struck the gong twice.

I found myself seized by my arms and lifted off the chair in which I had been seated! Two of his Chinamen—unheard, unsuspected—had entered behind me.

Brief, guttural words, and I was swung around, as Dr. Fu Manchu stood up, tall, gaunt, satanic, and from a hook upon the wall took down a whip resembling a Russian knout.

As I was swept about to face the door which communicated with the radio research-room, one horrifying glimpse I had in the palm-house, dimly lighted, of an ivory body hanging by the wrists. . . .

## CHAPTER XXXVII

## THE GLASS MASK

In a frame of mind which I must leave to the imagination, I paced up and down the little sitting-room of the apartment numbered eleven.

I was alone, and the door was unopenable; some ten minutes before I had heard the section-doors being closed, also. Whichever way my thoughts led me, I found stark madness lurking there.

Fleurette! What would be the fate of Fleurette? For Dr. Fu Manchu was not human in the accepted sense of the word. He was a remorseless intelligence. What he could not use, he destroyed. Perhaps he would spare Fleurette because of her remarkable beauty. But spare her—for what?

And Petrie! He was helpless indeed, desperately ill. As for myself, I suffered those hundred deaths which the coward is said to die, during the uncountable period that I paced up and down that small room.

My mad passion for Fleurette had brought this down upon all of us! In those feverish moments whilst I had been pleading with her, I should have been clear of this ghastly house. My freedom meant the safety of the world. I had sacrificed this to my own selfish desires. Only by wrecking the elaborate organization of the Si-Fan—the scope of which hitherto I had never suspected—could I hope to win Fleurette.

Fool—mad fool!—to have supposed that a newly awakened passion could upset traditions so carefully implanted and nurtured.

What was happening?

I tried to work out what Nayland Smith would be likely to do—to estimate the chances of a raid taking place, before it was too late. I could not forget the imperturbable figure in the yellow robe.

That Dr. Fu Manchu was prepared for such an emergency as this it was impossible to doubt. His manner had not been that of a criminal trapped.

I pressed my ear against the door and listened.

But I could detect no sound.

I crossed to the farther wall in which I knew there was another door, but one I had never been able to open. I listened there also, for I remembered that there was a corridor beyond.

Silence. I was shut into a narrow section of the house between barriers of steel.

I estimated that fully an hour elapsed. I knew from experience that these apartments were practically sound-proof. My brain was a phantom circus and I was rapidly approaching a state of nervous exhaustion. My frame of mind had been all but unendurable when I had thought that I was dead, when I had thought that I was in a state of delirium. But now, knowing that the horrors accumulated about me, the monstrosities, parodies of nature, the living-dead men, the incalculable machines, were real and not figments of fevered imagination—now, when I should have been most sane, I was more likely to lose my mental poise than at any time during the past.

A dream which I had scarcely dared to entertain had come true—only to be shattered in the very hour of its realization. That I should ever leave this place alive, I did not believe for a moment. But surely no man had ever held so much in his hands, ever needed life as I needed it at this moment, when I knew I faced death.

I dropped down into a little armchair—one in which I remembered miserably Fleurette had sat—and buried my face in my hands.

If only I could conjure up one spark of hope—find something to think about which did not lead to insanity!

Then, I sprang to my feet. It had reached me unmistakably . . . that dim vibration which told of the section-doors being raised!

What did it mean?

That my fate had been decided upon and that they were coming for me? I crossed and pressed the control button. There was no response.

Again, as in Fleurette's room earlier that night, I felt like a mouse in a trap. It could profit no one, myself least of all, but a determination came to me at this moment which did much to steady me.

I would die fighting.

I tested the weight of the little armchair in which I had been seated. It was about heavy enough for my purpose. I would hurl it at whoever entered.

I pulled open the drawers of a large cabinet which occupied a great portion of one wall. It contained laboratory appliances, presumably belonging to a former occupant, and including a glass mask and rubber gloves. But I found no weapon there.

A pedestal lamp stood upon the table. I wrenched the flex from it, removed the lamp and the shade, and realized that it made a very good club. Armed with this I would rush out and see what account I could give of myself in the corridors.

This useless plan made, I stood there waiting. At least, there would be action to come.

The muted rumbling of the doors continued. Once again,

setting the lamp-stand upon the carpet beside me, I tested the control—but without result.

That rumbling and the queer throbbing gong-note which accompanied it, could be heard quite distinctly when I pressed my head against the framework. But now, abruptly, it ceased.

The section-doors were raised.

Yet again I tried the control, but uselessly. I stood there waiting, dividing my attention between the wall with its hidden entrance and the door which I knew.

But silence prevailed; nothing happened.

For fully five minutes I waited, not knowing what to expect, but full of my plan for a fighting finish. At last, I determined that I could bear this waiting no longer. Again, I tested the control. . . .

The door slid noiselessly open.

What I could see of the corridor outside seemed to be more dimly lighted than usual. There was another white door nearly opposite. A faint, putrid smell reached my nostrils.

Cautiously I crept forward, and peeped out, looking along the passage.

A strange humming sound seemed to be drawing nearer to the light shining out from the room behind me. And then—

I sprang back, stifling a scream that was truly hysterical.

The passage was held by an army of flies, of ants, of other nameless things, which flew and crawled and scurried. . . . And, not three feet away, watching me with its hideously intelligent eyes, crouched that monstrous black spider I had seen in the glass case. . . .

## CHAPTER XXXVIII

# THE GLASS MASK—*concluded*

FRENZIEDLY, I closed the door, shutting out those flying and crawling horrors.

Then I began a grim fight—a fight to conquer shaken

nerves. That long period of waiting had been bad enough;
but the terrors of the corridor, crowned by the apparition of
that giant spider "capable of primitive reasoning", had taxed
me beyond the limit.

What had happened?

Was this a plan, premeditated?—or had some action on
the part of Nayland Smith resulted in a disturbance of this
ghastly household?

I dismissed the idea that Dr. Fu Manchu had released
this phantom army merely to compass my own death. I had
intruded—unwittingly as he had admitted—upon the delicate machinery of his purpose. But brief though my acquaintance had been with the Chinese doctor, I was not
preapared to believe him capable of stooping from that
purpose, even momentarily, in response to the promptings of
jealousy, or of any lower human impulse.

Therefore, if what I had seen conformed to some plan,
this plan was not directed against myself, although I might
be included in it. If it were the result of accident, of panic
on the part of a household disturbed by unexpected events,
it could only mean that the Doctor had departed—fled before the menace of Nayland Smith!

And by virtue of the fact that I was exercising my brain
in hard reasoning, I regained control of that courage which,
frankly, had been slipping. And a memory came.

In my frantic search for some weapon with which to put
up a fight for life, I had hauled out the drawers of a big
cabinet which occupied nearly the whole of one wall of the
sitting-room in which I now stood.

Among the objects, useless at the time, which I had discovered, had been a glass mask of the kind chemists wear.

I formed a desperate resolution. I ran to the drawer in
which the mask lay, and slipped it over my head. I saw now
that my white overalls, which were made of some unfamiliar material, were adapted to the wearing of this mask:
the collar could be turned up and buttoned to the equipment. I fixed it in place, bending before the mirror in the
bathroom and contemplating my hideous image.

The rubber gloves!

These also, I discovered, could be attached to my sleeves
in a certain manner so that nothing could penetrate between
glove and sleeve. My final discovery, that the trousers of
the white overalls might be tucked inside the tops of the shoes
to which a strap was attached for the purpose, convinced
me.

Courage returned. I was equipped to face the terrors of the corridor.

I would have given much for a gun, or even a handy club, but in the end I was reduced again to the lamp-standard.

Clutching this in my hand, I reopened the door. There was some system of ventilation in the curious mask which I wore—but nevertheless breathing was difficult.

I stood looking along the passage.

The black horror, the giant spider—which, for some reason, although it may have been comparatively harmless, I feared more than anything else—had disappeared. The air was thick with flies; I could hear them vaguely. Some had settled upon the walls. I saw that they were of various kinds.

One of the huge wasps flew straight against my glass mask. I ducked wildly, striking at it—not confident yet in my immunity.

The thing flew by—I heard the fading buzz of its passing. . . .

I came to the end of the corridor and looked down the stairs. My wits were far from clear. At all costs I must remember the route. I found as I stood there that I could remember only that by which Dr. Fu Manchu had first conducted me.

Another way there was, and I had gone by it. The route I remembered would lead me through the bacteriological research-room. From thence onward I knew my course.

All the doors were open.

At the entrance to the room where I had seen Sir Frank Narcomb, I pulled up. My knowledge of bacteria was limited; but if the insects were free—so presumably were the germs. . . .

I glanced down at my feet. Large ants, having glittering black bodies, were swarming up over the lashings of my overalls!

Stamping madly, I stooped, brushing the things off with my rubber glove. I saw a centipede wriggling away from my stamping feet. Panic touched me. I ran through the room and out into a short passage beyond.

In that dimly lighted place, surrounded by windows behind which the insects lived, I saw that the doors of the cases were open. Some of the things still hovered about their nests, but many of the cases were empty.

There was no one in the passage beyond—which was even more dimly lighted; but I stepped upon some wriggling thing and heard the crunch of its body beneath my rubber-shod foot.

The sound sickened me.

I pressed on to the botanical research-room. A glance showed that it had been partly stripped. I stared through the observation window into that small house where the strange orchids had been under cultivation. They had disappeared.

Looking about at the shelves, I realized that much of the apparatus had been taken away. The doors leading into the first of the big forcing-houses were open.

I passed through, and immediately grasped the explanation of something which had been puzzling me; namely, that the escaped insects were scarcely represented here, whereas the corridors beyond were thick with them, flying and crawling.

A sharp change in the atmosphere offered an explanation.

Windows, as well as doors, were open here, admitting a keen night air borne by a wind from the Alps.

Those things were seeking warmth in the interior of the place. And already, so delicate are such plants, I saw that many of the tropical flowers about me were drooping—would soon be dead.

What did this mean?

It was probably part of a plan to destroy such results of those unique experiments as could not be removed.

With every step I advanced the air grew colder and colder—and destruction amongst the *outré* products through which I passed was such that I could find time for a moment of regret in the midst of my own engrossing troubles. The palm-house, in common with every other place I had visited, was deserted. The doors leading into Dr. Fu Manchu's study were open . . . I could see light shining out.

Here was the crux of the situation. Here if anywhere I should meet with a check.

Despite the keenness of the air, I was bathed in perspiration, buckled up in my nearly air-tight outfit.

I advanced slowly, step by step, until I could look into the study. Then I stood still, staring through the glass mask—which had grown very misty—at a room stripped of its exotic trappings!

The furniture alone remained. This destruction, then, which I had witnessed, was the handiwork of Dr. Fu Manchu himself—or so I must suppose. For here was clear evidence that he had fled, taking his choicest possessions with him.

I paused there for only a few moments; then I ran out into the great radio research-room.

Of the masses of unimaginable mechanism which had cumbered the room, only the heaviest remained. The instruments had gone from the tables. Many shelves were bare. Three intricate pieces of machinery, including that which I had thought resembled a moving-picture camera, were there, but wrecked—shattered—mere mounds of metallic fragments upon a grey floor!

There were no insects visible in the big room, which was as cold as a cavern. Indeed, as Nayland Smith had pointed out, a cavern, practically, it was. Doors I had not known to exist were open in the glass walls, but I ran the length of the place and sprang up the stairs beyond.

The door did not close beind me. The whole of that intricate mechanism had been locked in some way.

Gaining the top corridor, I glanced swiftly to the right.

A cold grey light—the light of dawn—was touching the terrace.

CHAPTER XXXIX

# SEARCH IN STE. CLAIRE

I RAN forward.

"Hands up!" came swiftly.

And even as I obeyed that order, I groaned, filled with such bitterness of spirit as I had rarely known.

On the very threshold—freedom in sight—I was trapped again!

A group of semi-human figures, surrounded me in the half-light: creatures goggle-eyed, with shapeless heads, to which were attached trunk-like appendages! I raised my hands, staring helplessly about at the ghoulish party closing in upon me.

"Search him!" came the same voice, staccato, but curiously muffled.

But now, hearing it, I gasped the truth!

The hideous head-dresses of the men surrounding me were gas-masks!

147

"*Sir Denis!*" I cried, and knew that my own voice was at least as muffled as his.

The leader of the party was Nayland Smith!

Something very like unconsciousness threatened me. I had not fully appreciated how wrought-up I was until this moment. Sights and sounds merged into an indistinguishable blur. But presently, out of this haze, I began to apprehend that Nayland Smith was talking to me, his arm about my shoulders.

"Not a soul has left Ste. Clarie. Sterling; it's covered from the land and from the sea. When your first message reached me—"

"I sent no message! But what was it?"

"You sent no message?"

"Not a thing! Nevertheless, I think I know who did. What did you take it to mean?"

"According to the system we had arranged, it meant that Petrie was there—but dead. There was a second, much later, which quite defeated me—"

"I don't know who sent the second. But it's true that Petrie is here—and, when I saw him last, was *alive*."

"Sterling, Sterling! You are sure?"

"I spoke to him. And—by heavens! I had almost forgotten—"

I plunged a rubber-clad hand into the pocket of my overall, and pulled out the creased and folded sheet of paper.

"The formula for '654'."

"Thank God! Good old Petrie! Quick! give it to me."

Nayland Smith had discarded his helmet temporarily, and I my glass mask. He dashed away down the steps, leaving me standing there, looking about me.

Six or eight men were by the open door, their heads hidden in gas equipments, and I realized now that they must be French police. I felt very much below par, but the keen night air was restoring me, and after an absence of no more than two or three minutes, Sir Denis came running back.

"I don't think, Sterling," he said in his rapid way, "that the Doctor's campaign was ripe to open. It depended, I believe, upon climatic conditions. But in any event, '654' will be in possession of the medical authorities of the world to-night."

"Petrie's wish is carried out!"

"I should have raided an hour ago, if I had had the foresight to equip the party suitably. We were here before I realized the nature of the death-trap into which I might be leading them. I once saw a party of detectives in a Lime-house cellar belonging to Dr. Fu Manchu die the most dreadful deaths. . . .

"The Chief of Police was at the main gate, and I consulted with him. He quite naturally wanted to waive my objections; but I persisted. The delay was caused by the quest for gas-masks, of which there is not a large supply in the neighbourhood. When they were obtained, the men on duty reported that the door had been opened from the inside but that none had come out. I had rejoined them only a few minutes when you appeared.".

"Yet the place is deserted!"

"What?"

"Part of it is infested with plague flies and other horrors, but there is no trace of a human being anywhere."

"Come on!" he snapped, and readjusted his helmet. "Are you fit, Sterling?"

"Yes."

I buttoned myself up in my grim equipment. Followed by the police party I found myself again in the house of Dr. Fu Manchu.

Unhesitantly I began to run towards the green lamp at the end of the corridor which marked the position of Fleurette's room—when all the lights went out!

"What's this?" came a muffled exclamation.

The ray of a torch cut the darkness; then many others. Every member of the party was seemingly provided. Someone thrust a light into my hand, and I went racing along to the door of Fleurette's room.

One glance showed me that it was empty.

"I forgive you, Sterling," came hoarsely, "but you are wasting time."

The party clattered down the stairs, Nayland Smith and I leading.

"Petrie's room!" came huskily; "that first. . . ."

We dashed across the dismantled radio research-laboratory, eerie in torchlight, through the empty study where Dr. Fu Manchu, wrapped in a strange opium dream, had sat in his throne-chair, and on through those great forcing-houses where trees, shrubs and plants, to which Dame Nature had never given her benediction, wilted in the keen air sweeping through open doors.

Hoarse exclamations told of the astonishment experienced by the police party following us as we dashed through those exotic mysteries. Then, mounting the stair and coming to the corridor with its white, numbered doors, I became aware of a crunching sound beneath my feet.

I paused, and shone the light downward.

The floor was littered with dead and comatose insects, swift victims of this change of temperature! The giant spider had succumbed somewhere, I did not doubt; yet, even now I dreaded the horror, dreaded those reasoning eyes—

"We turn right, here!" I shouted, my voice muffled by the mask.

I ran along the passage and in at the open door of that room in which I had seen Petrie.

The room was empty!

"They have taken him!" groaned Nayland Smith. "We're too late. What's that?"

A sound of excited voices reached me, dimly. Then came a cry from the rear. The men under the local chief of police had joined us; they had come in by the main entrance.

Yet, neither group had discovered a soul on the premises!

"Spread out!" cried Nayland Smith—"parties of two! There's some Chinese rat-hole. A big household doesn't disappear into thin air. Come on, Sterling! our route is downward, not up."

We pressed our way through the throng of men behind us, Nayland Smith and the Chief of Police repeating the orders.

Sir Denis beside me, I raced back along the way we had come; and, although every door appeared to be open, there was seemingly none in that range of rooms other than those I knew. We searched the big forcing-houses, meeting only other muffled figures engaged upon a similar task.

But apparently the doors leading into Dr. Fu Manchu's study and those which communicated with the botanical research-room were the only means of entrance or exit!

Out into the big, dismantled laboratory we ran. There were two open doors in the wall opposite our point of entrance.

"This one first!" came in a muffled voice.

Sir Denis and I ran across to an opening in the glass wall.

"The Chinaman who arrived in the speedboat went this way," he shouted.

Shining our torches ahead, we entered—and found a descending stair. Our light failed to penetrate to the bottom of it.

"Stop, Sir Denis!" I cried.

Wrenching off the suffocating glass mask, I dropped it on

the floor, for I saw that in the darkness he had already discarded his gas helmet.

"We must assemble a party—we may be walking into a trap."

He pulled up and stared at me; his face was haggard.

"You are right," he rapped. "Get three or four men, and notify Furneaux—he's in charge of the police—which way we have gone."

I ran back across the great empty hall from which that curious violet light had gone, and shouted loudly. I soon assembled a party, one of whom I dispatched in search of the Chief of Police, and accompanied by the others, I rejoined Nayland Smith.

We left one man on duty at the door.

Nayland Smith leading, and I close behind him, we began to descend the stairs into the subterranean mystery of Ste. Claire.


CHAPTER XL

THE SECRET DOCK


"This is where the Chinaman went," he said. "It speaks loudly for the iron rule of the Doctor, Sterling, that although this man had presumably brought important news, not only did he avoid awakening Fu Manchu, but he even left the doors of the palm-house open. However, where did he go? That's what we have to find out."

A long flight of rubber-covered stairs descended ahead of us. The walls and ceiling were covered with that same glassy material which prevailed in the radio research-room. I counted sixty steps and then we came to a landing.

"Look out for traps," rapped Nayland Smith, "and distrust every foot of the way."

We tested for doors on the landing, but could find none. A further steep flight of steps branched away down to the right.

"Come on!"

The lower flight possessed the same characteristics as the

higher, and terminated on another square landing. A long corridor showed beyond—so long that the light of our torches was lost in it.

"One man to stand by here," came the crisp order—"and keep in contact with the man at the top."

We pressed on. We were now reduced to a party of four. There were several bends in the passage, but its general direction according to my calculations was southerly.

"This is amazing," muttered Nayland Smith. "If it goes on much farther, I shall begin to suspect that it is a private entrance to the Casino at Monte Carlo!"

Even as he spoke, another bend unmasked the end of this remarkable passage. Branching sharply down to the right, I saw a further flight of steps—rough wooden steps; and the naked rock was all about us.

"What's this?"

"We must be down to sea level."

"Fully, I should think."

Sir Denis turned; and:

"Fall out another man," he directed; "patrol between here and the end of the passage. Keep in contact with your opposite number, a shot to be the signal of any danger. Come on!"

A party of three, we pressed on down the wooden steps. There was a greater chilliness in the air, and a stale smell as of ancient rottenness. Another landing was reached, wooden planked; roughly-hewn rock all about us. More wooden stairs, inclining left again.

These terminated in an arched, crudely octagonal place which bore every indication of being a natural cave. It was floored with planks, and a rugged passage, similarly timbered, led yet farther south—or so I estimated.

"Stay here," Nayland Smith directed tersely. "Keep in touch with the man at the top."

And the last of the police party was left behind.

Sir Denis and I hurried on. Fully a hundred yards we went—and came to a yawning gap, which our lights could not penetrate. Moving slowly, now, we reached the end of the passage.

"Careful!" warned Sir Denis. "By heavens! what's this?"

We stood on a narrow wharf!

Tackle lay about; crates, packing-cases, coils of rope. And the sea—for I recognized that characteristic smell of the Mediterranean—lapped its edge.

But not a speck of light was visible anywhere. The water

was uncannily still. One would not have suspected it to be
there.

"Lights out!" snapped Sir Denis.

We extinguished our lamps. Utter darkness blanketed us:
we might have stood in a mine gallery.

"Don't light up!" came his voice; "I should have foreseen
this. But even so I don't see how I could have provided
against it. . . . My God! what's that?"

A dull sustained note, resembling that of a muted gong,
vibrated eerily through the stillness. . . . In fact, now that
he had drawn my attention to it, I believed that it had been
perceptible for some time, although hitherto partly drowned
by the clatter of our rubber soles upon wooden steps.

For one moment I listened—and knew. . . .

"You were right, Sir Denis," I said; "this place isn't deserted.
Someone is closing *the sections-doors!*"

"Quick! for your life! Back to the stairs. . . ."

We turned and ran into the wooden-floored tunnel; our
feet made a drumming sound upon the planks. The man left
on duty at the foot of the stairs was missing. Up we went
helter-skelter, neither of us doubting the urgency. We met
with no obstruction, and breathing hard, began to race up
the higher flight.

Neither patrol was to be seen. I suspected that they had
gone back along the corridor to establish contact with the
man at the farther end.

In confirmation of my theory, came the sound of a shot,
curiously muffled and staccato, from some point far ahead.

We pulled up, panting and—staring.

A section-door was descending, cutting us off from the
corridor! It was no more than three feet from the ground,
and falling—falling—inch by inch. . . .

"We daren't risk it!" groaned Nayland Smith. "If we did,
and weren't crushed, we should be shut in between this and
the next."

I heard shouting in the corridor beyond; a sound of racing feet. But even as I listened and watched, the dull grey
metal door was but fifteen inches above floor level, and:

"We must try back again," I said hoarsely. "There must
be some way out of that place, even if we have to swim for
it."

"There's no way out," Sir Denis rapped irritably. "The
entrance is below sea level."

"What!"

"You saw the patches of oil on the wharf?"

153

"I did. But—"

"Nevertheless, we'll go back. There may be some gallery communicating with another exit."

We began to descend again.

I was trying to think, trying to see into the future. An appalling possibility presented itself to my mind: that this might be the end of everything! So tenacious is the will to live in all healthy animals, that predominant, above every other consideration at the moment, towered that of how to escape from this ghastly cavern.

Nayland Smith's torch—he was leading by a pace—shone upon the oil-stained planking of the wharf.

"Lights out!"

In complete darkness we stood there. That warning note which indicated the closing of the section-doors had ceased.

They were closed.

Failing our discovery of another way out, rescue depended upon the forcing of many such obstacles!

Considering what I knew of the equipment of Ste. Claire, I realized that the whole of the party within its walls must be cut off one from another in the innumerable sections. Lacking intelligent work on the part of someone outside—and I believed the Chief of Police to be inside—it was a hopeless task to attempt to calculate how long we might have to wait for that rescue.

And now, a voice—a voice once heard never to be forgotten—broke the silence: it echoed eerily from wall to wall of the cavern.

"Sir Denis Nayland Smith. . . ."

It was Dr. Fu Manchu speaking!

My heart throbbed painfully and I choked down an exclamation.

"You are not called upon to answer if it please you better to remain silent, but I know that you are there. I may add that you will remain there for a considerable time. Apart from certain personal inconvenience, Sir Denis, do not congratulate yourself upon having altered my plans. Dr. Petrie's experiments were a menace more serious than any intrusion of yours. The impossibility of adapting my flying army to certain Russian conditions, was an obstacle which in any event I had not succeeded in surmounting. However, Dr. Petrie is with me now, and his proven genius in my own special province should be of some service in the future."

I could hear Nayland Smith breathing hard close beside me, but he spoke no word.

"Mr. Alan Sterling," the guttural, mocking voice continued, "I have reconstructed your brief romance with Fleurette. It is regrettable. I remain uncertain if I can efface your handiwork. . . ."

I doubted if any man had ever participated in so fantastic a scene; and now, as if to crown its phantasy, Sir Denis spoke out of the darkness beside me.

"Who built your submarine?" he asked in an ordinary conversational tone.

And with that courtesy proper between life-long enemies, Dr. Fu Manchu replied:

"My submersible yacht was designed by Ernst von Ebber, whose 'death' some ten years ago you may recall. But it incorporates many new features of Ericksen. It was built at my yard on the Irrawaddy, in your beloved Burma.

"I must leave you. If I do with a certain reluctance, this is due to the fact that I always pay my gambling debts. My life was at your mercy, Sir Denis, and you held your hand. . . ."

CHAPTER XLI

## " I  S A W  T H E  S U N "

SILENCE.

That guttural, imperious voice had ceased.

"No lights—yet!" came harshly from Nayland Smith. "He has paid the debt. He won't pay twice!"

And in that clammy darkness I stood waiting—and listening.

Sir Denis began speaking again, close to my ear, in a low voice:

"Where did you place him?"

"Almost directly opposite to where we stand—"

"But higher up?"

"Yes."

"I agree. There's some gallery there. We must move warily. I gather that you are a powerful swimmer?"

My heart sank. Keyed up though I was to the supreme

object—escape—contemplation of plunging into that still, cavernous water appalled me.

"Fairly good—but I'm rather below par at the moment!"

"That is understood, Sterling. Only vital issues at stake could demand such an effort. As a matter of fact, I believe this pool to be no more than fifty or sixty yards from side to side. My own powers as a swimmer being limited, I trust I am right. I might manage once across!"

"What's your plan, Sir Denis?"

"This: If we show ourselves again we may be shot down; but this we can test: I suggest that we place a light on the edge of the wharf, as a beacon, and that you slip quietly into the water. There's a ladder near to where we stand. Getting your direction from the light, swim across—"

"I'm game. What next?"

"Find out if there is any way of climbing up—"

"In this utter darkness!"

"Palpably impossible. But you have probably swum across a river before now, carrying your valuables under your hat?"

"I have seen it done."

"My rubber tobacco-pouch, which is unusually large, will comfortably accommodate the automatic which I am now slipping into it, and also one of the flash lamps. . . . Pass yours to me—"

Silently, I groped in the blackness, found Sir Denis's outstretched hand and transferred my lamp to him.

"I am tying up the pouch in a silk handkerchief," he murmured. . . . "Here we are—come nearer."

As I moved cautiously forward, I felt his grasp on my shoulder; some of the man's amazing vitality was imparted to me: I warmed to the ordeal.

"Tie the loose ends under your chin," he directed.

And as I endeavoured to the best of my ability to carry out his directions, he went on, speaking in a low voice but urgently:

"If you can get ashore, use the light to find a way up. Keep the gun in your other hand. If you can make no landing, swim back. Is it clear—and can you do it?"

"It's clear, Sir Denis; and failing interference I think I can do it."

"Good man! Now grab my arm, and when I move back move with me!"

I felt him stoop . . . then suddenly a light sprang up at my feet!

"Back!" he muttered.

He drew me back three paces, and, watching, I saw the light move . . . it moved slowly towards us . . . became stationary . . . moved again!

"I tied a piece of string to it," he murmured in my ear.

The silence, save for those low-spoken words, remained unbroken, until:

"No snipers!" rapped Sir Denis. "Dr. Fu Manchu retains his one noble heritage. His word is his bond. Get busy, now, Sterling! I'll place the light. . . ."

Of that swim across the cavern I prefer not to think; therefore I shall not attempt to describe it. The temperature of the water was much lower than in the open sea.

At a point which I estimated to be not more than fifty yards from the wharf, I touched a rock bottom. I experimented, cautiously; found a foothold; and began to grope forward.

Shelves of rock met my questing fingers. I managed to scramble out of the water. Then, half sitting on a ledge, I unfastened my curious head-dress, and, gripping the tobacco-pouch between my teeth, extracted the lamp. I continued to hold it so, the automatic still inside, whilst I directed a ray of light upward.

It was no easy climb, but I saw that there was a shelf of rock ten or twelve feet up. It sloped at an easy gradient to what looked like a small cave in the wall of the cavern.

I turned, looking back.

The faint beam of light from the lamp, gleaming on that still pool, pointed almost directly towards me.

I began to climb.

There were fewer difficulties than I had looked for. Without very great exertion, I gained the shelf and started for the gap in the rock. When I reached it, I hesitated for a moment. It was much higher and wider than I had thought it to be from below.

Taking the tobacco-pouch from between my teeth, I grasped Nayland Smith's automatic—and went foward.

I found myself in a rock passage not unlike that which we had negotiated on the other side of the pool, except that it was not boarded and that it sloped steeply downward.

Shining my light ahead, I followed this passage.

Its temperature was bitingly low for a naked man: but a tang of the sea came to my nostrils which drew me on.

The passage wound and twisted intricately, growing ever lower and narrower. I pushed on.

There was nothing to show that it was used: it looked like

untouched handiwork of Nature; untravelled, undiscovered. The gradient grew so steep as to resemble a crude stair. I stumbled to the foot of it. . . .

And I saw the sun rising over the Mediterranean!

I shouted, exultantly! I was a sun-worshipper!

I stood in a tiny, pebbly bay, locked in by huge cliffs. The sea lay before me, but neither to right nor to left could I obtain a glimpse of any coastline.

There was some hint of a path leading steeply upward on one side. I examined it closely. Yes! at *some* time it had been traversed!

Five paces up, I found a burned match!

I turned back, running in my eagerness. And, in a fraction of the time taken up by my outward journey, I found myself at the mouth of the passage, staring across the pool to where that feeble beacon beckoned.

"Sir Denis!" I cried, and waved my flashlight—"swim across! *We're out!*"

CHAPTER XLII

# THE RAID

I LOOKED out across the sea, shimmering under a cloudless morning sky, then turned and stared at my companion. He was hatless, but his crisp grey hair in which were white streaks was of that kind which defies rough usage and persistently remains well-groomed.

His tanned skin, upon which in that keen light many little lines showed, and the fact that he was unshaved, added to the gauntness of his features. He wore a grey flannel suit and rubber-soled shoes. The suit was terribly wrinkled, and his tie, which I had watched him knotting, was not strictly in place; but nevertheless I felt that Sir Denis Nayland Smith presented a better front to the world than I did at that moment.

In that keen profile I read something of the force which lies behind a successful career; and looking down at the dirty white overalls in which I was arrayed, a wave of ad-

miration swept over me—admiration for the alert intelligence
of my companion in this strange adventure. Who but Sir
Denis would have thought of bundling our scanty possessions into a small packing-case, and towing it behind him
on that same piece of string which had served in his test to
unmask a possible sniper?

He was examining the match upon the rock path which
alone had given me a clue to the fact that escape from this
secret spot was possible. Then I spoke:

"Sir Denis," I said, "it's a great privilege to have helped
you in any way. You are a very remarkable man."

He turned, and smiled; his smile was thirty years his
junior.

"I suppose you must be right, Sterling," he replied,
"otherwise, I shouldn't have survived. But—"

He stopped.

And blotting out the triumph of our escape from that
cavern which Dr. Fu Manchu had thought to be a Bastille,
came reality—memories—sorrow.

Petrie had gone to join the ranks of those living dead
men. . . .

Fleurette!

Fleurette was lost to me for ever! No doubt my change
of mood was reflected on my face; for:

"I know what you're thinking, Sterling," Sir Denis added,
"but don't despair—yet. There's still hope."

"What!"

"That this path leads somewhere and does not just lose
itself among the rocks, I have little doubt. My own impression is that it leads to the beach of Ste. Claire. But this
is not the chief point of interest—"

"To me, it seems to be."

"What do you regard as the most curious features of our
recent experience?"

I considered for a moment, and then:

"The mystery of Dr. Fu Manchu's motive in remaining
behind," I replied, "and the greater mystery of how and
when he joined his submersible yacht—whatever a submersible yacht may be."

Nayland Smith nodded rapidly.

"You are getting near to it," he rapped. "I am satisfied
that the opening above the water-cave at the top of the
rocks was the place from which he spoke to us. And I think
we are unanimous on the point that there is no other means
of exit but this. Therefore, I have been asking myself for the

last ten minutes: why did he come by this roundabout route when he could have boarded his craft at the wharf, as no doubt the other members of his household did. It's rather a hazardous guess, but one I like to make."

"What is it, Sir Denis?"

"I don't think he joined the submarine at all."

"What!"

"Whatever the construction of that craft may be, it would offer serious obstacles to the transporting of a sick man."

"Good heavens! You think—"

"It is just possible that Petrie has been taken another way, under the personal care of the Doctor."

"But," I protested, "that climb up the rocks?"

"Could easily be performed by native bearers carrying a stretcher or litter, and descent to this point is easy."

"But—" I pointed along the faintly pencilled track.

Nayland Smith shook his head.

"Not that way, Sterling," he admitted. "A motor-boat has been lying here. Look—there are still traces of oil at the margin of the water, and the beach slopes away very sharply."

"You think Dr. Fu Manchu has been taken to some landing-place farther along the coast, where a car awaited him?"

"That is the point we have to settle. Only one of two roads could serve—the Great Corniche or the Middle. All cars using them are being challenged and searched."

"Then, by heaven! we may have him yet!"

"Knowing him better than you do, I look upon that as almost too much to hope for, Sterling. However, suppose we begin our climb."

We set out.

A wild, eleventh-hour hope was mine, that not only Petrie, but Fleurette might be with Dr. Fu Manchu, and that this delay might prove to be his undoing. I did not know how far to take his words literally—but I remembered that he had said "Dr. Petrie is with me". Yes, there was still a ghost of a chance that all was not lost yet.

The path was one of those which would not have appalled a hardened climber, but mountaineering had never aroused my enthusiasm. One thing was certain: Dr. Fu Manchu and his party had never come this way.

It wound round and round great gnarled crags, creeping higher and ever higher. I was glad to be wearing rubber-soled shoes, although I am aware that experienced mountaineers reject them.

At one point, it led us fully a mile inland, climbing very

near to the rim of a deep gorge and at an eerie height above the sea. It was a mere tracing, much better suited to a goat than to a human being. Never once did it touch any practicable road, but now led seaward again, until we found ourselves high up on the side of a dizzy precipice, sheer above the blue Mediterranean.

"Heavens!" muttered Nayland Smith, clutching at the rocky wall at his right hand. "This is getting rather too exciting!"

"I agree, Sir Denis."

At a point which was no more than eighteen inches wide, I was tempted to shut my eyes, but knew that I must keep them open and go on.

"Heaven knows who uses such a path as this," he muttered.

We rounded the bluff and saw that our way lay inland again. The slope below was less steep, and there was dense vegetation upon its side. Nayland Smith pulled up, and under one upraised hand, stared hard.

"It is difficult to recognize from this point," he said, "but here is the bay of Ste. Claire as I suspected."

And now that crazy path began to descend, leading us lower and lower.

It was very still there, and the early morning air possessed champagne-like properties. And suddenly Sir Denis turned to me:

"Do you hear it, Sterling?" he snapped.

Distinctly, in the silence, although it seemed to come from a long way off, I had detected the sound to which he referred—a distant shouting and an almost incessant booming sound.

"It seems incredible," he continued, "but they are evidently still trying to force a way into the house! Come on, let's hurry—there's much to do, and very little time to do it."

We ran down the remaining few yards of the path, and found ourselves upon the beach—that beach of which I had dreamed so often—but always with the dainty, sun-browned figure of Fleurette seated upon it.

Sir Denis, whose powers of physical endurance were little short of phenomenal, ran across, making for that corresponding path upon the other side which led to the seven flights of steps communicating with the terrace of the villa. . . .

We mounted at the double.

I saw that the main door had been forced and the shutters torn from an upper window against which a ladder rested.

The booming sound, which had grown louder as we approached, was caused by the efforts of a party of men under a bewildered police officer, endeavouring to force the first of the section-doors, that at the top of the steps which led down to the radio research-room.

Sir Denis made himself known to the man—who had not been a member of the original party. And we learned the astounding fact that with the exception of four, the whole of that party, including the Chief of Police, remained locked inside the house—nor had any sound or message come from them!

A man was at work with a blow-lamp, supported by others with crowbars.

Expert reinforcements were expected at any moment; and—a curious feature of the situation—although there was a telephone in the villa, no message had come over it from within, nor had any reply been received when the number was called. . . .

## CHAPTER XLIII

# KÂRAMANÈH'S DAUGHTER

In the course of the next few minutes I had my first real sight of Ste. Claire de la Roche.

A paved path encircled the house. There were ladders against several windows; ways had been forced into the outer rooms, and the villa proper was in possession of the police. But I knew that the real establishment was far below, and that it was much more extensive than that more or less open to inspection.

Crashing and booming echoed hollowly from within.

The front of the villa, by which I mean that part which faced towards the distant road, was squat and unimpressive. An entrance had been forced from this point also, and there were a number of police hurrying about.

A little cobbled street, flanked by a house with an arched entrance, presented itself. Beside the house, in a cavern-like opening, a steep flight of steps disappeared into blackness. The top of a ladder projected above the parapet on my right, and, looking over, I saw that part of the glass roof of one of the forcing-houses visible at this point had been smashed and a ladder lowered through the gap.

Dim voices reached me from far below. I wondered if any of the raiding party had been found in that section.

But Nayland Smith was hurrying on down the slope. And now we came to a long, sanded drive. There was a wall on the left, beyond which I thought lay a kitchen-garden, and a sheer drop on the right.

Sweeping around in a northerly direction, the drive led to gates of ornate iron scroll-work, which were closed, and I saw that two police officers were on duty there.

The gates were opened in response to a brief order, and we hurried out into a narrow, sloping lane. I remembered this lane. It wandered down to the main road; for I had penetrated to it in my earliest attempt to explore Ste. Claire de la Roche, and had been confronted with a "No thoroughfare" sign.

"There's a police car at the corner," said Nayland Smith; "we must take that."

No cars had been found in the stone garage attached to the villa, and I wondered what had become of that which had once belonged to Petrie, and which must have been hidden on the night of my encounter with the *dacoit* on the Corniche road.

A sergeant of police was standing by the car. He reported that a motor-cyclist patrol had just passed. All cars using both roads had been challenged and searched throughout the night in accordance with Sir Denis's instructions. But no one had been detained.

Nayland Smith stood there twitching at the lobe of his ear; and my heart sank, for I thought that he was about to admit defeat.

"He may have gone by sea down to Italy," he said; "it is a possibility which must not be overlooked. Or, by heavens!—"

He suddenly dashed his fist into the palm of his left hand.

"What, Sir Denis?"

"He may have had a yacht standing by! He got away from England in that manner on one occasion."

"It's also just possible," I began. . . .

"I know," Sir Denis groaned. "My theory lacks solid foundation—he may have joined the submarine?"

"Exactly."

"His delay might be due merely to his sense of the dramatic—which is strong. Get in, Sterling."

He turned to the sergeant in charge of the car.

"Office of the Préfet," he rapped and jumped in behind me.

To endeavour to reconstruct the ideas which passed through my mind during that early-morning drive would be futile, since they consisted of a taunting panorama of living-dead men; the flower-like face of Fleurette appearing again and again before that ghostly curtain, and set in an expression of adoration which formed my most evil memory. I could not banish the image of Petrie, could not accept the fact that he had joined the phantom army of Dr. Fu Manchu.

Nayland Smith sat grimly silent, until at last:

"Sir Denis," I said, "this is no time to talk of my personal affairs, but—something which happened in Petrie's room has been puzzling me."

"What is that?" he snapped.

"Fleurette kept watch at the door—she had led me there—whilst I slipped in to see him. Just before I left, he caught a glimpse of her, and—"

"Yes?" said Sir Denis, a sudden keen interest in his eyes. "What did he do?"

"He sat up in bed as though he had seen an apparition. He asked in a most extraordinary voice who it was that had looked into the room. I had to leave—it was impossible to stay. But there is no doubt whatever that he recognized her—although, as she told me afterwards, she had never seen Petrie in her life."

I paused, meeting his eager regard; and then:

"You also thought you recognized her, Sir Denis," I went on, "and evidently you were not wrong. I can't believe I shall ever see her again, but, if you know, tell me: who is she?"

He drew a deep breath.

"You told me, I think, that you had never met Kâramanèh—Petrie's wife?"

"Never."

"She was formerly a member of the household of Dr. Fu Manchu."

"It seems impossible!"

"It does, but it's a fact, nevertheless. I seem to remember telling you that she was the most beautiful woman I have ever known."

"You did."

"On one side she's of pure Arab blood, of the other I am uncertain."

"Arab?"

"Surely. She was selected for certain qualities of which her extraordinary beauty was not the least, by Dr. Fu Manchu. Petrie upset his plans in that direction. Now, it is necessary for you to realize, Sterling, that Petrie, also, is a man of very good family—of sane, clean, balanced stock."

"I am aware of this, Sir Denis; my father knows him well."

Sir Denis nodded, and went on.

"Dr. Fu Manchu has always held Petrie in high esteem. Very few people are aware of what I am now going to tell you—possibly, even your father doesn't know. But a year after Petrie's marriage to Kâramânèh, a child was born."

"I had no idea of this."

"It was so deep a grief to them, Sterling, that they never spoke of it."

"A grief?"

"The child, a girl, was born in Cairo. She died when she was three weeks old."

"Good heavens! Poor old Petrie! I have never heard him even mention it."

"You never would. They agreed never to mention it. It was their way of forgetting. There were curious features about the case to which, in their sorrow, they were blind at the time. But when, nearly a year later, the full facts came into my possession, a truly horrible idea presented itself to my mind."

"What do you mean, Sir Denis?"

"Naturally, I whispered no word of it to Petrie. It would have been the most callous cruelty to have done so. But privately, I made a number of inquiries; and whilst I obtained no evidence upon which it was possible to act, nevertheless, what I learned confirmed my suspicion. . . .

"Dr. Fu Manchu is patient, as only a great scientist can be."

He paused, watching me, a question in his eyes. But as I did not speak:

"When I entered that room, which I described to you as the Palace of the Sleeping Beauty, I received one of the great shocks of my life. Do you know what I thought as I looked at Fleurette asleep?"

"I am trying to anticipate what you are going to tell me."

"I thought it was Kâramânèh—*Petrie's wife!*"

"You mean—"

"I mean that even with her eyes closed, the likeness was

uncanny, utterly beyond the possibility of coincidence. Then when you described to me their unusual quality—and Kâramanèh's eyes are her crowning beauty—I knew that I could not be mistaken."

Positively I was stricken dumb—I could only sit and stare at the speaker. No words occurred to me.

"Therefore, poor Petrie's recognition does not surprise me. It may seem amazing, Sterling, almost incredible, that a child less than three weeks old could be subjected to that treatment upon which much of Fu Manchu's monumental knowledge rests: the production of artificial catalepsy; but a fact which by now must have dawned upon you. He is not only the greatest physician alive to-day, he is probably the greatest physician who has ever been."

"Sir Denis—"

The car was just pulling up before the police headquarters.

"There's no doubt whatever, Sterling!" He grasped my arm firmly. "Think of what the Doctor has told you about her—think of what she has told you about herself—so much as she knows. There isn't a shadow of doubt. Fleurette is Petrie's daughter, and Karâmanèh is her mother! Buck up, old chap, I know how you must feel about it—but we haven't abandoned hope, yet."

He sprang out and ran in at the door, brushing past an officer who stood on duty there.

## CHAPTER XLIV

## OFFICE OF THE PRÉFET

In the large but frigid office of M. Chamrousse, Préfet of the Department, that sedate, grey-bearded official spoke rapidly on the telephone, and made a number of notes upon a writing-block; Sir Denis snapping his fingers impatiently and pacing up and down the carpet.

I had no idea of his plan, of what he hoped for. My state of mental chaos was worse than before. Fleurette, Petrie's daughter! From tenderest infancy she had lived as those others lived whom he wanted for his several purposes: a dream-life!

And now—Petrie himself. . . .

In upon my thoughts broke the magisterial voice of the man at the big table.

"Here is the complete list, Sir Denis Nayland Smith," he said. "You will see that the only private vessel of any tonnage which has cleared a neighbouring port during the past twelve hours is this one."

He rested the point of his pencil on the paper. Nayland Smith, bending eagerly over him, read the note aloud:

"M.Y. *Lola*, of Buenos Ayres; four thousand tons; owned by Santos da Cunha."

He suddenly stood upright, staring straight before him.

"Santos da Cunha?" he repeated. "Where have I heard that name?"

"Curiously enough," said M. Chamrousse, "the villa at Ste. Claire was formerly the property of this gentleman, from whom it was purchased by Mahdi Bey."

Sir Denis dashed his fist into the palm of his hand.

"Sterling!" he cried—"there's hope yet! there's hope yet! But I have been blind.. This is the Argentine for whose record I am waiting!" He turned to the Préfet. "How long has the *Lola* been lying in Monaco?"

"Nearly a week, I believe."

"And she left?"

"Soon after dawn, Sir Denis—as I read in this report—"

"You see, Sterling! you see?" he cried.

He turned again to the Préfet, and:

"The *Lola* must be traced," he said rapidly—"without delay. Please give instructions for messages to be sent to all ships in the neighbourhood, notifying the position of this motor yacht when sighted."

"I can do this," said the other gravely, inclining his head.

"Next, is there a French or British warship in port anywhere along the coast?"

M. Chamrousse raised his eyebrows.

"There is a French destroyer in the harbour of Monaco," he replied.

"Please notify her commander to be ready to leave at a moment's notice—in fact, the instant I get on board."

That peremptory manner, contempt for red tape and routine, which characterized Sir Denis in emergencies, had the effect of ruffling the French official.

"This, sir," he replied, taking off his spectacles and tapping them on the blotting-pad, "I cannot do."

"Cannot?"

The other shrugged.

"I have no such powers," he declared. "It is in the province of the Naval authority. I doubt if even the Admiral commanding the Mediterranean Fleet could take it upon himself to do what you ask of me."

"Perhaps," rapped Nayland Smith, "in these circumstances, you will be good enough to put a call through to the Ministry of Marine in Paris."

M. Chamrousse shrugged his shoulders and looked mildly surprised.

"Really—" he began.

"My authority from the British Foreign Office," said Sir Denis, with a sort of repressed violence, "is such, that any delay you may cause must react to your own discredit. The interests of France as well as those of England are involved in this matter. Damn it, M. Chamrousse! I am *here* in the interests of France! Must I go elsewhere, or will you do as I ask?"

The Préfet resignedly took up the telephone and gave instructions to the outer office that Paris should be called.

Nayland Smith began again to pace up and down the carpet.

"You know, Sir Denis Nayland Smith," M. Chamrousse began in his dry, precise voice, "it is perhaps a little unfair to me that I am so badly informed regarding this matter. All the available police have been rushed to Ste. Claire, and according to my latest reports, are locked up there. I am in the dark about this—I am tied hand and foot. Paris instructed me to place myself at your disposal, and I have done so, but the reputation of Mahdi Bey, whom I have met several times socially, is quite frankly above suspicion. To me, the whole thing is incomprehensible; and now you demand—"

In this unemotional outburst I saw the reason of the Préfet's coldness towards Sir Denis. He resented the action of Paris. Sir Denis realized this also; for checking his restless promenade, he turned to face the little bearded man.

"Such issues are at stake, Mr. Chamrousse," he said, "and my own blunders have so confounded me, that perhaps I have failed in proper courtesy. If so, forgive me. But try to believe that I have every reason for what I do. It is of vital importance that the yacht *Lola* should be detained."

"I accept your assurances upon these matters, Sir Denis," said M. Chamrousse.

But I thought from the tone of his voice that he was somewhat mollified.

Conversation ceased, and unavoidably I dropped back into that valley of sorrowful reflection from which this verbal duel between Sir Denis and the French official had temporarily dragged me.

Fleurette was Petrie's daughter!

This was the amazing face outstanding above the mist and discord which ruled my brain. It might be that they were together; but, once Petrie should have fully recovered from his dangerous illness, I did not doubt that he would be forced to accept that Blessing of the Celestial Vision from which I had so narrowly escaped: and then. . . .

If my influence had "not tarnished the mirror"—in Dr. Fu Manchu's words—a ghastly union of unknown age and budding youth would be consummated!

I could not face the idea. I found myself clenching my fists and grinding my teeth.

At which moment, the connexion with Paris was made; M. Chamrousse stood up, bowed courteously, and handed the receiver to Sir Denis.

The latter—in voluble, but very bad, French—proceeded to tread heavily on the toes of the Paris official at the other end of the line. I had learned that he, in moments of stress, was prone to exhibit a truculence, an indifference to the feelings of others which underlay and may have been the driving power behind that brusque, but never uncourteous, manner which characterized him normally.

He was demanding to speak to the Minister in person and refusing to be put off.

"At home and asleep? Be so good as to put me through to his private number at once!"

M. Chamrousse had taken his stand on the carpet upon which Nayland Smith so recently had paced up and down; listening to the conversation, he merely shrugged, took out a cigarette and lighted it with meticulous care.

However, it must be recorded to the credit of Sir Denis that his intolerant language—which was sometimes frankly rude—achieved its objective.

He was put through to the sleeping Minister. . . .

No doubt there is much to be said for direct methods in sweeping aside ill-informed opposition. In the Middle West of America, my father's home, I had learned to respect the direct attack as opposed to those circumlocutionary manoeuvres so generally popular in European society.

To the unconcealed surprise of M. Chamrousse, Sir Denis's demands were instantly conceded!

I gathered that authoritative orders would be transmitted immediately to the commander of the destroyer lying in the harbour at Monaco; that every other available unit in the fleet would be dispatched in quest of the submarine. In short, it became evident during this brief conversation that Sir Denis wielded an authority greater than even I had suspected.

When presently he replaced the receiver and sprang to his feet, the effect upon M. Chamrousse was notable.

"Sir Denis Nayland Smith," he said, "I congratulate you—but you fully realize that in this matter I was indeed helpless!"

Sir Denis shook his hand.

"Please say no more! Of course I understand. But if you would accept my advice, it would be this: proceed personally to Ste. Claire, and when you have realized the difficulties of the situation there, you will be in a position to deal with it."

Some more conversation there was, the gist of which I have forgotten, and then we were out in the car again and speeding along those tortuous roads headed for Monaco.

"Much time has been wasted," said Nayland Smith; "only luck can help us now. Failing a message from some ship which has sighted the yacht *Lola*, it's impossible to lay a course. Probably the *Lola* has a turn of speed which will tax the warship in any event. But lacking knowledge of position, we can't even start."

"I don't doubt she will have been sighted. There's a lot of shipping in those waters."

"Yes, but the bulk of it is small craft, and many of them carry no radio. However, we are doing all that lies in our power to do."

## CHAPTER XLV

## ON THE DESTROYER

FROM the bridge of the destroyer I looked over a blue and sailless sea. The speed of the little warship was exhilarating, and I could see from the attitude of her commander beside me that this break in peace-time routine was welcome rather than irksome.

I glanced towards the port wing of the bridge where Nayland Smith was staring ahead through raised glasses. Somewhere astern of where I stood, somewhere in the slender hull, full out and quivering on this unexpected mission, I knew there were police officers armed with a warrant, issued by the Boulevard du Palais, for the arrest of Dr. Fu Manchu.

And as the wine of the morning began to stir my blood, hope awakened. The history of Fleurette lay open before me like a book; and all that had seemed incomprehensible in her character and her behaviour, lover-like, now I translated and understood. She had been cultivated as those plants in the forcing-houses had been cultivated.

The imprint of Dr. Fu Manchu was upon her.

Yet through it all the real Fleurette had survived, defying the alchemy of the super-scientist: she was still Petrie's daughter, beautiful, lovable, and mine, if I could find her.

I set doubt aside. Definitely, we should overtake the South American yacht. News had come from a cruising liner ten minutes before we had reached Monaco harbour; the *Lola*, laid on a southerly course, was less than twenty miles ahead.

But, since the *Lola* also must have picked up the message, we realized that the course of the motor yacht would in all probability have been changed. Nevertheless, ultimate escape was next to impossible.

Yet again, that damnable thought intruded: the *Lola* might prove to be a will-o'-the-wisp; Fu Manchu, Fleurette and Petrie not on board!

It appeared to me that the only thing supporting Nayland Smith's theory and his amazing reaction to it, was the fact that the *Lola* had not answered those messages sent out by the French authority.

At which moment, Sir Denis dropped the glasses into their case and turned.

"Nothing!" he said, grimly.

"It is true," the commander replied; "but they have a good start."

A man ran up to the bridge with a radio message. The commander scanned it.

"They are clever," he reported. "But all the same they

171

have been sighted again! They are still on their original course."

"Who sends the report?" asked Nayland Smith.

"An American freighter."

"The Air arm is strangely silent?"

"We must be patient. Only two planes have been dispatched; they are looking also for a submarine: and there are many miles of sea to search."

He took up the glasses. Nayland Smith, hands thrust in his pockets, stared straightly ahead.

The destroyer leaped and quivered under the lash of her merciless engines, a living, feverish thing. And this reflection crossed my mind: that the Chinese doctor, wherever he might be at that moment, was indeed a superman; for he is no ordinary criminal against whom warships are sent out. . . .

Another message was brought to the bridge; this one from a flying officer. The *Lola* was laid-to, less than five miles off and nearly dead on our course!

"What does this mean?" rapped Nayland Smith. "I don't like it a bit."

I was staring ahead, straining my eyes to pierce the distance. . . . And, now, a speck on the skyline, I saw an airplane flying towards me.

"Coming back to pilot us," said the commander; "they know the game is up!"

A further message arrived. The *Lola* was putting a launch off at the time that the airman had headed back to find us. No submarine had been sighted.

"By heavens!" cried Nayland Smith, "I was right. His under-water craft *is* waiting for him in the event of just such an emergency as this! Instruct the plane to hurry back!"

The order was dispatched.

I saw the pilot bank, go about and set off again on a course slightly westward of our own.

The commander spoke a few more orders rapidly and we crept into line behind the swiftly disappearing airman. We must have been making thirty-five knots or more, for it was only a matter of minutes before I saw the yacht—dead ahead.

"The launch is putting back!" said Nayland Smith. "Look!"

The little craft was just swinging around the stern of the yacht! And now we were so near that I could see the lines of the *Lola*, a beautiful white and silver ship with a low, graceful hull and one squat, yellow funnel with a silver band.

"By heavens!" I shouted, "we're in time!"

The Naval air pilot was circling now above the yacht. That the submarine was somewhere in the neighbourhood it seemed reasonable to suppose, unless it had been the purpose of the launch's crew to head for shore: a possibility. But no indication of an under-water craft disturbed the blue mirror of the Mediterranean.

The commander of the destroyer rang off his engines.

CHAPTER XLVI

# WE BOARD THE *LOLA*

WE watched the launch return to the ladder of the yacht and saw her crew mount. The launch was already creeping up to her davits when the boat from the destroyer reached the ladder.

A lieutenant led with an armed party, Nayland Smith followed, then came the French police, and I brought up the rear.

A smart-looking officer—Portuguese, I thought—took the lieutenant's salute as he stepped on deck. Never, I think, in the experiences which had come to me since I had found myself within the zone of the Chinese doctor, had I been conscious of quite that sense of pent-up, overpowering emotion which claimed me at this moment.

Fleurette! Petrie! Were they here?

The sea looked like a vast panel which some Titan craftsman had covered with blue enamel, and the French warship might have been a gaunt grey insect trapped in the pigment.

"Sir Denis," I said suddenly, in a low voice—"if the submarine is really in our neighbourhood—"

"I had thought of it," he rapped. "It was impossible to identify the man in the stern of the launch. But unless it was Dr. Fu Manchu, in which event he's on board here, our safety is questionable!"

"Take us to the captain," said the lieutenant sharply.

The yacht's officer saluted, and led the way.

Armed men were left on duty at the ladder-head and at the foot of the stair leading up to the bridge. The bridge

173

proved to be deserted. Two men were posted there, and we followed on into the charthouse.

This was small, but perfectly equipped, and it had only one occupant: a tall man wearing an astrakhan cap and a fur-collared overcoat. His arms folded, he stood there facing us as we entered.

Emotion almost choked me; triumph, with which even yet a dreadful doubt mingled. Nayland Smith's jaw squared as he stood beside me staring across the room.

No greetings were exchanged.

"Who commands this yacht?" the lieutenant demanded.

And in that cold guttural voice, so rarely touched by any trace of human feelings:

"I do," Dr. Fu Manchu replied.

"You failed to answer an official call sent out to all shipping in these waters."

"I did."

"You are accused of harbouring persons wanted by the police, and I have authority to search this vessel."

Dr. Fu Manchu stood quite still; his immobility was mummy-like.

Nayland Smith stepped aside to make way for the senior police officer from Nice. As the man entered, Sir Denis merely pointed to that tall, dignified figure. The detective stepped forward.

"Is your name Dr. Fu Manchu?"

"It is."

"I hold a warrant for your arrest. You must consider yourself my prisoner."

## CHAPTER XLVII

## DR. PETRIE

"COME in," said a low voice.

Sir Denis stood stock-still for one age-long moment, his hand resting on the door knob. Then he pulled open the white cabin door.

In the bed under an open porthole, Petrie lay! His eyes,

darkly shadowed, were fixed upon us. But his expression as
Nayland Smith sprang forward was one I shall never forget.

"Petrie! Petrie, old man. . . ! Thank God for this!"

Sir Denis's face I could not see—for he stood with his
back to me grasping Petrie's upstretched hand. But I could
see Petrie; and I knew that he was so overwhelmed by
emotion as to be incapable of words. Sir Denis's silence told
the same story.

But when at last that long, silent hand-grasp was relaxed:

"Sterling!" said the invalid, smiling—"you have done more
than merely save my life. You have brought back a happiness I thought I had lost for ever. Smith, old man"—he
looked up at Sir Denis—"get a radio off to Kara in Cairo
at the earliest possible moment! But break the news gently.
She will be mad with joy!"

He looked at me again.

"I understand, Sterling, that what you have found you
want to keep?"

At that Nayland Smith turned.

"I trust your financial resources are adequate to the task,
Sterling?" he rapped, but with a smile on his tired face—
and it was a smile of happiness.

"Does she know?" I asked, and my voice was far from
steady.

Petrie nodded.

"Go and find her," he said. "She will be glad to see you."

I went out, leaving those life-long friends together. I returned to the deck.

What must there not be that Petrie had to tell Sir Denis,
and he to tell Petrie? It was, I suppose, one of the most
remarkable reunions in history. For Petrie had died and had
been buried, and was restored again to life. And Sir Denis
had crowned his remarkable career with the greatest ac-
complishment in criminal records—the arrest of Dr. Fu
Manchu. . . .

The attitude of the members of the crew of the *Lola*
strongly suggested that the vessel was used for none but
legitimate purposes. One by one they were being submitted
to a close interrogation by the French detective and his assistant in a forward cabin.

I had heard the evidence of the chief navigating officer
and of the second officer. The vessel belonged to Santos da
Cunha, an Argentine millionaire, but he frequently placed
it at the disposal of his friends, of whom Dr. Fu Manchu
(known to them as the Marquis Chûan) was one. It was

the Marquis's custom sometimes to take charge, and he, according to these witnesses, was a qualified master mariner and a fine seaman!

His personal servants, of whom there were four, had come on board at Monaco; from this dehumanized quartet I anticipated that little would be learned. The ship's officers and crew denied all knowledge of a submarine. When the engines had been stopped by Dr. Fu Manchu and the launch ordered away, they had obeyed without knowing for what purpose those orders had been given.

Personally, I had no doubt that the under-water craft lay somewhere near, but that the Doctor had decided to sacrifice himself alone rather than to order the submarine to the surface when the coming of the French airman had warned him that his movements were covered.

Why?

Doubtless because he had recognized his own escape to be impossible.

I reached the cabin in which I knew Fleurette to be, rapped, opened the door and went in.

She was standing just inside—and I knew that she had been waiting for me.

I forgot what happened immediately afterwards; I lived in another world. . . .

When, at last, and reluctantly, I came to earth again, the first idea which I properly grasped was that of Fleurette's almost insupportable happiness, because she had learned that she really possessed a father—and had met him!

Her eagerness to meet her mother resembled a physical hunger.

It was not easy to see these strange events through her eyes; but, listening to her, watching her fascinatedly, tears on her dark lashes as she sometimes clutched me, nervously, excitedly, it dawned upon me that there is probably a great void in the life of one who has never known father or mother.

Her happiness was clouded by the knowledge that she had gained it at the price of the downfall of Dr. Fu Manchu. I tried to divert the tide of her thoughts; but it was useless.

She, and she alone, was responsible. . . .

It was clear to me that Petrie—sensing that exalted estimate which Fleurette had made of the character of the incalculable Chinaman—had done nothing to disturb her ideals.

How long we were there alone I don't know; but at last:

"Really, darling," said Fleurette, "you must go back. I am not going to move. I dare not face—"

I tore myself away; I returned to Petrie's cabin.

Nayland Smith was there. The two were deep in conversation: they ceased speaking as I entered.

"I have solved a mystery for you," Sir Denis began, looking up at me. "You recall, when Petrie lay in the grip of the purple plague and Fah Lo Suee was there, the voice which warned you to beware of her?"

"Yes."

"I was the speaker, Sterling!" said Petrie.

Save for that queer blanching of his hair, he seemed to me now to be restored to something almost resembling his former self. Happiness is the medicine of the gods. He had met a beautiful girl, in whom, as in a mirror, he had seen his wife; had known that this was the daughter snatched from them in babyhood. Then, within a few hours, he had been rescued from a living death to find Nayland Smith at his bedside.

"I suspected it; but at the time I found it hard to believe."

"Naturally!" Sir Denis was the speaker. "But I have just learned a remarkable, and at the same time a ghastly thing, Sterling. Victims of the catalepsy induced by Dr. Fu Manchu remain *conscious.*"

"What!"

"It is difficult to make you understand," Petrie broke in, "what I passed through. Evidently my preparation '654' is fairly efficacious. If you had known what to do next, I should have survived all right. I was insensible, but the injection of Fu Manchu's virus to induce catalepsy restored me to consciousness!

"How long after it had been administered, I don't know. Incidentally, that hell-cat made the injection in my thigh, under the sheet, whilst she sat beside the bed. Oh! you're not to blame, Sterling."

"She inherits her father's genius," Sir Denis murmured.

"As I saw her last," I said savagely, "she was suffering for it."

"What? I don't know about this."

"He flogged her. . . ."

Sir Denis and Petrie exchanged glances.

"Details can wait," rapped the former. "Inhuman though the sentiment may be, I cannot find it in my heart to be sorry."

"Can you imagine, Sterling," Petrie went on, "that from

the time I recovered consciousness and found Fah Lo Suee in the room, I was aware of everything that happened?"

"You don't mean—"

Sir Denis nodded, shortly.

"Yes . . . even that," Petrie assured me. "Somehow, when I saw that she-cat coiling herself about you, I forced speech —I tried to warn you. It was the last evidence of which I was capable to show that I still lived!

"I heard myself pronounced dead; I saw Cartier's tears. I was hurried away—a plague case. The undertakers dealt with me and I was put into a coffin."

"My God!" I groaned, and wondered at the man's fortitude.

"Do you know what I thought, Sterling, as I lay there in the mortuary?—I prayed that nothing would interfere with the plans of Dr. Fu Manchu! For the purpose of it all was clear to me; and I knew—try to picture my frame of mind!— that if my friends should upset his plans I should be—"

"Buried alive!"

Nayland Smith's voice sounded like a groan.

"Exactly, old man. You have noticed my hair? That was when it happened. When I heard the screws being removed, and saw two evil-looking Burmans bending over me—or rather, I saw them at rare intervals, for it was impossible to move my eyes—I sent up a prayer of thankfulness!

"They lifted me out—my body, of course, was quite rigid; placed me in a hammock and hurried me out to a car in the lane beyond. Of the substitution of which you have told me, I saw nothing. I was taken by road to Ste. Claire, carried to the room in which you found me, Sterling, and placed in the care of a Japanese doctor, who informed me that his name was Yamamata.

"He gave me an injection which relaxed the rigidity, and then a draught of that preparation which looks like brandy but tastes like death.

"You and I, Smith"—he glanced aside at Sir Denis—"have met with it before!"

"Is Dr. Yamamata on board?" I asked.

"No. I was carried in a sort of litter down to that water-cave which Smith tells me you have visited, across it in a collapsible boat which I assume is part of the equipment of the submarine; and from there up to a rock tunnel and down to the beach. A launch belonging to this yacht was waiting, in which I was brought on board, Dr. Fu Manchu

in person superintending. Fleurette was with us. We joined
the yacht in sight of Monaco. I resigned myself to becoming
a subject of the new Chinese Emperor of the World."

## CHAPTER XLVIII

# "IT MEANS EXTRADITION"

I HAD rarely, if ever, seen a display of Gallic emotion to
equal that of Dr. Cartier when he entered Petrie's room in
the Hôtel de Paris in Monte Carlo.

He beheld before him a man whom he had certified to
be dead; whom he had seen buried. Perhaps his behaviour
was excusable. Brisson, who was with him, controlled himself better.

"Because I am the cause of this," said Petrie, "I naturally
feel most embarrassed. But you may take it, Cartier, that
weakness now is the only trouble. It's a question of getting
on my feet again."

"I will arrange for a nurse."

The door opened, and Fleurette came in.

As her accepted lover, the incense of worship which the
Frenchmen silently offered should perhaps have been flat-
tering. Oddly enough, I resented it.

"This is my daughter, gentlemen," said Petrie—with so
much pride and such happiness in his voice that all else
was forgotten.

She crossed and seated herself at his side, clasping his
outstretched hand.

"This, dear, is Dr. Cartier—Dr. Brisson, my friends and
allies."

Fleurette smiled at the French doctors. That intoxicating
dimple appeared for a moment in her chin, and I knew
that they were her slaves.

"I shall require no other nurse," Petrie added.

It was hard to go; but a nod from Fleurette gave me my
dismissal. With a few words of explanation I left the room.

Sir Denis was waiting for me in the lobby.

"I hate to drag you away, Sterling," he said; "but if any

179

sort of progress has been made at Ste. Claire, you can probably help."

We joined a car which was waiting. I could not fail to recall in the early stages of the journey, that night when learning at Quinto's that Petrie was dead, I had launched what was meant to be a vendetta.

I had set out to seek the life of any servant of Dr. Fu Manchu who might cross my path!

And even now, when the fact had become plain to me that the unscrupulous methods of the great Chinaman, his indifference to human life, were not dictated by any prospect of personal gain, but belonged to an ideal utterly beyond my Western comprehension, I did not regret the death of that Burmese strangler with whom I had fought to a finish on the Corniche road.

"The big villa at Ste. Claire," said Nayland Smith, "has obviously been a European base of the group for many years past. It's impossible to close one's eyes to the fact, Sterling, that this Si-Fan movement, whatever it may embody, has gained momentum since the days when I first realized the existence of Dr. Fu Manchu. You have told me that he claims to be responsible for that financial chaos which at the moment involves the whole world. That he has defeated age, I know. And I gather that he professes to have solved the mystery of the Philosopher's Stone."

We were clear of Monaco now, and mounting higher and higher.

"In all this, there is one thing which we must bear in mind: it has taken me many years to learn as little as I know of the Mandarin Fu Manchu. But at last I have discovered his term of official office, and with many blanks have built up something of his pedigree."

"Tell me," I said, eagerly.

"He administered the Province of Ho Nan, under the Empress. Judging by the evidence which I have accumulated, he appeared to be of the same age in those days, as he appears now!"

"Whatever age *is* the man?"

"Heaven only knows, Sterling! This I doubt if we shall ever find out. He is affiliated to those who once ruled China. His place in the scheme of things, I take it, may be compared to that once held by the Pretender in England. But he has a legitimate claim to the title of Prince."

"Sir Denis, this is amazing!"

"Dr. Fu Manchu is the most amazing figure living in the

world to-day. He holds degrees of four universities. He is a Doctor of Philosophy as well as a Doctor of Medicine. I have reason to believe that he speaks every civilized language, with facility; and I know that he represents a movement which already has pushed Europe and America very near to the brink—and which, before long, may push both of them right over."

"You have prevented that, Sir Denis. An army is helpless without its leader."

I glanced aside at him as we sped along the Corniche road; he was tugging at the lobe of his ear.

"How do we know that he *is* the leader?" he snapped. "Think of the living-dead whom we chance to have identified. How many more belong to the Si-Fan whose identities we don't even suspect? His 'submersible yacht', the existence of which, even if I had doubted Dr. Fu Manchu's word (and this I never doubted), is established by the disappearance of every member of his household! The French authorities have never had so much as a suspicion that such a vessel was on their coasts!

"That pool may have been known to the monks in the old days; but you will search for it in vain in Baedeker. Do you grasp what I mean, Sterling? We in the West follow our well-trodden paths; no one of us sees more than the others see. But under the street along which we are walking, at the back of a house which we have passed a hundred times, beyond some beach on which we sun ourselves, lies something else—something unsuspected.

"These are the things that Dr. Fu Manchu has discovered —or re-discovered. This is the secret of his influence. He is behind us, under us, and over us."

"At the moment," I said savagely, "he is in a French prison!"

"Why?" murmured Nayland Smith.

"What do you mean?"

"His submersible yacht, for a sight of which I would give much, is almost certainly armed—probably with torpedoes, improved by Ericksen or some other specialist possessing a first-class brain stolen from the tomb to work for Dr. Fu Manchu. Therefore, why did he submit to arrest?"

"I don't follow."

"I agree that the circumstances were peculiar, and possibly I am pessimistic. But I am not satisfied. I have been in touch with the Foreign Office. The Naval resources of Europe already will be combing the Mediterranean for the

181

mysterious submarine. But—" he turned, and I met the glance of the steel-grey eyes: "do you think they will find it?"

"Why not?"

He snapped his teeth together and pulled out from his pocket a very large and dilapidated rubber pouch, and at the same time a big-bowled and much-charred briar. I recognized the pouch, remembering when and where I had last seen it.

"I thought I had lost that for you, Sir Denis!" I said.

"So did I," he rapped; "but I found it on my way down. It's an old friend which I should have hated to lose. Hello! here we are."

As he began to charge his pipe, the driver of the car had turned into that steeply sloping lane which led up to the iron gates of the Villa Ste. Claire.

"I don't expect to learn anything here, Sterling," said Sir Denis, "which is worth while. But there's no other line of investigation open at the moment. Dr. Fu Manchu's arrest is a very delicate matter. He has already applied to his Consul, and demanded that the Chinese Legation in Paris shall be notified of the state of affairs! To put the thing in a nutshell: unless there is some evidence here—and I don't expect to find it—to connect him with the recent outrages in the neighbourhood or to establish his association with the epidemic, which is frankly hopeless, it means extradition."

"Have you arranged for it?" I asked eagerly.

"Yes. But even if we get him back to England—and I know his dossier at Scotland Yard from A to Z—"

He paused and stuffed the big pouch into his pocket; some coarse-cut mixture which overhung the bowl of his briar, lent it the appearance of a miniature rock-garden—

"What!"

"The law of England has many loopholes."

CHAPTER XLIX

# MAÎTRE FOLI

THE absence of reporters from Ste. Claire, the gate of which was guarded by police, amazed me.

"There are some things which are too important for publicity," said Sir Denis. "And in France as well as in England we have this advantage over America: we can silence the newspapers. The only witnesses of any use in a court of law which we have captured so far are the four Chinese body-servants of the Doctor's, who were on board the yacht. Some of these you can identify, I believe?"

"Three of them I have seen before."

Sir Denis opened the door of the car. We had reached the end of that sanded drive which swept around the side of the villa and terminated near the southerly wing of the terrace.

"Have you ever tried to interrogate a Chinaman who didn't want to commit himself?" he asked.

"Yes, I have employed Chinese servants, and I know what they can be like."

Nayland Smith turned to me—he was standing on the drive.

"They are loyal, Sterling," he snapped. "Bind them to a tradition and no human power can tear them away from it. . . ."

Many of the section-doors had been forced, but more than half the party remained imprisoned. Under instructions from Sir Denis, I gathered, a party had been landed in that tiny bay, which was the sea-bound terminus of the exit from the water-cave. Suitably prepared, they had landed there, and were operating upon the first of the section-doors in order to liberate members of the raiding party trapped in that long, glass-lined corridor. The local Chief of Police was still amongst the missing.

"I think," said Sir Denis, "we can afford to overlook infection from the hybrid flies, and even from other insects which you have described to me. Those used experimentally by Dr. Fu Manchu—for instance the fly in Petrie's laboratory—seemed to have survived the evening chill. But you may have noticed that there has been a drop in the temperature during the past two days. I think it was these eccentricities of climate which baffled the Doctor. His flying army couldn't compete with them."

We spent an hour at Ste. Claire; but it was an hour wasted. When, presently, we left for Nice where Dr. Fu Manchu was temporarily confined, I reflected that if Ste. Claire was a minor base of the Si-Fan, as Fleurette had given me to understand, then the organization must be at least as vast as Sir Denis Nayland Smith believed.

Ste. Claire was a scientific fortress; its destruction in one way and another represented a loss to human knowledge which could not be estimated. His section-doors had checked pursuit of the Doctor so effectively that, failing my adventurous swim across the pool and discovery of that other exit, the fugitive could conveniently have landed from the motor yacht *Lola* at any one of many ports before radio had got busy with his description.

I wondered if the measures taken to ensure secrecy would prove to be effective.

The very air was charged with rumours; the Nice police had caught the infection. Such suppressed excitement prevailed that the atmosphere vibrated with it.

Dr. Fu Manchu had declined to be transported to Paris until he had had an opportunity of consulting with his legal adviser. In this he was acting within his rights, as he had pointed out; and the departmental authorities, at a loss, welcomed the arrival of Sir Denis.

M. Chamrousse awaited us, his magisterial dignity unmistakably disturbed.

There was a guard before the doubly-locked door; but in due course it was opened. The Préfet conducted Sir Denis and myself into the apartment occupied by Dr. Fu Manchu.

This, officially, was a cell; actually, a plainly-furnished bed-sitting-room.

At the moment of my entrance I thought that the scene was unreal—wholly chimerical. During my acquaintance with the Chinese doctor I had formed the opinion, reinforced later by what I had heard from Sir Denis, of the monstrous tentacles of the organization called Si-Fan, that ordinary, frail, human laws did not apply to this man who transcended the normal.

And, as I saw him seated in a meanly-furnished room, this feeling of phantasy, of unreality, claimed me.

It was just as fantastic, I thought, as the mango-apple; the *tsetse* fly crossed with the plague flea; the date-palms growing huge figs; the black spider which could reason. . . .

He had discarded his astrakhan cap and fur coat, and I saw that he wore a yellow robe of a kind with which I was familiar. Chinese slippers were upon his feet. Something strikingly unusual in his appearance at first defeated me; then I realized what it was. He did not wear the little cap which hitherto he had worn.

For the first time I appreciated the amazing frontal development of his skull. I had never seen such a head. I had thought of him as resembling Seti the First; but that great king had the skull of a babe in comparison with that of Dr. Fu Manchu.

He sat there watching us as we entered. There was no expression whatever in that wonderful face—a face which might well have looked upon centuries of the ages known to man.

"I shall be glad to see you, Sir Denis," came the guttural, imperturbable voice, "and Mr. Sterling may also remain. Pray be seated."

He fixed a glance of his emerald green eyes upon the Préfet, and I knew and sympathized with the effect which that glance had upon its recipient. The dignified official backed towards the door. Sir Denis saved his dignity.

"It may be better if you leave us for a few moments, M. Chamrousse," he whispered. . . .

When we were alone:

"Alan Sterling," said Dr. Fu Manchu.

And prisoner though he was, he was not so truly a prisoner as I; for he had caught and held my glance as no other man in the world had ever had power to do. I knew that my will was helpless. A dreadful sense of weakness possessed me, which I cannot hope to make clear to anyone lacking experience of that singular regard.

"I speak as one," the guttural voice continued, "who may be at the end of his career. You lack brilliance, but you have qualities which I respect. You may look upon Dr. Petrie's daughter as your woman, since she has chosen you. Take her, and hold her—if you can."

He turned his eyes away. And it was as though a dazzling light had been moved so that I could see the world again in true perspective; then:

"Sir Denis," he continued—

I twisted aside and looked at Nayland Smith. His jaws

were clenched. It was plain that every reserve of his enormous vitality, mental energy, his will, was being called upon as he stared into the face of the uncanny being whom he had captured, who was his prisoner.

"In order that we may understand one another more completely," the imperious voice continued, "I desire to make plain to you, Sir Denis Nayland Smith, that the laws of France, the laws of England, the laws of Europe, are cobwebs which I blow aside. It is your wish that I shall be carried to Paris and thence to London. You believe that your English Courts can end my labours. . . .

"I have this to say to you: the work of a world reformer is a work in which there is no sleep—no rest. That which he achieves is always in the past as he moves forward upon his endless path. Himself, he is alone—always looking into the future. You have fought me; but because you are untiring as myself, you have stimulated, you have checked me. But you cannot hold back the cloud-burst nor stifle the volcano. I may fall—thanks to you. But what I have made stands granite fast.

"Ask me no questions: I shall answer none."

I stared again at Sir Denis. His profile was as grimly mask-like as that of the Chinaman. He made no reply.

"Maître Foli," Dr. Fu Manchu continued, "my French legal adviser, has been detained unavoidably, but will be here at any moment."

## CHAPTER L

## "THE WORK GOES ON—"

WHEN presently we left the apartment of Dr. Fu Manchu, Nayland Smith's face was very stern.

"He was rather obscure," I said.

"Obscure?"

He turned his piercing grey eyes upon me with a glance almost scornful.

"I thought so."

Whereupon Sir Denis smiled, that rare smile which, when it came, must have disarmed his bitterest enemy. He grasped my arm.

"Dr. Fu Manchu is never obscure," he said; "he spoke the plain truth, Sterling. And truth is sometimes a bitter pill."

"But—Maître Foli! He is one of the greatest advocates in France!"

"Certainly. What did you expect? Surely you know that Dr. Fu Manchu never looks below excellence—living or dead! I warned you that Fu Manchu arrested and Fu Manchu convicted were totally different matters—"

We returned to the office of the Préfet, and:

"Hello!" Sir Denis exclaimed—"he's here!"

A stooping but imposing figure was seated in the leathern arm-chair before the table of the Préfet. M. Chamrousse, not yet entirely his own man, following his encounter with the formidable Chinaman, was listening with every mark of deference to his distinguished visitor. The latter ceased speaking and the Préfet stood up as we entered.

"Sir Denis," said Chamrousse, "this is Maître Foli—Dr. Fu Manchu's legal adviser."

Maître Foli stood up and bowed very formally.

I had recognized him immediately from his photographs published during the progress of a Paris *cause célèbre* in which he had secured the vindication of his client—a distinguished officer accused of espionage. I judged his age to be close on seventy; his yellow face was a map of wrinkles rendered more conspicuous by a small, snow-white moustache and a tiny tuft of beard under his lower lip.

He was buttoned up in a black, caped, overcoat, from the lapels of which bulged a flowing tie; and a wide-brimmed hat lay on the carpet beside a bulky portfolio. A close-fitting silk skull-cap lent him a mediaeval appearance, which was lost when he adjusted large, slightly tinted spectacles in order more closely to survey us.

It was a memorable situation.

"Your reputation is well known to me, Maître Foli," said Sir Denis.

"Indeed, yes," M. Chamrousse murmured, bowing to the famous lawyer.

"But the identity of your present client surprises me."

"Sir Denis Nayland Smith," Maître Foli replied in a harsh, strident voice, "I have acted for Dr. Fu Manchu over a period of some forty years."

"Is that so?" Sir Denis muttered dryly.

"You and I do not see eye to eye in the matters which we know about. You have behaved, and behaved honourably, in accordance with your principles, Sir Denis. Dr. Fu Manchu has followed another star. His codes are those of a civilization different from ours—and older. A day will come, must come, when you will recognize your outlook—as I have recognized mine—to be limited. His manner of warfare appalls you—yet I can only regret, Sir Denis, that a man of your great capacity should have been called upon to oppose the inevitable over a period of so many years."

He stood up.

"Thank you," said Sir Denis.

"Will you be good enough"—Maître Foli bowed to the Préfet and to Nayland Smith—"to grant me an interview with my client? I desire that this interview should not be interrupted—a desire which I am entitled to express."

The French official glanced at Sir Denis, who nodded. Maître Foli took up his bulky portfolio and went out, walking very slowly and much stooped. M. Chamrousse followed him.

I stared at Nayland Smith, who had begun to pace up and down the carpet, restlessly.

"This man Foli is going to oppose extradition!" he rapped. "If he succeeds—and he rarely fails—Fu Manchu will slip through our fingers!"

Presently, M. Chamrousse returned, shrugging apologetically.

"Such is the law," he said, "and the eminence of Maître Foli offers me no alternative. This Dr. Fu Manchu is a political prisoner. . . ."

A messenger entered to announce the arrival of the Chinese consul.

"Do you mind, M. Chamrousse," said Sir Denis, "if I see this gentleman privately for a few minutes?"

"But not at all."

Sir Denis nodded to the speaker and walked rapidly out of the room. Five to ten minutes elapsed, during which there was little conversation between M. Chamrousse and myself, and then:

"The appearance of the great Foli in this case gives me a heavy sense of responsibility," M. Chamrousse declared.

"I fully understand."

A further interval of silence; and then, heralded by the sound of a bell and the unlocking of doors, Maître Foli rejoined us, portfolio under his arm.

188

M. Chamrousse sprang to his feet.

"Gentlemen," said the famous lawyer, groping for that wide-brimmed hat which he had left upon the floor beside his chair, "I am returning at once in order to get in touch with the Chinese Legation in Paris."

"The Chinese consul is here, Maître Foli—

That stooping but dignified figure turned slowly.

"I thank you, M. Chamrousse; but this affair is outside the sphere of minor officialdom—"

M. Chamrousse rang a bell; a clerk appeared, who showed Maître Foli out of the office. At the door he turned.

"Gentlemen," he said, "I know that you look upon me as your enemy; but your enemy is my client. I am merely acting for him."

He bowed, and went out. The door closed.

Perhaps half a minute had elasped when it was flung open again and Nayland Smith hurried in.

"Was that Maître Foli who left a moment ago?" he rapped.

"Yes," M. Chamrousse replied. "He is anxious to get into immediate touch with the Chinese Legation in Paris."

Sir Denis stood stock-still, then:

"Great heavens!" he said in a low voice—and looked at me almost wildly—"It's not impossible! It's not impossible—"

"What do you mean, Sir Denis?"

"The Blessing of the Celestial Vision!"

His words were a verbal thunderbolt; his meaning was all too clear—

"Sterling! Good God! Follow me."

He rushed from the room, along the passage to the cell occupied by Dr. Fu Manchu. A guard was on duty at the door. He opened it in response to Sir Denis's order. We entered. M. Chamrousse was close behind.

A man was seated where Dr. Fu Manchu had sat; one in figure not unlike whom we had come to seek. But. . . .

"Great heavens!" cried Nayland Smith. "He wasn't relying on loopholes of the law! He was relying on his genius as an illusionist!"

The man in the yellow robe bowed.

*It was Maître Foli!*

"Sir Denis," he said, in his harsh, strident voice, "I have served my purpose—the purpose for which I have been retained by Dr. Fu Manchu for a period of more than thirty years. I am honoured; I am happy. I crown a successful career with a glorious deed. . . ."

189

The light in his eyes—their wild fanaticism—told me the truth. Maître Foli was a Companion; a victim of those arts which I had so narrowly escaped!

"I shall be committed to a French gaol—my sentence may be a long one. I am too old for Devil's Island; but in any event what does it matter? The Prince is free! The work goes on. . . ."